PRAISE FOR

A SEAN MCPHERSON NOVEL, BOOK ONE

"Buchanan's narrative is well-paced, flying right along. . . . the author has delivered an exciting beginning to an intriguing series."
—*KIRKUS REVIEWS*

"The author of this impressive novel has poured elements from radically different genres into the blender and set it on high spin . . . The last page promises further surprises in a sequel, which Buchanan better deliver soon."
—*BOOKLIST*

PRAISE FOR *ICONOCLAST*

A SEAN MCPHERSON NOVEL, BOOK TWO

"An involving thriller with compelling characters. This propulsive novel ably expands Buchanan's entertaining series, which is built primarily on engaging characterization."
—*KIRKUS REVIEWS*

"Buchanan shows a sure hand as an action writer. . . . A smooth, ultra-professional read."
—*BOOKLIST*

"An absolute page-turner . . . Not the one to be missed. With its atmospheric setting, page-turning suspense, and luminous insights into trauma, resilience, recovery, and friendship, this thriller will hook readers and keep them hooked."
—*THE PRAIRIES BOOK REVIEW*

"I devoured every page of *Iconoclast*, turning the pages viciously because I couldn't wait to find out what would happen next."
—*ONLINE BOOK CLUB*

PRAISE FOR *IMPERVIOUS*

A SEAN MCPHERSON NOVEL, BOOK THREE

"Don't miss this engaging story filled with an intricate plot, realistic characters, and mesmerizing suspense!"
—DEBBIE HERBERT, *USA Today* best-selling author

"Buchanan keeps you turning pages until the end."
—CHRIS NORBURY, author of the Matt Lanier mystery-thriller series

"Buchanan has a fresh, very different and fast-paced style. And somehow makes a chef's meal integral to the thrilling suspense. I go from salivating to shocked, chapter by chapter."
—CHRISTINE DESMET, novelist and screenwriter

"At Pines & Quill, the deadliest writers retreat in the Northwest, Buchanan delivers one knockout punch after another, leaving the reader reeling."
—SHEILA LOWE, author of the Beyond the Veil paranormal suspense series

"Hitchcockian suspense and tension reign in this page turner."
—SHERRILL JOSEPH, author of The Botanic Hill Detectives Mysteries

"Buchanan's writing tantalizes all your emotions: there are sweet moments to savor and descriptions for all the senses. But, lurking in the shadows, the dark mind of a devious killer drives the plot, threatening every character you've come to call your friend."
—JOY RIBAR, author of the Deep Lakes Cozy Mystery series

"Buchanan has done it again—kept me on the edge of my seat until the end as I follow the twists and turns of Sean 'Mick' McPherson's life as an ex-cop turned PI. Based at Pines & Quill, a quiet writers retreat in Bellingham, Washington, *Impervious* plunges readers deeper into a national crime web that Buchanan has masterfully created, and takes us on a wild ride to New Orleans, San Francisco, and back to Bellingham for the explosive ending. Peppered in the book are more mouth-watering meals from the kitchen at Pines & Quill and the ever-present delight of Hemingway, the retreat owners' loveable Irish Wolfhound. Can't wait for the next book!"
—ASHLEY E. SWEENEY, author of *Hardland*

"I'm hooked on Buchanan's Sean McPherson novels!"
—PAMELA WIGHT, author of *The Right Wrong Man*

"Buchanan delivers another knockout punch! I love this series!"
—SUZANNE SIMONETTI, author of
The Sound of Wings

"Buchanan's third Sean McPherson novel hits every note we've come to expect—tight tension, sympathetic characters, delicious menus, and high-stakes danger. She leads readers through the gamut of emotions from fear to joy. Whether you love thrillers or romance, you'll love *Impervious!*"
—SARALYN RICHARD, author of The Detective Parrott Mystery Series

IMPERVIOUS

IMPERVIOUS

A SEAN McPHERSON NOVEL

BOOK THREE

LAURIE BUCHANAN

This book is dedicated to authors,
their creative muses, and the craft of writing.

Published by SparkPress, a BookSparks imprint,
A division of SparkPoint Studio, LLC
Phoenix, Arizona, USA, 85007
www.gosparkpress.com

Published 2022
Printed in the United States of America
Print ISBN: 978-1-68463-194-0
E-ISBN: 978-1-68463-195-7

Library of Congress Control Number: 2022919506

Interior design by Tabitha Lahr

AUTHOR'S NOTE

While Bellingham and Fairhaven are
real towns in the state of Washington,
I've added fictitious touches to further the story.

"Nobody's ever been arrested for a murder; they have only ever been arrested for not planning it properly."

—TERRY HAYES

↑

Vancouver
British Columbia
Canada

Much like a
brilliant, multi-
faceted gem
nestled on the
ragged hemline
of the northern
Pacific coast,
Pines & Quill,
a wooded retreat
for writers, sits
Zen-like
overlooking
Bellingham Bay
in Fairhaven,
Washington.

Pines & Quill

↓ Seattle

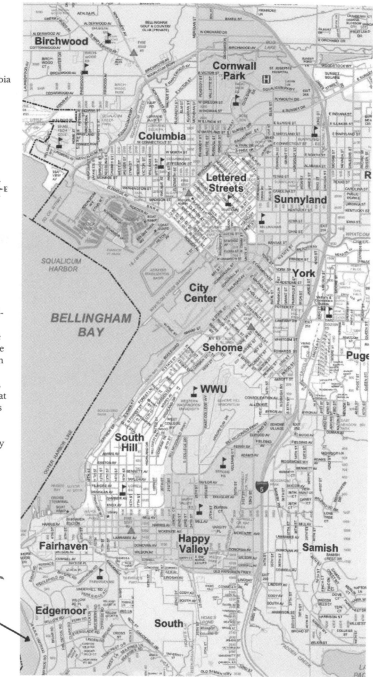

Bluff, Cliffs, &
Bellingham Bay

Dickens Cottage

Bellingham &
Fairhaven Historic District

Garage & Workshop

Entrance Gate

Austen Cottage

Back View of Main House
& Mudroom Door

PINES & QUILL

Niall's Garden

Bronte Cottage

Tai Chi Pavilion
& Event Center

McPherson Cabin

Bellingham Bay
National Park & Reserve

Thoreau Cottage

N
W · E
S

PROLOGUE

> *"Murderers are not monsters, they're men. And that's the most frightening thing about them."*
>
> —ALICE SEBOLD

Georgio "The Bull" Gambino sits in closed-eye contemplation, his thoughts a nonstop loop of his sinister achievements, his invincibility, his criminal genius. The only visible movement is in his hands. They rest on his stomach, where his thumbs circle the middle distance between his laced fingers.

Professor Moriarty and I are similar in that we're both Machiavellian criminal masterminds. His creator, Arthur Conan Doyle, once said of the professor, "He sits motionless, like a spider in the center of its web, but that web has a thousand radiations, and he knows well every quiver of each of them. He does little himself. He only plans."

Gambino reflects on their similarities:

Moriarty wields power over a London-based crime web. He controls and benefits from crimes committed by those in his hire.

I wield power over New Orleans, San Francisco, and my latest acquisition, Seattle-based crime webs. I control and benefit from crimes committed by those in my hire.

So gradual and widespread my infiltration, it's far too late for anyone to stop me. I'm impervious to my enemies' efforts. Untouchable.

Like a self-satisfied spider, Gambino mentally circles the prey trapped in his sticky web. In his mind's eye, he injects his quarry with neurotoxic venom. *It will immobilize my victims and ensure cooperation; it will dissolve their backbones, making them spineless creatures. Making them mine.*

He stops circling his thumbs. Raising both hands before his slit eyes, he envisions them as pincers. He flexes them. *Where to inflict pain next?*

Gambino picks up his cell phone and makes a call. Low and menacing, he utters three words, "Make it happen," then disconnects and goes back to his ruminations.

A faint smile appears on his line-bracketed face. Experiential knowledge informs him that his bidding is as good as done.

———

Officer Toni Bianco pulls into a space in the employee parking lot at the Bellingham Police station just as "The Bull" ends the call. She cuts the engine, collects her things, and exits the car. Intent on the task at hand, she barely notices the vapor trails crisscrossing the electric-blue June sky. *Just a little over a week until the Fourth of July. But there'll be plenty of fireworks before then.*

Fobbing the car locked over her shoulder, she scans the lot as she crosses it. The hydraulic whoosh of the building's door bids her entrance to an air-conditioned hallway, its icy draft a relief. Toni heads toward the "Prairie Dog Farm"—the bullpen where uniforms sit back-to-back in low-walled cubicles.

"Hey, Bingham," she says as she sits in her chair.

Joe raises his mug of home-brewed coffee. "Hey, Bianco."

"I wish I'd had time to bring coffee from home. Now I've got to drink that sludge." Toni nods toward the coffee station down the hall.

Toni stows her things in the bottom desk drawer and taps her workstation out of sleep mode. After entering her username and password, she's greeted by the Bellingham Police logo—an indigo background featuring a snow-covered mountain with green trees in the foreground, the same logo that's emblazoned on every squad car in town.

Toni turns toward Joe. "I still can't understand why you didn't change desks when you were promoted to homicide detective."

"I told you," he says, swiveling his chair to face her, "one change is enough for now."

Turning back to her desk, Toni opens the center drawer and rummages her hand inside. "I'm heading to the supply closet. My Post-it Notes keep growing legs. Need anything?"

"No, I'm good." Joe sips his coffee. "But thanks."

On the way back from her errand, Toni stops to pour herself a cup of station house coffee—wretched, but welcome.

Walking down the hallway to her cubicle, she makes one more stop. To the casual observer, it looks like she's dropping a block of yellow Post-it Notes on Officer Accardi's desk.

Toni smiles at Emilio and nods as she sets them down.

"Hey, thanks, Toni," he says, fanning the little stack.

Emilio sees that they're blank—nothing is written on them. But the message is loud and clear. It's the prearranged signal that sets everything into motion.

It reminds Toni of playing the game Mouse Trap with her cousins when she was a kid. *Like the boot kicking the marble,* she thinks. She pushes off from Emilio's desk and heads to her own. *It was fun collecting and stealing cheese from the other players. But in this case, the end game's different. Gambino will have all the cheese, and the other players will all be dead.*

Toni sits down in her desk chair and catches her reflection on her computer screen. She looks immensely pleased with the destruction she just engineered.

CHAPTER 1

"At first, I see pictures of a story in my mind. Then creating the story comes from asking questions of myself. I guess you might call it the 'what if—what then' approach to writing and illustration."

—CHRIS VAN ALLSBURG

Scan "Mick" McPherson's stomach feels queasy. *Wedding day jitters? No. I'm not nervous about getting married. But being at the center of attention makes me nauseous.* Mick absently touches his stomach. *I'm so relieved that Emma said, "I want a small wedding, one that's casual, down-to-earth, and intimate."*

Mick peers through the windshield to a slowly spreading stain of light on the eastern horizon before shifting his gaze to the rearview mirror. He looks into the dark eyes of his back-seat companion and smiles. "Hemingway, Emma and I are getting married today."

He hears a tail thump the leather upholstery.

Mick reaches around to rough the hair on the Irish wolf-hound's head. "That's right, buddy."

Taking that as an invitation, the big dog inserts his chest and front legs between the two front seats. Easing down, he lies his head on his front paws on the middle console. His hair, wiry and rough, is especially long under his chin and over his eyes.

Mick pats the head of his four-legged companion. "Hey, buddy. We've got to look our best." His tone rises and falls to instill enthusiasm. "That's why I'm bathing you this morning."

Hemingway lifts his head, pricks his ears, and stares at Mick.

"We're going to have company at Pines & Quill. Not a lot. Just our families, closest friends, and the priest. The other people—the florist, band, caterer, and the baker who's delivering the wedding cake—will stop by briefly and then leave again."

Mick's fingers thrum the steering wheel while he thinks through the list of people. "Oh, and there's Dean and Kevin. They're two students I hired from Western Washington University to valet the cars, port the guests to the pavilion in the ATV, and bartend. But it still means way more cars than we usually have on the property. I'm moving the Jeep out here now, so Emma and I can make an easy getaway later."

Mick strokes the top of Hemingway's head and continues in an exaggerated happy voice. "Now there's room in the drive-way for me to hose you down, lather you up, and rinse you off."

Hemingway nudges Mick's arm with his wet nose.

"I'll make it as fast and painless as I possibly can, big guy. But you've got to cooperate."

Hemingway's long, pink tongue lolls out the side of his mouth.

Mick sees Hemingway's tail wave back and forth in the rearview mirror, scraping the overhead interior.

"It sounds fun, doesn't it? But we both know," Mick says, "that getting a bath is one of your least favorite things." He pats the top of Hemingway's giant paw. "That's why I'm going to put a leash on you and hook it to the side of the garage before we start. That way, you can't run away and roll in the dirt, dead leaves, and rabbit poop like last time."

———————

Emma's nostrils take in the delicious aroma of the ham-laced breakfast casserole that Niall popped into the oven before leaving to join the other men for their wedding-morning festivities. She loves the spacious kitchen in the main house at Pines and Quill. She's in it as often as she's in the one she shares with Mick in their cabin, just walking distance down the tree-canopied lane.

Emma gets a treat out of the biscuit jar on her way to the Dutch door to pet a disgruntled, still-damp Hemingway. He stretches his neck as far over the ledge as he can. She obliges by stroking him lightly on his head. "Hey, handsome. Mick said you have to stay here so you can't roll in the dirt and get filthy."

Hemingway's tail beats against the washing machine on the mudroom side of the half-open door.

Emma gives him the biscuit. "Lie down now and get some rest. We've got a big day ahead of us."

Libby sets a pitcher of orange juice on the table. "He'll be just fine. He's playing on your sympathies."

Emma looks at Libby and the rest of the pajama-clad women who've gathered around the enormous pine table Libby acquired at an auction in Seattle. Said to have seated a dozen threshers at mealtime in the early 1900s, it now serves the writers who come to Pines & Quill to escape the distractions of life and write.

Through eyes filled with happy tears, Emma sees her mother, Maureen Benton, Mick's mother, Maeve McPherson, and Mick's sister, Libby MacCullough. She turns to see her best friend, Sally Newson, Fiona O'Meara, fiancée to Mick's nephew Ian, Marci Bingham, wife of Mick's best friend, Joe, and Linda Washington, a professional photographer who graciously agreed to stay at Pines & Quill a little longer to photograph the wedding. Linda's staying in Brontë cottage, where she's been working on her manuscript.

Emma wiggles her bare toes. "I'm so excited about today. Thank you for being with me." She looks at her mother. "My mom can tell you that I've always wanted a small, intimate wedding."

"Ever since she was little," Maureen agrees.

Emma raises her cup of coffee. "Here's to you, the women who mean the world to me. Thank you for being here to support me on my wedding day."

Pressing her hands together in front of her chest, Fiona asks, "Can we see your dress now?"

Emma beams. "Absolutely."

"I'll get it for you, dear." Maureen leaves the table and gathers a dress bag from the back of the room. She carries it to the side and hangs it from the rod above the window overlooking a profusion of color on the flower-strewn patio.

Emma walks over and unzips the bag, revealing a champagne-colored sleeveless floral jacquard dress.

There's an audible intake of breath from the women.

Linda tiptoes around the room, capturing their dewy-eyed faces on film.

"I didn't want a formal, floor-length gown. I wanted something simple, something perfect for the last week in June."

"It's perfect," Marci sighs.

Maeve sets down her coffee cup. "I love the bateau neckline."

Fiona leans forward. "The fitted bodice on top of the gathered, full skirt is gorgeous."

Emma looks at the newly engaged Fiona and smiles. She imagines planning wheels spinning in the young woman's head.

Sally tucks a wayward strand of hair behind her ear. "Even though it's backlit by the early morning sun, we can't see through the fabric."

Emma nods. "You're right. That's the last thing I wanted to worry about with an outdoor wedding. So I made sure to get a dress that's lined." She takes the hanger down and turns the dress around so the women can see the back.

Libby sets down her coffee mug. "I love that the zipper's hidden." She walks over to Emma and hugs her soon-to-be sister-in-law. "You're a beautiful bride inside and out. My brother's a lucky man."

Emma returns the hug. "Thank you. I'm looking forward to being part of *two* families now—the Bentons and the McPhersons."

Mick and the other men walk to the pavilion, each carrying two chairs. Thankful for today's perfect weather forecast, Mick notices the occasional puffy clouds are wedding-gown-white under the soft blue sky. He looks at his family and friends and scratches his cheek. *None of us has shaved yet, so we look a bit rough around the edges.*

Mick's grateful to his brother-in-law, Niall, for putting two delicious-smelling breakfast casseroles in his cabin's oven to bake this morning. Just thinking about the woodsy scent of smoked sausage makes his mouth water. *We'll be starving by the time we finish.* His dad, Connor McPherson, and Emma's dad, Philip Benton, are just as game as the younger guys. Emma's brothers, the three E's—Eric, Ethan, and Ellery—will be great brothers-in-law. Ian, his nephew, is just months away from graduating from veterinary school.

Then there are his two best friends: Joe Bingham, who just accepted a homicide detective position in Bellingham, and Rafferty, a special agent with the FBI in town to investigate multiple deaths and other crimes attributed to crime boss Gambino.

As the men draw near the pavilion, Mick can't help but appreciate the pagoda-style copper roof, patinated with age, and corners that flare out over Chinese-red supports. Its design is distinctly Asian. In addition to teaching, discussing the writing process, and offering feedback on the writers in residence manuscripts, his sister, Libby, offers tai chi classes in the pavilion as a way for them to loosen up for a productive day of writing.

When they reach the pavilion steps, Mick turns to the guys. "Thank you for helping me make quick work of setting up for the wedding. After we put the chairs in three rows of four on each side, I'll go load more stuff on the ATV." He turns and points. "The lectern goes there, and the bar and catering tables go over there."

Eric, Emma's oldest brother, taps his two younger brothers on their shoulders. "We'll come with you and help load up."

Mick nods. "That'll be great. I've hitched a small trailer to the back. We should be able to do it in one trip, two at the most."

When they're all done, Mick hangs a sign that Libby had calligraphed—*PICK A SEAT, NOT A SIDE.*

———

After devouring Niall's breakfast casseroles loaded with ham, cheese, and eggs, and downing umpteen cups of coffee, the men grab their gear and walk across the property. They stop to pick up Tom Gordon at Austen cottage on their way to the makeshift shooting range Mick, Connor, and Philip set up on the bluff the night before.

"Guys, I'd like you to meet Tom Gordon. He's covering for me while Emma and I are on our honeymoon." Mick introduces each of the men in turn.

"Nothing like a little shooting to vent wedding day jitters," Tom jokes.

Mick scratches his unshaved jawline. "All kidding aside, when Tom was in Afghanistan, he braved enemy fire to evacuate two wounded Marines and carry out the body of a third. He was awarded the Navy Cross, second only to the Medal of Honor."

Connor steps forward and shakes Tom's hand. "Thank you for your service."

Tom dips his head in acknowledgment.

Aware that Tom is still getting used to his prosthetic legs, Mick and the other men ease their pace toward the bluff.

"You've got fine shooting skills, Eric," Mick says to Emma's oldest brother after Eric shoots four of the six cans off the makeshift stands fifty yards in the distance.

"Thanks, but that's nothing compared to Emma."

"That's right," Ethan and Ellery say.

Mick, Niall, Connor, Ian, Joe, Rafferty, and Tom turn, their eyebrows raised, to look at the four Benton men.

Philip Benton stands even taller. "That's right. My daughter's been shooting with her brothers and me since she was little. Emma can shoot the whiskers off a gnat at fifty yards."

Mick knows his eyebrows are flirting with his hairline.

A wicked grin splits Rafferty's face. "You didn't know?"

Mick shakes his head. "I had no idea."

Ellery, Emma's middle brother, tucks his hands into the front pockets of his jeans. "It's probably best if you watch your p's and q's."

It's obvious Joe's trying not to laugh. "I wonder why she never told you?"

"I guess the subject never came up," Mick says, joining their merriment. "But it's good to know she's got my back."

CHAPTER 2

"Exercise the writing muscle every day, even if it is only a letter, notes, a title list, a character sketch, a journal entry. Writers are like dancers, like athletes. Without that exercise, the muscles seize up."

—JANE YOLEN

After introducing herself to the Jason Parker Quartet, who are warming up in the back corner of the pavilion, Libby turns to watch her brother, Mick. He's talking with Father Burke from St. Barnabas Catholic church, the priest who's officiating Mick's and Emma's wedding.

Dread clenches Libby's heart. *Are they discussing Paddy MacCullough, Father Burke's best friend? He was found shot to death in a confessional at St. Barnabas church, where he'd been a priest for decades. I'm glad Mick got his private investigator's license and is helping the local police and the FBI to find Paddy's killer.*

Libby relaxes her shoulders and exhales deeply. *There's been so much death. First, there was Jason Hughes, who turned out to be Alex Berndt. Then Vito Paglio at The Scrap Heap wrecking yard, who turned out to be Salvatore Rizzo. The third person was our very own writer in residence, Pam Williams, who turned out not to be Pam Williams at all. Unfortunately, the real Pam Williams and her brother, Kyle, are missing. Finally, the sniper who tried to kill Emma while she and Mick were on a whale-watching cruise. It turns out he was a relatively new recruit at the Bellingham Police station.*

Libby shakes her head in disbelief. Except for Paddy MacCullough, the common denominator is that each person who died had a "Family First" tattoo on their lower back, tying them to Georgio "The Bull" Gambino—head of the Gambino crime family.

Nostalgia grips her throat, sinking her into fond memories of her brother-in-law, Paddy. *Just a couple of weeks ago, we held his memorial service in this very place. Who would murder a priest? And equally important, why?*

Libby watches Linda Washington orbit gracefully around the guests taking candid photos. *I'm so glad she agreed to stay a few extra days and photograph the wedding. I think she was delighted to have a chance to spend more time with Tom Gordon too.*

Her gaze travels back to her brother. *Mick's black suit is cut to precision, bold across the shoulders with gentle lines around his slender waist—the perfect inverted triangle.*

Libby feels adrift. *I love being needed, but Mick and Emma thought of everything.* She watches Kevin Pierce—doing double-duty with Dean Hampton as parking valet and bartender—porting guests in the ATV from the parking area to the pavilion. *Mom was great to suggest this idea so that the women's heels don't sink into the grass.*

The florist, Bella Flora, did an excellent job. The big sprays of greenery and colorful wildflowers with a delicate floral scent are perfect for this natural setting.

Libby smiles as Joe's wife, Marci, places an eco-friendly, biodegradable birdseed favor on each seat. *The Wild Bird Chalet did a great job creating them for the guests to open and toss at Emma and Mick as they step out of the pavilion.*

As the chairs fill, everyone bobs their head in time to the jazz and rhythm-and-blues music that the Seattle-based Jason Parker Quartet is known for. *A perfect choice for a couple who's honeymooning in New Orleans.*

Libby turns to the back of the room where the buffet is set out in metal chafing dishes. *I'm glad that Mick and Emma wanted Niall to fully enjoy this day and went with A Taste of Elegance to cater their wedding instead of him.*

Walking closer to the buffet, Libby inhales the delicious aromas. Emma had asked her and Niall to help select the menu. They decided on glazed New Orleans barbecue shrimp and sausage kabobs in Paddy's honor and grilled beef and chicken kabobs with cherry tomatoes, button mushrooms, and asparagus spears. The side dishes include rice pilaf, green bean almondine, steamed broccoli and baby carrots, Caesar salad, a Cajun pasta salad, and French bread with whipped garlic butter.

Beyond the buffet tables, Libby sees the distressed white plantation dressing screen, an accent piece she and Niall use as a divider in their guest room. Mick placed it in the back of the pavilion for Emma to wait behind before the ceremony.

Libby walks over and lightly taps. "Emma, it's Libby. Are you doing okay?"

"I'm fine. Please come around. Sally's here with me."

Libby clasps her hands together in front of her chest when she sees the bride. "You're beautiful, Emma. Absolutely beautiful."

Mick nods at the band. *I'm glad I got to select the song Emma walks down the aisle to.*

All of the guests turn in their seats when the quartet starts playing "Perfect" by Ed Sheeran. Mick stands up even straighter. His heart slams in his chest when Emma steps out from behind the plantation shutters.

The epitome of radiance, Emma walks toward Mick at the front of the pavilion. The skin at the outside corners of her eyes crinkles from her wide smile.

Over the thunder of his heartbeat, Mick hears the female guests sighing. He sees his mother and sister holding hands, happy tears shining on their cheeks.

Father Burke scans the pavilion. *I wish more than anything that Paddy was here today. Why was Paddy murdered?* The priest's eyes well with sorrow at the loss of his friend. His fingers caress the well-worn leather on Paddy's Bible, a gift from Niall MacCullough. *So many have died. How many more? I'm afraid for Niall, Libby, Mick, and Emma.* He looks out at the brilliant blue summer sky and feels close to the Almighty. *Oh, God, please protect this family.*

Father Burke clears his throat. "Good afternoon, everyone. We're glad you're here. From this beautiful pavilion at Pines & Quill, we take ourselves out of our daily living routines to witness a unique moment for Emma and Mick. Today they join their lives in the union of marriage. You're the ones who've supported them and know them so well. It's only fitting that you're the ones to share this once-in-a-lifetime moment with them."

The priest turns his attention to the bride and groom. "Emma and Mick, you both look to a shared future that includes a richly lived life together. The years will come and go, and you won't take each other for granted. You'll laugh a lot. You'll grow older and wiser together. It's a good story, and the ending's not in sight."

In his peripheral vision, Father Burke sees Linda Washington taking candid photos. He makes sure to smile. "We come now to the words Emma and Mick want to hear the most today, the vows that take them across the threshold from being engaged to being married."

The wedding guests lean forward in their seats.

A soft breeze rustles leaves in the surrounding trees. A bird calls. Though distant, the distinctive *cuck* informs Father Burke it's a robin.

The priest scans the group in the pavilion and continues. "But before they declare their vows to one another, I want to hear them confirm that it is indeed their intention to be married today."

Father Burke looks at the bride. "Emma, do you come here freely and without reservation to give yourself to Mick in marriage? If so, answer 'I do.'"

Emma looks up into Mick's deep green eyes. "I do."

Next, the priest turns his attention to Mick. *I remember when Paddy confided that Mick was like a son to him. He would have loved to officiate his wedding.* "Mick, do you come here freely and without reservation to give yourself to Emma in marriage? If so, answer 'I do.'"

Mick looks down into Emma's moss-green eyes. "I do."

"Emma and Mick, having heard that you intend to be married to each other, I now ask you to declare your marriage vows. But before you do that, please call your ring bearer."

Mick gives a short, two-fingered whistle. Everyone turns as Hemingway struts up the aisle and stops in front of two of his favorite people. The wedding guests laugh when he does a full-body wag.

As Mick and Emma lean forward and each unties a platinum band from Hemingway's collar, Mick whispers, "He's eating this up."

"With a spoon," Emma whispers back.

"Good boy," Mick says. He gives a hand signal. "Now sit."

Hemingway sits, but his tail swishes back and forth like a turbo-boosted metronome dusting the pavilion floor.

Father Burke chuckles. "Emma and Mick, please face each other and hold hands. Your wedding rings are the outward and visible sign of the inward and invisible bond which already unites your two hearts in love.

"Mick, place the ring on Emma's finger and state your vows."

The priest sees an expectant look on the big dog's face as he watches the exchange between two of his favorite people.

Mick clears his throat. "Emma, I feel overwhelmingly lucky and proud to be standing beside you today. I knew from the moment I laid eyes on you and your 'pumpkin spice' colored luggage at the airport that you were my forever. I will encourage your compassion and creativity. I promise to love you unconditionally and support you in achieving your goals. I will cherish you for as long as I live."

Soft sniffles ripple through the audience.

"Emma, place the ring on Mick's finger and state your vows."

Emma beams up at Mick. "Mick, I take you to be my partner for life. I will encourage your pursuit of justice as you create change for fairness in the world because that's what makes you unique and wonderful. I promise to stand by you and comfort you in times of trouble, and to cherish you as we grow and build our lives together. I give you my love. I give you myself."

Father Burke leans forward. A slight breeze carries the aroma of Creole seasoning from the New Orleans barbecue shrimp and sausage kabobs. His stomach growls. *Paddy's favorite. He would have smothered them in Louisiana hot sauce.*

"May the wedding rings you exchange today remind you always that you're surrounded by enduring love. Emma and Mick, I offer you these good wishes on your wedding day. May all of your years be filled with moments to celebrate and renew your love. May your love be a lifelong source of excitement, contentment, affection, respect, and devotion for one another.

"Now, by the power vested in me by the state of Washington, it's my honor and delight to declare you husband and wife. You may seal this declaration with a kiss."

Mick collects Emma into his arms and takes his time, kissing her slowly.

Hemingway can't contain himself any longer. He stands and adds his excited yips with the whoops from the wedding guests.

Father Burke raises his voice. "I'm pleased to present the newlyweds, Mr. and Mrs. McPherson."

Mick and Emma accept hearty congratulations as they mingle with their guests. Some are eating; others are visiting. They see Hemingway watching the buffet with laser focus—the hope of table food evident in his eyes.

Mick squeezes Emma's hand. "He's waiting for food to drop on the floor. His name should be Hoover."

"'The big lug,' as you call him, did well," Emma says. "I was afraid he might do something awful after you gave him a bath this morning."

"Nah. He got to be in the limelight. That's not to say he won't punish us for leaving him for nine days while we're honeymooning in New Orleans."

Mick sees Jason from the quartet wide-eye him, silently asking if they should start playing the song for the bride and groom's first dance.

As Mick is about to nod his assent, Kevin, one of the two students he hired from Western Washington University to valet the cars and bartend, rushes up. "Mr. McPherson, the delivery van from Pure Bliss Desserts just arrived. Unfortunately, with the way everyone parked, they can't make it through. The easiest way is to move just one vehicle—that would be yours. I'm happy to do it. I just need your keys."

Mick extracts his keys from the suit jacket he'd draped over the back of a chair. "Thanks, Kevin. Please bring them back when you're done. Emma and I want to make a quick getaway later. We've got a plane to catch."

"Yes, sir. I'll bring them right back."

Mick turns back to Jason and nods.

The guests clear the center of the pavilion and gather around to watch the newlyweds when they hear the quartet start playing "You Are the Reason" for the first dance.

Despite his limp, Mick is an excellent dancer. His mouth finds Emma's, gentle yet urgent, as he wraps her in his arms. He feels the softness of her body pressed against his. It seems that he exists only in the gliding circle they make.

"I love you, Emma McPherson."

———

Kevin whistles as he jog-walks to Mick's Jeep. *When Jessie saw me dressed in these black slacks, tie, vest, and white dress shirt, she said, "You're so handsome, you make me melt."*

The wedding makes him think about their date tonight. *I hope a beautiful woman looks at me one day the way Mr. McPherson's bride looks at him.*

Kevin presses the button on the fob to unlock the Jeep's door. Slipping into the leather seat, he looks at the dash. *Man, this must have cost a chunk of change.*

He puts the key into the ignition and turns it. It's the last thing he ever does.

CHAPTER 3

*"I kept always two books in my pocket, one to read,
one to write in."*
— ROBERT LOUIS STEVENSON

"Get down!" Mick shouts as an explosion rents the air.
The blast shakes the ground as a tsunami of air hits the
pavilion. The reverberation is felt throughout Pines & Quill.

Shoes pound the pavilion's wood floor as people scatter—
most of them running away from the sound.

Mick grabs Emma's shoulders. "Stay here."

Fear bathes Emma's ashen face. "Oh, my God, Mick.
Please be careful."

"I'll come and get you once I know it's safe."

Before she can respond, Mick joins his dad, Joe, and
Rafferty as they run toward where the blast originated. His
uneven gait doesn't slow him down, even as they pass through
smoking debris scattered on the ground.

Mick pats his pockets. *My cell phone's in my suit coat in the pavilion.* He glances at Rafferty, who presses a cell phone to his ear. *I bet he's calling first responders.*

Mick looks over his shoulder to make sure Emma hasn't followed. One hand is fisted on her chest, the other is holding fast to an agitated Hemingway who's straining at his collar, his ears pricked forward. *He's watching my every move because he's worried about me.* Mick gives a hand signal for Hemingway to stay with Emma. *Just a minute ago, I was the happiest man on earth. And now this. What's going on?*

Tom strides toward him. His trekking poles help him maintain balance on his new prosthetic legs.

A breeze pushes an aggressive cloud of smoke toward Mick, stinging his eyes. Barely discernible, the smell of burnt flesh creeps into his nostrils. *Oh, my God!* From the black haze comes the wail of car alarms. *The concussive shockwaves hit the surrounding vehicles.*

The four men—Mick, Connor, Joe, and Rafferty—come to a standstill as another smell reaches them—gasoline.

When the choking cloud begins to clear, they see a fiery hulk of metal—the remains of Mick's Jeep. "We need to get back. I filled it up yesterday. The gasoline's fueling the fire."

The explosion's force destroyed the windows in most of the surrounding cars. The ones parked closest to the Jeep are blown out; the ones further away, shattered. Side mirrors dangle from several vehicles. A rooftop luggage carrier hangs from the back of a car.

Tom catches up and stands next to the four men. Like the rest of them, he's shaken to his core. "I was an EOD—explosives ordinance disposal—specialist. I'd know that sound anywhere. It came from a VBIED, a vehicle-borne improvised explosive device. No one could have survived that blast."

Connor shakes his head. "That car bomb was meant for you, son. You and Emma were going to drive it to the airport shortly. Didn't I see you give your keys to the valet just a few minutes ago?"

Mick's chest constricts. He feels like he's about to retch. "Yes. Kevin said that the van with the wedding cake couldn't get through with the way everyone parked. He said the easiest way was to move just one vehicle—mine."

Mick pinches the bridge of his nose in an attempt to stop the prickling in his eyes. "Oh, my God. What have I done?"

Connor places a hand on his son's shoulder and squeezes. "You had no way of knowing that this was going to happen. None."

The sirens coming closer overlay the car alarms. Two police cruisers and a firetruck speed up the lane from the Pines & Quill entrance gate. Newspaper and television vans follow.

"The press has caught wind of the explosion," Mick says. "Probably from their police band radios."

The men hear the unmistakable whir of chopper blades and look up at the sky. They see a news helicopter hovering like a fat bumblebee through the dissipating smoke.

Joe says, "I called in a crime unit. They'll be here soon."

Officers Chris Lang and Herb Johnson exit their squad car. "What the hell happened?" Johnson asks.

Before anyone can answer, Lang says, "The last time I was out here, I had to be buzzed in."

Officer Toni Bianco approaches from the second unit. She looks at Mick and then nods down the lane. "You must have engaged 'party-mode' on the entrance gate today so that your guests and the wedding vendors could come and go."

In his peripheral vision, Mick sees Joe clench and unclench his fists. *He's livid. The four of us know that Bianco's a dirty cop working for Gambino. But we agreed to keep it to ourselves while we investigate and find iron-clad evidence to bust her and any other minions he has planted in the precinct.*

Mick pauses before answering. "Yes. Anyone can gain

access to Pines & Quill this afternoon. Got any ideas who might have done this?"

Bianco shakes her head. "Nope. None." She takes a deep whiff, then wrinkles her nose. She strolls over to the still-smoking remains of the Jeep. Covering her mouth with her arm, she bends down and peers through the frame. "Looks like we need to call the meat wagon too."

———

Joe holds up his hands at the stunned wedding guests making their way en masse toward the devastation that Officers Langley and Johnson are cordoning off with yellow crime scene tape. Many of them are crying.

"Let's all head to the pavilion and have a seat. Unfortunately, this is a crime scene now. We need to interview each of you and get your statements."

Wringing a white bar towel, Dean—one of the two college students Mick hired to do double-duty as parking valet and bartender—asks, "Hey, where's my buddy, Kevin?"

"What do you mean, 'interview' us?'" someone from the gathering crowd interjects.

"You might have seen something that's helpful," Joe says. "Don't hold back. Every detail, even seemingly insignificant, is important."

"What happened?" one of the quartet members asks.

The Crime Scene Unit is bagging evidence and snapping photos. Some of them have the emotionally arduous task of recovering human remains. *The last thing they need is onlookers.* Joe's attention returns to the question. "I'll share what little we know once we're seated in the pavilion."

Joe turns to the guys. "Let's divide and conquer. Mick, you take people who aren't your family—the photographer, the quartet, catering personnel, the florist, the person driving the bakery van, and the valet.

"Rafferty, if you'd also take people who aren't your family—the priest, my wife Marci, Mick's nephew and his fiancée, Ian and Fiona, Mick's sister and brother-in-law, Libby and Niall, and his parents, Maeve and Connor. I'll take people who aren't my family—Emma, her parents, Philip and Maureen, her brothers, Eric, Ethan, Ellery, her friend Sally, and Tom. I think that's everyone. Now let's go."

"What about me?" Bianco asks.

Joe lowers his voice so the wedding guests can't hear. He points at his ex-partner. "Wait here for the Crime Scene Unit, the ME, and the 'meat wagon' as you so crudely put it. Make sure that nobody crosses the tape."

Marci looks across the pavilion to where her husband, Joe, is interviewing his group of people. *I'm so glad we didn't bring the girls with us today. At thirteen and eleven, Carly and Brianna have a broad idea of what their dad does—law enforcement— but they don't know the extent of how unsafe and ugly it can get.*

She turns back to her group. Seated on her left is Father Burke, Ian, and Fiona. On her right are Libby and Niall, and Maeve and Connor.

After fifteen years of being married to a cop, Marci has learned to observe details. She's come to appreciate how important they are.

She looks at Rafferty facing them from the front of their half-circle. Before he takes a seat, Marci guesses that he's just over six feet tall. His black pants, peach button-down shirt, and tie complement his firm-looking build. *He wears his age well. He could be anywhere from his late thirties to his mid-forties. But from the dusting of gray at his temples, it's probably the latter. Either that, or it's from the stress from his job. His short brown hair is unruly. Behind wire-rimmed glasses are intense, brown eyes. But there's a sadness in them too.*

Rafferty removes his glasses and rubs his eyes. *I've seen a lot of terrible stuff go down in my time at the bureau, but a car bomb at a wedding beats it all.* His head aches. *I'm glad I didn't wear contacts today.*

"Father Burke, you had the advantage of standing at the front of the pavilion, giving you the best view of everyone. Did you see anything that struck you as even remotely unusual?"

The priest rubs his ears. "Can you please repeat the question? My ears are still ringing from the blast."

Rafferty's repeated question sparks a lively conversation between his eight interviewees. He pulls his chair closer, making notes on his cell phone. Every time he hears something that might be a hint of a lead, he follows it with more questions.

Joe sits backward on his chair, facing his group. *I'm sick about what's happened. And on today of all days.* He looks at Emma first. Hemingway's lying protectively on the floor at her feet. They're in the center of a semicircle of chairs.

On Emma's left are her friend Sally and her parents, Philip and Maureen. Her brothers, Eric, Ethan, and Ellery, on her right.

Joe's gaze travels back to Emma. *Most brides would be hysterical at what happened today. She reminds me of my Marci. She may fall apart afterward, but she exudes calm and focus when it counts. Mick's a lucky man.*

Joe doesn't have to ask too many questions before his group begins talking among themselves, comparing what they observed. He absorbs every detail. Unfortunately, nothing seems to have a loose thread he can pull and follow where it leads.

Emma's heartsick. *I didn't get close enough to see for sure, but it looked like it was Mick's Jeep that got blown up.* "Joe, was it Mick's Jeep that exploded?"

Joe looks into Emma's green eyes and nods. "Yes, Emma. Unfortunately, it was."

Was the bomb meant for me? For Mick? Or for both of us? If it was meant for me, then this is the third time. Jason Hughes would have killed me in El Cañón del Diablo—The Devil's Canyon—if Mick hadn't shot him first. A sniper tried to shoot me on the whale-watching tour. The only reason he missed is that Mick pushed me onto the deck. And now a car bomb. What is it they're afraid I know?

Emma's oldest brother, Eric, leans forward. His face is painted with disbelief at what's happened at his baby sister's wedding. "Why on earth would anyone blow up Mick's car?"

"That's what we're going to find out," Joe answers before asking more questions.

Emma feels Hemingway nudge her with his wet nose. Cupping his whiskered face, she looks into his dark-brown, almond-shaped eyes. He whines. Well-versed in "dog," Emma knows that though the blast scared Hemingway, his fear isn't so much for himself but for the "pack"—his people. *He wants to herd us together to keep track of us and protect us.* "We need to stay here right now." Emma motions for him to lie down. Once he settles, she reaches down and roughs the fur around Hemingway's neck.

Emma returns her attention to Joe. *He's a good listener. I appreciate the way he respectfully considers everyone's answers before moving on. He has an ease about him that cuts through even the worst tension. And though he's good at his job, I'm glad that Mick's on the case too. Between the three of them—Mick, Joe, and Rafferty—they'll get to the bottom of this.*

Mick takes a seat in front of his group—the wedding vendors and Linda Washington, their wedding photographer.

"Thank you for everything you've done on Emma's and my behalf. I'm so sorry this happened." He looks into their faces—all except one. A musician in the Jason Parker Quartet is trying to keep it together with his head between his legs. "I'm going to start by asking about the parking. I understand that the last vehicle to arrive was Pure Bliss Desserts."

The driver nods. "That's right. When I got here, I couldn't get through."

"Why didn't you park where you were?" Mick asks.

"There's no way I could carry a multitiered cake that far without losing it. I needed to get closer."

Mick nods his understanding.

"A young man who said he was the valet told me not to worry, that he'd take care of it right away. It wasn't but a few minutes later that he came back, smiled and gave me a thumbs-up, and then got into the Jeep. That's when it exploded." He shivers. "I'm glad I'd backed the van up to readjust my angle. Or I'd probably be dead too."

Dean looks at Mick, horror on his face. "Oh, my God. That's why I haven't seen Kevin. He's—" The young man's face melts in tears.

Mick lowers his gaze to his hands, giving the young man a moment.

Linda walks over and puts an arm around Dean's shoulders. "Besides you and Kevin, where's the other valet? I'm sorry, I didn't get his name."

Mick's head snaps up. "What other valet?"

"The young man in the parking area who asked me not to take any photos of him. He said he was camera shy."

Mick looks at Dean. "Did someone else come with you and Kevin?"

"No, it was just the two of us."

Mick stands up. A surge of excitement flows through his veins. "Thank you, everyone, that'll be all for right now. Linda, please stay a moment. I need to speak with you about your cameras."

"Those?" She points to the two cameras on the seat she'd vacated. "What would you like to know? They're both Hasselblads. One's film and one's digital."

"Did you get *any* photographs of the young man who asked you not to?"

Mick sees the heat rise in her cheeks. "Yes. I got a few candid shots before he said he was camera shy. But he didn't know I'd taken them. I didn't say anything because he seemed so angry. I took them with the digital and was going to delete them tonight."

"Thank God you didn't. You may have photographed the person who rigged the car bomb."

CHAPTER 4

"The secret of getting ahead is getting started. The secret of getting started is breaking your complex, overwhelming tasks into small, manageable tasks, and then starting on the first one."

—MARK TWAIN

Dr. Jill Graham, the chief medical examiner, pulls her head and shoulders out of the smoking skeleton of Mick's Jeep. *My son, Jim, is a student at Western Washington University. They'd be about the same age.* She looks up at the June blue sky to collect herself. *I hate this part of my job.*

She mentally removes her heart from her sleeve, then looks at Mick, Joe, and Rafferty. All business now, she says, "In this instance, you don't need my professional opinion. But I'll give it to you anyway. The blast killed the victim. It blew him apart."

After peeling off her latex gloves, she drops them into a biohazard bag. Breaking eye contact, she gestures at the surrounding area dotted with smoldering debris. "The young man you say was Kevin Pierce is literally scattered in pieces. It's a good thing you know who he was because there's not much left for his family to identify."

Mick watches the last of the guest and vendor vehicles drive down the tree-arched lane toward the entrance. Two of the cars are on transport trucks because they're not drivable. Libby arranged Uber rides for the owners of those vehicles. Mick shakes his head. *The insurance paperwork is going to be a nightmare.*

After extracting promises from the arson investigators, the ME, and the CSI team to keep him abreast of their findings, Mick trails behind their vehicles on foot to the entrance gate, where he closes and secures it.

He lowers his shoulders on the walk back, trying to ease the bow-tight tension between his scapulas. *A news crew was escorted off the property earlier by Joe, who'd made a brief statement. "There was an explosion. Bruce Simms, the chief of police, will update you when we have more details."*

Mick's grateful that he and Emma booked rooms at the MoonDance Inn for the overflow of family and friends who wouldn't fit into Dickens and Thoreau—the two empty cottages at Pines & Quill. *The July group of writers in residence arrives in less than a week.*

Emma and Hemingway rush out to meet him when he reaches the circular drive in front of the main house. *She's the most beautiful woman I've ever seen.* Mick gathers her close to his chest. Emotion closes his throat. *It could have been her. It could have been us. Who wants us dead? Why?*

Emma's doctor said that her "selective amnesia" is a common condition for people who've suffered a traumatic event—in Emma's case, being held hostage by Jason Hughes, also known as Alex Berndt. Whatever her subconscious mind is protecting her from is what the killer thinks she knows, and it's somehow incriminating to them.

Hemingway circles the couple, trying to wedge his bearded muzzle between them so he can get in on the attention. After several unsuccessful attempts, he trots away, his attention caught by tantalizing scents in the nearby bushes.

Emma leans back and looks up into Mick's eyes. "That bomb was for us, wasn't it?"

Mick pulls her back in close and speaks into her hair. *It smells fresh and citrusy, like lime, with a hint of vanilla.* "My dad thinks so, and I do too. We were the only people who were supposed to be in the Jeep." Mick glances at his watch. "And it wouldn't have been too long from now."

Emma places her palm on Mick's chest. "I'm going to our cabin. I need to change the flight and hotel reservations."

"Emma, I don't want you to be alone. The person who rigged that bomb could be hiding somewhere on the property."

"You don't need to worry, Mick. My parents and brothers are there. By the way, do you have a feel for how long I should push out our reservations?"

"I need to talk with the guys about the next steps in the ongoing investigation of Gambino. And after our honeymoon in New Orleans, I need to work on Pam and Kyle Williams's disappearances. I promised their parents. They live there, so it's the perfect opportunity. But I'd like to be here for Kevin's funeral."

Mick's gaze locks onto Hemingway in the distance. "I feel responsible for Kevin's death. Just like I'm responsible for Sam's death."

Emma wraps her arms around Mick's neck. "If the daily coin flip with your partner, Sam, had come up tails, *you* would have been the one driving the squad car. Not Sam. *You* would have been the person the sniper killed. Not Sam. Mick, you had no way of knowing. Just like today. You couldn't possibly have known that someone put a bomb in the Jeep. If it hadn't needed to be moved so the bakery van could make it through, we—the intended target—would have gotten in it to drive to the airport."

Linda Washington, the photographer, approaches Mick and Emma. "I'm sorry to interrupt. I know you want to look at the photos I took. I just want you to know that I'll be back in a few minutes. I want to check on Tom. He looked sick when I saw him heading to Austen cottage."

"If there's anything I can help with or that he needs," Mick says, "just let me know. Otherwise, we'll see you back at the main house in a little while."

They watch Linda walk toward Austen cottage.

Emma's brow furrows. "I hope everything will be okay."

"Tom was a munitions expert in the Marines. I'm sure the explosion has surfaced unpleasant memories."

Mick pulls back a little way from Emma to see her better. "Speaking of munitions, this morning, your dad and brothers told me you could 'shoot the whiskers off a gnat at fifty yards.'"

"I've been shooting with them since I was a little girl, so I'd better be a decent shot by now." Emma stands on her tiptoes and kisses the end of Mick's nose. "I might as well tell you right now that I'm pretty darned good at fishing too." She grins. "Now, to get back to our honeymoon. Do you think if I push everything out two weeks, that will work?"

"How about one week? We can always change the reservations again if needed."

"I love you, Mr. McPherson," Emma says against his lips.

"I love you too, Mrs. McPherson."

Joe releases his wife from a bear hug, then leans down and puts his forehead on hers. "I'm not sure what time I'll be home tonight."

Marci tips her head up and looks into his dark, pain-filled eyes. "How are you going to get there if I take the car?"

"I'll catch a ride with Rafferty."

"And here I thought your promotion to homicide detective would keep you safer."

"I nev—"

Marci places a finger across Joe's lips. "Shh, I love you, no matter what. And I understand your need to find whoever's behind all of the killings. Just come home to me and our girls alive and well." She blinks—a long, slow flutter of dark eyelashes against her cheeks. "That's all I ask."

She grabs him by the back of his head, pulls him in, and kisses him soundly.

Joe returns the kiss, his hands on her face, gripping her tightly, holding her close, determined never to lose her.

Tension drains from Mick's body when he smells Niall's homemade chicken soup and yeasty biscuits. The delicious aroma threads the air in the main house's kitchen. *This is what "home" smells like.*

Mick kneels to unlace his shoes. Every scratch and divot, a history of purpose and bustling activity, reads like braille in the wide, buttery pine boards of the floor in his brother-in-law's sanctuary.

His gaze shifts to the exhausted faces of the people seated around the oak table. His parents Maeve and Connor McPherson, and his sister Libby, sit on one side of the table. Across from them are his best friends. Joe Bingham is a Bellingham homicide detective. Sean Rafferty, a Seattle-based special agent with the FBI. The three of them are working on

Paddy MacCullough's murder case—the tip of the iceberg in a string of other deaths and possibly the disappearances of Pam and Kyle Williams. The common denominator is the crime boss, Georgio "The Bull" Gambino, with help from Toni Bianco, a dirty cop. Seated next to Joe and Rafferty is the writer/photographer Linda Washington.

Emma takes a seat next to Libby.

Hemingway joins her, laying his bearded chin across her feet.

Mick turns when his apron-clad brother-in-law joins them with a pot of fresh-brewed coffee. "That smells delicious, Niall. Thank you."

Niall fills the thick, sage-colored mugs at each place setting around the large oak table. Handcrafted by Emma, a gifted potter, they were a present to him and Libby. "You're welcome. I'm putting together a simple meal. It'll be ready soon."

Mick looks at Emma. "Speaking of food. Thank you for arranging with the caterer to pack up the wedding food and have their van follow Father Burke to St. Barnabas to set up a buffet in the soup kitchen."

Emma looks up from stroking the wiry hair on Hemingway's back. "You're welcome. I didn't want it to go to waste, and I know it'll get put to good use."

Turning his attention to Linda, Mick asks, "How's Tom doing?"

"He's not doing well. I think the blast triggered his PTSD. He said it brought back strong memories, and he feels like he's living through the explosion that took his legs all over again. He asked me to come back and stay with him when we finish."

"We won't keep you long then. Thank you for bringing your cameras. You said that you took a few photographs of the unknown valet—the one who asked you not to take his photo because he's camera shy."

Linda tucks a strand of ash brown hair behind her ear. "That's right."

"Would you please find those shots and transfer them to Libby's laptop?" Mick asks. "That way, we can save time by looking at them as a group on the larger laptop screen."

Libby heads to her office to get her laptop.

Linda rummages through her camera bag and extracts a USB cord.

When Libby returns, she sits in the chair next to Linda.

It only takes a minute for Linda to transfer the photos from her camera to the laptop. "Those three are the only photos I took of the guy. If you wouldn't mind, I'd like to get back to Tom."

"Thank you so much, Linda. This is what we need. Libby can take it from here."

After Linda leaves, Joe says, "We seem to have caught a lucky break."

"With the photos?" Rafferty asks.

"That too," Rafferty says. "But I got a call earlier. We got a lead on the 'Family First' tattoos."

Mick leans in. "What is it?"

"A dead body, for starters," Joe says. "Angelo—'Angel'— Romano, the owner of Tit 4 Tat Tattoo Studio in Bellingham, was found dead in his office this morning. According to Lang and Johnson, the first officers on the scene, the file drawers were open. It looked like someone used an egg beater on them. But that's not all." Joe rubs the palms of his hands together. "The Vic has a tattoo on his lower back. I'll give you one guess what it says."

"Family First," they say in unison.

Emma stands up. "I wonder who did his ink?"

Mick arches an eyebrow. "His *ink?*"

"Hey, I'm a potter. We get our hands dirty. We know things." Emma hides a smile behind the rim of her coffee mug.

"We're getting close," Joe says, "or they wouldn't have killed one of their own."

"You said, 'for starters.' What else have you got?" Rafferty asks.

Joe looks at Emma. "This may answer your question about his *ink*. It appears that 'Angel' had connections with two other tattoo studios. One of them is Hell or High Water Tattoo in New Orleans."

Mick's head snaps up. "Where the missing siblings, Pam and Kyle Williams, live. And where the person posing as Pam Williams flew in from for her writing residency at Pines & Quill."

"That's right. And where you and Emma are going for your honeymoon," Joe says. "You need to hightail it out of here and follow up on this lead while it's still hot."

Mick pushes his hands deep into his pockets. "Right after Kevin's funeral."

"You said 'connections with *two* other tattoo studios.' Where's the other one?" Rafferty asks.

"Black Heart Tattoo in San Francisco."

Mick shakes his head. "Well, it's come full circle then. It all started there with the death of my partner, Sam."

"I've got this one," Connor says. "Maeve and I fly back to San Francisco in the morning. I may be retired from the FBI, but you never forget how to follow a lead."

Joe nods. "That would be great, Connor. Thank you."

Libby tucks a strand of hair behind her ear. "The photos are ready."

Once everyone gathers behind her chair, Libby expands the first shot to fill the screen. The image was taken from the back as the valet opens the car door for a smiling Father Burke. The second photo captures the valet's right profile. In it, he's stepped back to let Father Burke get out of the car.

Mick senses Joe tense. He watches him lean in closer, squint, and adjust his glasses.

The third photo captures the valet seated in the car. His left profile is to the camera.

"Can you enlarge that a bit and home in on what looks like a tattoo behind his ear?" Joe asks, his voice taut with excitement.

Libby's fingers make a few keyboard strokes. "How's that?"

"Well, I'll be damned," Joe says.

They all turn to Joe, whose white-knuckled hand grasps the back of Libby's chair.

Mick puts a hand on his shoulder. "Who is it?"

CHAPTER 5

"Where secrets are concerned, the idea is to dole them out like pieces of Thanksgiving pumpkin pie. If you do so thoughtfully, readers won't mind waiting a year for another slice."

—TESSA WEGERT

Joe strokes his throat and grimaces. "To answer your question, Mick, the 'valet' in the photo is Emilio Acardi, a Bellingham Police officer. Like Bianco, he must be on Gambino's payroll too."

Shifting his gaze from Mick to Emma, Joe continues. "And he wants one or both of you dead."

All heads lift in unison as the landline in the kitchen rings, startling everyone.

Niall wipes his hands on his apron. "I'll get it."

"This isn't the end of it," Connor says. "If Gambino's ordered the hit, he can't lose face. He'll make certain that someone sees it through."

Maeve places a hand on her husband's. "I wish it weren't true, but your dad's right, Mick. This isn't the end of it."

Joe mulls over her words. *Who else is on Gambino's payroll? How deep is his presence rooted into the precinct? Is Bruce Simms, the chief of police, in "The Bull's" pocket?* Joe mops his forehead with the crisp handkerchief Marci tucked into his suit coat this morning for the wedding. *Was the wedding just this morning? It seems like days ago.*

Niall returns to the dining area. "That was Linda. The explosion has taken a toll on Tom. She feels it would be better if he wasn't alone, so she's staying the night with him in Austen cottage. He's decided to fly home tomorrow, and she's going with him to make sure he gets there okay and help settle him back in. She said they'd both feel better if there was a police presence at Pines & Quill tonight. She even offered her cottage if that would help."

"I wondered where we were going to stay tonight," Emma says. "We were supposed to fly to New Orleans, so we gave our cabin to my brothers for the night. My parents are in Thoreau, and Sally's in Dickens. They all fly back to San Diego in the morning."

Libby looks at her parents. "The guest room here in the main house is taken too. Mom and Dad are staying with us."

"Our flight back to San Francisco is in the morning," Maeve says.

Mick pushes up his sleeves. "It looks like we're staying in Brontë tonight."

Hemingway lifts his chin from Emma's feet and thumps his tail against the floor.

"No way, mister," Niall says. "You're staying here."

Rafferty looks from Joe to Niall. "I don't have a wife and family to get home to. I'll stay and patrol the grounds. Can I bunk on the couch in the Ink Well?"

Joe rubs the whiskers on his jawline. *I do have a wife and family to go home to. I wonder how hard my being a homicide detective is on them? I don't know about the girls, but Marci's aware that I could get killed any day. That has to be hard on her, but she never complains.*

Joe shifts his gaze to Emma. *I wonder how well she'll stand up to the emotional strain of being married to a private investigator who helps law enforcement solve crimes?*

"Our home is your home," Niall says to Rafferty.

Joe turns to Rafferty. "Then can I borrow your car? Marci took ours. I'd planned on hitching a ride with you."

"Sure. Just pick me up in the morning. But wait until *after* breakfast. I don't want to miss Niall's cooking."

Joe claps Rafferty on the back. "I'll make sure to be here *in time* for breakfast."

Toni presses the cell phone to her ear to hear better.

"Well?" Gambino asks.

"The car bomb went off, exactly as you ordered."

"Do I hear a 'but' coming?" Gambino asks.

"Unfortunately, Mick and Emma weren't in the Jeep. A val—"

"What do you mean they weren't in the goddamn Jeep? If it wasn't them, who was it?"

"A valet needed to move the car so the bakery van with the wedding cake could get through."

"So you're saying the job was botched. *You* were in charge of overseeing this hit, Bianco. What do *you* intend to do about it?"

Toni clears her throat. "There's more, sir. Emilio Acardi said a photographer was all over the place taking candid shots. He doesn't think she got any of him, but he's not sure. What he knows is that she got a good look at his face. She's a potential witness who can identify him."

"Do I need to do *all* of your thinking?" Gambino barks. "What are *you* going to do about this royal fuckup?"

"I'm going to have Acardi go back to Pines & Quill tonight, sneak into Brontë cottage where Linda Washington, the photographer, is staying, get her cameras and eliminate the potential witness."

"Good. Make sure he doesn't screw this up. I'd have *you* do it, but the risk's too great. No one, and I mean *no* one, can know that you're on my payroll. Having a mole like you inside the station house of Bellingham's finest allows me access to information I wouldn't otherwise have. And it helps me make the police look like bumbling idiots."

"He'll do it right," Bianco says. "If he doesn't, I'll dispose of him myself."

———

Mick works at keeping the worry from his face. *I'm afraid for my family. There have been three attempts on Emma's life—in the cave in El Cañón del Diablo, onboard the Odyssey, and now a car bomb.* Mick realizes his fists are clenched and relaxes his hands. *And the person posing as a writer in residence, Pam Williams, was killed right here at Pines & Quill, what's supposed to be a haven.*

Mick jams his hands into his pockets. *I need to protect my family.* "Rafferty, we'll patrol in shifts. Each of us will take watch two hours on and two hours off."

His gaze shifts to Hemingway, and Mick pats his thigh.

With an expectant look on his face and his tail waving, the massive Irish wolfhound comes to his side. Hemingway's ready for whatever's next.

Mick roughs the wiry hair on the dog's back. "And we'll take this big lug on our rounds. Not only is he good company, but he can also see, hear, and smell what we can't."

Rafferty leans forward. "It sounds good to me."

"After we eat," Mick says, "I'll head to the cabin to get my gun and one for Emma."

Libby raises one of her eyebrows. "One for Emma?"

"Trust me, sis. Her father and brothers informed me this morning that my bride can 'shoot the whiskers off a gnat at fifty yards.'"

Libby turns to look at Emma. She sees a smile pull at her sister-in-law's lips. "I was already impressed with you, but this raises the already high bar even higher."

"Rafferty, I don't suppose you brought your gun," Mick says.

The FBI agent opens the left side of his suit coat, revealing a leather cross-draw holster and the butt of a Sig Sauer P229. Rafferty gives Mick a white-toothed smile. "You suppose wrong."

Just then, Niall enters the dining area with a steaming tureen of homemade chicken soup and sets it in the table's center. "It's self-serve, so dig in, and don't be shy. I'll be right back."

Mick's nostrils flare in appreciation as they take in the chicken's heady fragrance combined with herbs and vegetables.

Joe pats his stomach. "Oh, man. That has to be one of the most comforting smells that come out of a kitchen."

Niall returns a moment later. The heat from the stove flushes his cheeks. In one hand, he holds a platter piled high with homemade biscuits. In the other, a bowl of freshly whipped honey butter.

Libby shakes her head; amusement sparkles her sapphire blue eyes. "I don't know, Joe. I think it's a close call with the yeasty smell of Niall's biscuits."

Conversation ebbs and flows around the table as they enjoy a meal of comfort food—Niall's specialty.

"This is delicious, Niall," Maeve, his mother-in-law, says.

"I second the motion," Connor says around a bite of soft, flaky biscuit he'd slathered with sweet butter. Turning to his daughter, he continues. "By the way, Libby, what's the plan for transportation to the airport in the morning. Should we call Uber? By my count, there's ten of us flying out."

Libby's eyebrows raise. "Ten?"

"Your mom and me, Emma's parents, her three brothers, her best friend Sally, and now Tom and Linda."

"Oh, my gosh, Dad, you're right. And the Pines & Quill van can only seat eight, plus luggage."

"I'd offer the Jeep," Mick says, but—" He holds up his empty hands.

"When Joe picks me up in the morning," Rafferty says, "we'll use my rental and take Tom and Linda to the airport."

Libby walks around the table and gives Rafferty a big hug. "Thank you. Thank you. Thank you," she says, each thanks punctuated by a kiss on alternating cheeks.

Everyone laughs when they see the tips of his ears heat up.

Mick scoots his chair back and looks out the window. Dusk is setting in, making it dark in the shadow of the trees. He looks at his watch, then shoots a glance over his shoulder. "Rafferty, I'll meet you in the circular drive in ten minutes. The three of us"—he nods toward Hemingway—"will walk the property so you can refamiliarize yourself with the location of each cottage while there's still a bit of light. Right now, I'm heading to the cabin for those guns."

Emma tips her head back and takes a deep breath of cool night air. The sky is that deep velvet blue that speaks of midnight or close to it. She squeals with delight as Mick whisks her into his arms and carries her over the threshold of Brontë cottage. She laughs into his neck. "I wasn't expecting that."

"Who wouldn't carry their bride over the threshold on her wedding night?" Mick asks as he toes the door shut behind them and takes Emma to the bedroom, laying her on the freshly made bed.

Emma wraps her arms around Mick, pulling him close. His hands seem to be everywhere at once. His lips hot on her skin, raining kisses on her neck, the hollow of her throat. She closes her eyes and strokes his back, which is warm, smooth, and incredibly inviting. The tension in her body is wired so high her limbs start shaking. Then her body turns to fire as stars burst behind her eyelids.

Afterward, they lie together beneath the tangled covers, and he holds her as they enjoy the shared silence.

Emma feels Mick start when she nudges his shoulder. "You need to get going," she whispers, nodding toward the nightstand. "According to the clock, you need to relieve Rafferty in ten minutes." Emma concentrates on her breathing. *Inhale through my nose, exhale through my mouth to keep from shaking like a leaf in a windstorm. I don't want Mick to go. We were both targeted today. I'm afraid that someone's going to try again.*

"But I don't want to go," Mick groans. He collects her back into his arms and kisses her slowly.

I want to be a good wife. I want to show Mick that I'm strong, courageous, and support his work even if I'm scared that he might not come back. "I don't want you to go either," Emma says, "but it's your turn to make the rounds. I'll be right here when you get back." *Please return to me.*

Mick nods toward his holdout gun next to the clock on the nightstand—a P938 that's small enough for an ankle carry. "Don't hesitate to use it."

"I won't," Emma promises while watching Mick dress by moonlight at the foot of the bed.

He returns to Emma in the shadow of pillows and warm blankets and kisses her soundly before leaving. "I'll be back in two hours," he says, his voice low and husky all at once.

"I'll be waiting," Emma says, hoping her smile covers the dread she feels at her core.

Toni places a manicured hand on Emilio Acardi's solid arm. "Stop the car here." Nodding through the windshield toward the line of trees in the far distance, she continues. "Let's go over it one more time. Tell me what you're going to do."

"Again?" Emilio whines.

"Again," Toni says.

"I'm going to cut through those trees on the north side of Pines & Quill and then head east, staying clear of the lit pathways. The first building I come to is a workshop. The second building is the cottage where the photographer's staying. I'll know it's the right cottage because there's a carved sign to the right side of the door on each cottage. I'll verify it's 'Brontë' before entering."

"So far, so good," Toni says. "Then what?"

"I'll let myself in. If the door's locked," Emilio says, patting his shirt pocket, "I'll pick it. Then I'll locate the cameras, slit the photographer's throat, grab the cameras on my way out, and meet you back here." His chest puffs up a bit. "I bet I can do it in under fifteen minutes."

Toni's fingernails—like tiny hot-pink bayonets—dig into Emilio's flesh. "Don't get cocky. Arrogance breeds mistakes."

Moonlight spills over the hood of Emilio's black muscle car—a 1982 Camaro Z28 he'd rebuilt. Before he touched it, it accelerated from 0 to 60 mph in 9.4 seconds, finished the quarter-mile in 17.10 seconds at 80 mph, and stopped from 60 mph in 149 feet. After working his magic, it practically flies.

Toni looks at her watch. *It's almost 3:00 a.m.—The Devil's Hour*, she muses. "It's time."

Emilio reaches for his keys in the ignition.

Toni places her hand on his. "Leave them. I'll slip into the driver's seat in the event we need to haul ass when you return."

Emilio shrugs. "Have it your way."

Toni smiles. *I always do.*

A floorboard squeaks. Emma cocks her head. *Mick can't be back already.* She looks toward the bedroom doorway. A man's silhouette fills the frame.

Slants of moonlight sneak in between the vertical blinds on the bedroom window, painting stripes across a man's face. Not Mick's.

Emma's eyes lock onto the glint of a knife blade in his hand. Stinging prickles start in her extremities and spread over her body, setting every nerve on fire. Her breathing turns shallow, and her heart beats erratically. The skin on her face draws tight, and her chest feels like it's in a vice.

"Where are the cameras?" the man growls.

"What cameras?" she asks from the darkness of the bed. Then it dawns on her. *This guy thinks I'm Linda.*

The man steps closer, raising the blade.

Fighting hard to keep the tendrils of panic from taking hold, Emma rolls and grabs the pistol from the nightstand. Arms outstretched, she flicks the safety off. In her mind's eye, she's at the range, hands steady, the target square in her sight. She hears her dad, "On the exhale, gently squeeze the trigger." Calm now, she says, "Drop the knife."

"Or what?" the man taunts.

"Or I'll shoot."

"Oh, right. Like you've got a gun," the man sneers into the shadows and steps closer.

Emma pulls the trigger.

The man grabs the left side of his head. Startled surprise wipes the sneer from his face. "You bitch. You shot my fucking ear off!"

"Just the lobe," Emma says. "That was a warning. Now get out before I shoot to kill."

The man doesn't hesitate. He turns and bolts.

At the sound of a gunshot, Toni turns the key in the ignition and guns the engine. It roars to life. She lets it idle, purring like a lion.

She opens the driver's door and steps out. Easing the pistol from her shoulder holster, Toni positions herself—arms straight out—over the top of the car, one foot braced on the door frame.

In the distance, a man dashes from the tree line into the clearing. *It's Emilio.* Like steel coupling rods on an express train of days gone by, his arms pump rapidly. *He's empty-handed— the fool.*

A minute later, a large beast—*that goddamned dog, Hemingway*—launches into the clearing. In a heartbeat, two men are on his tail.

Toni gets Emilio in her sight. She savors the moment: her favorite one—the delicious blink of time before squeezing a trigger.

Mick and Rafferty race behind Hemingway. His powerful strides devour the distance between him and the man he's chasing. *Oh, my God,* Mick thinks, *the last time Hemingway chased a man off the property, he was shot at.* Before they catch up to him, a gunshot reverberates, and the man drops to the ground.

Hemingway positions himself over the man.

An engine roars. Red taillights grow smaller in the distance.

When Mick and Rafferty reach Hemingway and his quarry, Mick signals him to stand down.

Rafferty trains his gun on the man as Mick toes him over.

The man's eyes—with a bullet hole in between—stare blankly at the moonlit sky. Blood oozes from what remains of his left ear.

"It's the guy in the photos Linda took," Mick says. "The third valet."

CHAPTER 6

"Over the years, I've found one rule. It is the only one I give on those occasions when I talk about writing. A simple rule. If you tell yourself you are going to be at your desk tomorrow, you are by that declaration asking your unconscious to prepare the material. You are, in effect, contracting to pick up such valuables at a given time. Count on me, you are saying to a few forces below: I will be there to write."

—NORMAN MAILER

"This damn 'smart phone' isn't so smart," Toni growls as the latex gloves on her hands prevent touch recognition on the keypad. "Siri," she says. "Call Bobby's cell."

Even though it's the middle of the night—Toni checks her watch. *Correction. Make that extremely early morning—* the recipient picks up after the second ring.

"I suspect you need help," says a neutral voice. "Who do you want this time? Bobby with a 'y' or Bobbi with an 'i'?

"With an 'i,'" Toni says. "I need you to be me again."

"That's easy," the voice, now distinctly female, says. "You're a dead ringer for Liza Minnelli in her younger years— only with curly hair. She was part of my repertoire at the Baton."

Toni rolls her eyes. *I don't want to hear the whole damn spiel.* "You don't have to remind me, Bobbi. I'm aware of your fame." She's well aware that Bobbi headlined at the Baton Show Lounge in Chicago—America's premiere drag showcase. The nightclub features the best of the best female impersonation and male revue.

Bobbi can be such a bitch. To assure his agreement, Toni decides to butter him up. "The first time I saw the show, I couldn't believe my eyes. The men look more like women than most women. And to top it off, there's the singing and acting talent. You, of course, were the star."

Toni hears Bobbi purr with inflated delight.

"By the way, do you still have copies of my ID?"

"I do, Toni. But *your* kind of gorgeous is going to take some time."

"I'm going to book morning flights, so you don't have time. Be at the Departures terminal at Bellingham International by nine. I'll send electronic round-trip tickets to your phone. It's vital we aren't seen together."

"No problem, honey. If I lay eyes on you, I'll make sure our paths don't cross. By the way, where am I headed? And how long am I going to be gone? I need to know what kind of clothes to pack and how many outfits I'll need."

"You're flying as me to San Francisco for two weeks to stay with my mother. Poor dear, she fell and broke her hip. And don't worry, I'll cover all of your expenses."

"Oh, I do love me some Frisco," Bobbi squeals with delight. "Hey, I thought your mother was dead."

"She is," Toni says. "But that little nugget of information is only on a need-to-know basis, and nobody needs to know. By the way, do you have any ink on your body?"

"What, you mean like tattoos?"

"Yes, do you have any tattoos?"

"I have two. Why?"

"Is either one of them on your lower back?"

"No, girlfriend," Bobbi sounds affronted. "I do *not* have a tramp stamp."

"There's an extra ten thousand dollars in it for you if you'll get one. One that I specify."

"What's it a tattoo of?" Bobbi asks, caution lacing his voice.

"It's of a butterfly. An extremely intricate butterfly that's seven inches wide and five inches tall."

"Damn, that's a lot of ink."

"I'll send you a photo. It must be this *exact* tattoo. No exceptions. If you agree, I'll make the arrangements with the artist at Black Heart Tattoo in San Francisco." Toni hears the *whoosh* of the photo leaving her phone.

"Got it. Hold on a sec."

Toni hears Bobbi's intake of breath.

"Oh, honey. This is *gor-geous*. And you're paying *me* ten thousand dollars to get this tattoo?"

"That's right."

"What's the catch?"

"There is no catch. I have one on my back, and as my impersonator, you need to have one too. *He doesn't need to know I'm lying through my teeth. It'll be true soon enough.* "I'll send you half the money upfront, and the other half when the tattoo artist sends me a photo of it on your back."

"Consider it done." Bobbi's silent for a moment. "Am I going as you, the good cop with a stick stuck up her ass? Or the *real* you?"

"You're going as the good cop, minus the stick, wise ass.

I have a reputation to keep, Bobbi. You're my decoy. All eyes will be on you, so don't screw up."

"Honey, when I'm in the limelight, I never miss a beat," Bobbi says. "Where are you going, girlfriend?"

"That's on a need-to-know basis, too," Toni says. "And you don't need to know."

———

Mick speed dials Joe.

"This better be good," Joe mumbles.

"Remember the third valet?" Mick asks.

"Yes. Emilio Acardi. A dirty cop."

"His days of being dirty are over. He's dead."

The volume of Joe's voice escalates. "What do you mean, he's dead?"

"Hemingway chased him off the property with Rafferty and me on his heels. Just as he cleared the tree line, he was shot between the eyes. The only thing we saw were red taillights heading away in the distance."

"I'll call the ME and CSI team, and then I'm on my way. You realize this is the *second* body at Pines & Quill in less than twelve hours."

"We're going to get to the bottom of this, Joe. Hang on a second."

Mick turns to Rafferty. "I need to go to Emma. Will you stay here with Hemingway?"

Rafferty nods. "Sure. I sure wish I hadn't given up smoking. I could use a cigarette about now."

Mick gives Joe the gate code. "If you wait for the ME and CSI at the entrance gate, then you can let them in. I'll meet all of you at Brontë cottage. Then we'll head out to Rafferty and the body together."

Joe agrees. "Will you do me a favor?"

"Sure. What is it?"

"Check Acardi's lower back. I want to confirm my hunch."

"Hold on." Mick hands his cell phone to Rafferty, then rolls Acardi back over. He untucks the shirt from Acardi's waistband and tugs the leather belt, pulling the fabric away from the body.

"Hit the light on your cell phone, Rafferty."

Rafferty turns the light on and directs the beam beneath the pants' fabric.

Mick takes his cell back from Rafferty. "Your hunch was right, Joe. He's got a tattoo. It says, 'Family First.'"

When Mick rounds the bend in the pathway toward Brontë cottage, it's lit up like a lighthouse. Emma's standing on the front porch with a blanket wrapped around her shoulders.

Mick leaps the steps and pulls her against his chest. He wraps his arms tight around her. "Are you okay?"

She nods and manages a muffled "I shot his ear off" against his shirt.

Astonished, Mick leans back and looks at her.

"Your heart is racing," she points out, her hands splayed on his chest.

"That gunshot scared the life out of me."

"After he dropped the knife," Emma says, "I ran out here to see which way he went."

Mick pales. "The *knife?*"

"Yes. I heard a floorboard squeak and knew it was too soon for you to be back. When I looked, I saw a man in the bedroom doorway. The moonlight from the window illuminated his face, so I knew it wasn't you. He raised the knife and said, 'Where are the cameras?' That's when I realized he thought I was Linda. He'd come to take the wedding photographer's cameras.

"When he stepped closer, I rolled over and grabbed your pistol from the nightstand. I flicked the safety off and told him to drop the knife. He couldn't see me in the dark and didn't realize I had a gun aimed at him. I told him not to come any closer."

"Or what?" he said.

"That's when I told him I'd shoot. When he took another step, I aimed for his left ear and pulled the trigger. I told him it was a warning, and the next one would be a kill shot. That's when he turned and ran."

Mick pulls Emma even tighter into his embrace and buries his face in her hair. "Have I told you lately how much I love you, Mrs. McPherson?"

Joe rolls down his car window as Dr. Jill Graham, the chief medical examiner, steps out of the crime scene van and walks toward him. She looks at her watch. "Do you know what time it is?" she asks.

Joe glances at the dashboard and grimaces. "Looks like it's close to three o'clock in the morning."

She shakes her head. "Haven't you ever heard of office hours?"

"You know as well as I do that crime happens anytime without notice—day, night, and on the weekends." He frowns. "Even at weddings."

"Will the MacCulloughs and the McPhersons ever catch a break?" Jill asks. "First, it was Father Paddy, Niall's brother, shot to death in the confessional at St. Barnabas. Now they're after Emma, or Mick, or both."

"We're working on it," Joe says.

The doctor turns and walks back toward the team waiting in the van. "Lead the way," she calls over her shoulder.

Joe starts the ignition. *I'm afraid for Mick and Emma. Hell, I'm worried for everyone here. It's as if Pines & Quill and everyone associated with it has a target on their back.*

Headlights catch Mick's and Emma's attention. They turn to see Joe's car and the CSI van in the distance. Their beams wash over what looks like a scene from a zombie movie, people walking toward them en masse, their arms hanging loose at their sides.

Mick whispers. "We're not the only ones who heard the gunshots."

"Are you okay, honey?" Philip Benton, Emma's father, calls out.

"I'm okay, Dad."

"What happened, son?" Connor McPherson asks.

"There was an intruder in Brontë cottage." Mick turns to his brother-in-law, Niall, his eyes pleading an unspoken request.

Niall raises a hand. "I tell you what, folks. Let's all head up to the main house. I'll make some coffee and muffins while these folks"—he nods toward the ME and CSI team—"do what they've come to do." He turns to Joe. "I suspect Detective Bingham will have some questions for us, and it might be helpful if we're all in the same place at the same time."

"Thank you. That would be terrific," Joe says. "Once we finish, we'll join you at the main house."

Joe steps over to the newlyweds and leans toward Emma. "Until I've had a chance to talk with you, will you keep what happened to yourself?"

"That'll be easy," Emma says, "because I'm coming with you."

Joe looks to Mick. His eyebrows lift a fraction.

"She just went toe-to-toe with a killer. I wouldn't stand in her way."

———

Emma's pace is slow as she and Mick make their way through the woods toward Rafferty, Hemingway, and the body. When she trips on an exposed root, Mick catches her. "Are you okay, honey?"

Emma nods. "I'm just tired." She straightens and arches her back to relieve the pain. *Dr. Timmerman warned me about overdoing it. She said, "If you're not careful, you could find yourself back in your wheelchair. Slow and easy is the ticket."*

When Hemingway spots Emma stepping through the distant tree line, he breaks from Rafferty's side and bolts to her. Because of his height, he starts sniffing her above the waist and works his way around, assuring himself that she's okay. He wags his tail and shifts from side-to-side on his front paws. His eyes watch her every move.

Emma leans down and hugs his neck. *I don't want anyone to know how scared I am. I want Mick to be proud of me, so I need to appear strong, confident, and in control. But after that intruder, I'm a whisper away from coming unglued.* "I'm okay, big guy. Come on, let's go see Rafferty."

When Emma, Mick, Joe, the ME, and the CSI team reach Rafferty, Dr. Graham asks for details and then sends the techs to check for tire tread. "I've got this guy," she says, nodding toward the body on the ground.

Emma takes a deep breath of pine-scented air. *I wonder if this event is going to have any effect on my memory lapses? Dr. Timmerman explained that traumatic events trigger them, and tonight, I was scared out of my wits.*

The ME slips on evidence gloves then squats down, sitting on the back of her heels. She scans the prone body with a light, then turns to Mick and Rafferty and quirks a brow.

Mick holds his hands up. "Okay, you got me. I checked to see if he has a 'Family First' tattoo. He does."

"I'd appreciate it if you'd leave my job to me." When she turns back to the body, Rafferty mouths to Mick, "You're in trouble now."

Over her shoulder, Dr. Graham asks, "I don't suppose you know the identity of *this* victim like you did this morning's victim?"

Joe pipes up. "As a matter of fact, I do."

"*Really?*" she asks, surprise evident on her face. "I was being facetious."

"Unfortunately, he was a Bellingham Police officer."

Dr. Graham stands and snaps off her gloves. "Will someone please tell me what's going on?" She nods toward Emma and Mick. "This morning, a car bomb meant for one or both of you kills a college student instead. Now there's a dead police officer."

"A police officer who was going to kill me," Emma says. "I know you haven't gotten to it yet, but I shot his left earlobe off."

Graham steps over the body, squats down, and shines the light on the left side of the victim's head. She whistles. "That's a clean shot. Are you responsible for the kill shot too—the one between his eyes?"

Rafferty steps forward. "No. When Mick, Hemingway, and I were chasing him, a shot came from over there." He points toward where the techs are searching the ground with high-powered lights. "He fell to the ground, then a moment later we heard a car engine roar and saw red taillights fading in the distance."

"Hey, I found a shell casing," one of the techs call out.

The doctor nods toward Mick and Rafferty. "Obviously the shooter was in a hurry with you and Hemingway rushing from the tree line and didn't have time to find the casing after the shot."

"I wonder if the shooter was careless *before* that?" Emma says.

"How so?" the ME asks.

Emma points to the latex gloves in the doctor's hand. "Maybe they didn't wear gloves when they loaded their gun. If you dust the shell casing for prints, we might get lucky."

"*We?*" the doctor asks.

Emma looks into the ME's eyes and nods. In the hint of a smile on the doctor's face, Emma sees her approval level ratchet up a notch.

———

When possible, Toni takes backstreets and residential streets to avoid street cams as she drives Emilio Acardi's Camaro to his apartment complex and parks it. She leaves the keys in the ignition, exits the car, and takes care closing the driver's door.

After pulling her hat low and her collar up, she peels off her latex gloves and shoves them into her pockets, then brisk-walks twelve blocks where she gets into her own car and drives home. Again, avoiding street cams. *It's good being a cop. You know where all the "eyes" are.*

After an hour of keystrokes, a few phone calls, and two fingers of scotch, Toni sits back satisfied. *New Orleans is two cities, one gentrified and grand, the other devastated and despairing, both within a single municipal boundary.*

She raises her glass. *Gentrified and grand, here I come.* Toni yawns and stretches like a content cat. *I'm not about to have my "Family First" tattoo modified in squalor.*

CHAPTER 7

> *"And by the way, everything in life is writable about if you have the outgoing guts to do it, and the imagination to improvise."*
>
> —SYLVIA PLATH

L ibby backs into the comfortable shape of Niall's body under their covers and spoons against his warm embrace. "We just got into bed, and it's almost time to get up again."

"I know, dear. Before Joe, Mick, and Rafferty questioned our guests, they were tired. By the time they left, they were dog-whipped exhausted."

Hemingway thumps his tail against the floor on Niall's side of the bed.

"Our guests or the guys?"

Niall feels Hemingway's nose in his back. "Both."

"Poor Emma looks like a wrung-out dishrag," Libby says. "She can't take any more."

"I noticed that too." Niall shifts his weight. "Hemingway, lay back down. It's time to sleep."

Libby scoots toward the middle of the bed and rolls onto her back. "When we're up here in our bedroom, it seems like we're untouchable—like nothing bad can happen to us."

Niall takes her hand. "I wish that were true."

The second-floor master bedroom in the main house at Pines & Quill has two enormous skylights that drench the room in sunlight by day but allow them to peek at the stars at night. Bathed in moonlight, their upstairs haven beckons her to snuggle deeper under the lavender-scented sheets. Libby loves the lofty treehouse feel of this room—her favorite in the whole house. But in the wee hours of this morning, it's not enough to assuage her fears.

"I'm scared for Mick. He can't shoulder any more loss, Niall. He pulled me aside tonight and, with tears in his eyes, told me he feels responsible for *three* deaths."

"I know he's carrying a heavy burden over Sam's death. But he didn't have anything to do with it. Jason Hughes, a.k.a. Alex Berndt, admitted that it could have been *anyone* at the wheel of that squad car. All he needed to do was to kill a cop. Who on earth are the other two?"

Libby rolls over and looks into her husband's face. "Mick feels responsible for your brother's death and for Kevin, the young man who died in the car bomb after the wedding ceremony."

Niall pushes himself up onto his elbow and scowls. "He had *nothing* to do with Paddy being shot to death in the confessional. So far, it appears that crime boss, Gambino, thought Jason Hughes told Paddy something—a deathbed confession of sorts—in the ICU when Paddy sat with him on chaplaincy duty. Whatever it was, he had to be silenced.

"Whoever put a hit on Paddy also thinks Jason Hughes told Emma something when he held her hostage in the cave. Jason told Emma he was going to kill her and didn't have anything to lose. Whatever that information is must be incriminating."

Libby nods in agreement. "Mick's sick with worry that Emma's going to be the fourth person. The car bomb makes the third attempt on her life."

Niall's eyes droop shut. Enervated, he lays his head on his pillow. "I can't think about it anymore tonight, sweetness. And worrying isn't going to change anything. Let's try to get some sleep."

"You're right. Worrying won't change a thing. This day feels like a week, and I'm exhausted." Libby wiggles back into their spooning position, closes her eyes, and lets out a bone-weary sigh.

———

Bleary-eyed, Rafferty looks out the window. The morning is just beginning to glitter with freshly rinsed sunshine. He turns his wrist—*six o'clock. Only a few hours ago, there was another murder.* A sense of urgency kicks his heart rate up a notch. He starts thinking about today's tasks. *Check in with the ME. Get Linda and Tom to the airport by nine.* His nostrils flare. The delicious scent derails his train of thought. He follows the smell of bacon from the couch he was sleeping on in the Ink Well, to the dining area in the massive open-plan kitchen.

Joe unfolds himself from an overstuffed chair and follows suit.

Libby hands them each a steaming mug of fresh-brewed coffee. "Good morning. I heard a nasty rumor," she says, nodding toward Mick, "to never get between you gentlemen and your first cup of coffee in the morning."

Despite its heat, Rafferty takes a drink from his mug. "It's not a rumor. It's a fact." His eyes close in deep satisfaction, and his shoulders relax. "I think this is as close to heaven as we can get on this earth."

Still in his stocking feet, Joe sits at the table next to Maeve and nods his agreement.

Rafferty sees the keen worry on Joe's face. Dark crescents bruise the skin below his eyes. The line between his brows is trench-deep.

Rafferty runs a hand over his own face. What feels like a three-day beard graces his jaw. *Was it only twenty-four hours ago that I shaved, showered, and got dressed for Mick's and Emma's wedding?* He looks down at his clothes. His tie is open and pushed to the side of his untucked, wrinkled dress shirt. His pants look corrugated. He takes a seat at the table next to Connor. "How are you doing this morning?"

Connor clinks Rafferty's proffered mug. "I'd guess about the same as you. Hellish."

Shell-shocked, the men sip their coffee.

As Rafferty looks at the faces around the table—Mick, Emma, Connor, Maeve, Joe, and Libby—he does mental triage on his nerves. Gnawing anxiety grips his chest. *A car bomb went off yesterday that was meant for Mick, Emma, or both. It killed a college student instead. In the early hours of this morning, the dirty cop who planted the bomb was killed. The owner of Tit 4 Tat Tattoo Studio, Angelo Romano, was found dead. Vito Paglio, a.k.a. Salvatore Rizzo, was found dead at The Scrap Heap wrecking yard.*

Hemingway nudges Rafferty's leg for attention. Rafferty absently rubs one of the big dog's ears. *And that's only the tip of the iceberg. What lurks beneath the surface is even bigger. Twin brothers Alex and Andrew Berndt are both dead—one killed in prison, the other died in the hospital. As Jason Hughes, Alex was the tipping point for the entire fiasco when he killed Mick's partner, Sam. The sniper who tried to kill Emma on the Odyssey was found dead. The person impersonating Pam Williams was shot and killed right here at Pines & Quill. The real Pam Williams and her brother Kyle are both missing.*

Rafferty runs a hand through his hair. *That's nine deaths, and other than Kevin, the young man who died in the car bomb, the common denominator between the dead people is Gambino. I'm worried sick; we've got to figure this out before anyone else gets killed. After breakfast, Mick, Joe, and I need to strategize. Maybe it would save time if we split up, take the divide-and-conquer route.*

Apron-clad, Niall enters with two heaping platters. One is mounded with crisp bacon strips and scrambled eggs with chives, crème fraîche, and grated cheese, the other with warm, flaky buttermilk biscuits, a crock of whipped honey butter, and a little glass jug of warm maple syrup. The delicious scent of Niall's kitchen wizardry fills the air.

The sound of Hemingway's tail comes from under the massive table. It goes into overdrive, thumping against the buttery-colored pine boards of the floor.

Niall sets the platters on the table then looks at his watch. "Dig in, folks. In a *very* short amount of time, we've got to get ten people and their luggage to Bellingham International."

Rafferty nods. "Joe's with me, and we said we'd take Tom and Linda in my rental."

Libby nods. "The rest will easily fit in the van."

Niall rubs his hands together. "The day after tomorrow is the first of July, and a new group of writers in residence arrives for a three-week stay. We thought Tom was staying at Pines & Quill while Mick and Emma are on their honeymoon. But as you know, in light of what's happened, he's going back to Philadelphia."

Libby stands up and walks over to Niall. She slips an arm through his. "Rafferty, we thought that instead of you staying out at the MoonDance Inn, it would be easier for you guys to brief and debrief"—She nods toward Mick and Joe—"if you stay here."

Rafferty sets his mug down, then covertly slips a piece of bacon under the table, where it disappears from his fingers.

Libby tucks a phantom strand of hair behind her ear and turns to Niall. Everyone at the table watches as they think out loud. "Since Tom won't be in Austen," Libby says, tapping a finger on Niall's forearm, "we'll put Ivy Gladstone in it. It's more spacious because it's wheelchair-friendly. And though Ivy doesn't use a wheelchair, she's blind and is bringing her Seeing Eye dog."

Hemingway pricks his ears forward and leans around Rafferty's legs to look at Libby.

Niall pats his wife's hand. "That's a good idea."

Libby turns to Rafferty and presses her palms together. "And you'll stay in Thoreau where Ivy was going to be." Over Rafferty's shoulder, she notices the wall clock. "Oh, my goodness! Everyone's waiting by the van. We've got to go. *Now!*"

Rafferty ruffles the hair around Hemingway's neck, then joins the others bustling from the table. *Well, I guess that settles that. And besides, I'd rather be here in the thick of it with my friends than anywhere else.*

———

Toni has to go through two underlings before she's able to speak with Gambino. After laying out her plan, there's silence on his end of the phone. Just when she thinks they've lost the connection or he disconnected it, she hears, "I don't like it. Not one little bit." More silence. "But I understand your point. If anyone sees that tattoo on your back, it'll confirm you're part of my family." A sigh plays out on Gambino's end of the phone call. "There's more than one way for me to mark my property, to show ownership. I'll take care of that when you return."

Toni presses the phone against her ear to hear better. *His voice has changed, almost to a whisper.* She shudders when she realizes what he means—at the thought of his hands on her. She's heard rumors about what he's done to women, to girls. Just this morning, *The Seattle Times* proclaimed, "Crime boss—Georgio 'The Bull' Gambino—accused of racketeering, extortion, murder, sex trafficking, pedophilia, gun-running, and of presiding over a multi-billion-dollar narcotics operation has slipped through authorities' fingers. *Again.*

"Authorities allege that Gambino, 60, the head of the Gambino crime family, is arguably one of the most notorious drug-trafficking operations in history. Experts say he is in the same league as notorious drug lords El Chapo and Pablo Escobar."

And though Toni's never met "The Bull" in person, she remembers the one time she saw him. It was at the end of Paddy MacCullough's funeral. *I looked across the distance as mourners made their way through headstones to their cars. Blending with the shade of a tree, dressed in a dark suit—with two men behind him in sunglasses and suits—stood a man in his sixties. A bulbous nose dominated his ruddy face, and a heavy brow countered it. He had a thick mat of white hair and a matching mustache. An imposing figure, he looked to possess great physical strength. Viscerally, I knew it was my boss, Georgio "The Bull" Gambino.*

His voice interrupts her thoughts. "I'm going to switch to the video feature on my phone. Switch yours, too, and pay close attention. You're going to see a small example of what happens to people in my employ who fail. Before I begin the demonstration, tell me what you see."

Toni brings the phone closer to her face. Center stage in what appears to be fluorescent lighting, she sees the brittle glare of glass on an aquarium. "I see a large water-filled tank with fish in it."

"That's right. What you're looking at is a three-hundred-gallon tank with red-bellied piranha swimming back and forth, waiting to eat. When they're hungry—and I let mine get hungry—they have a reputation for feeding frenzies."

Toni swallows. Her heartbeat accelerates, not from fear, but in excited anticipation of what might happen next.

With a signet ring on its pinkie, Gambino's hand gestures toward the tank. "The red-bellied piranha is considered one of the more dangerous and aggressive species of piranha. And while they're predominantly carnivorous, they eat vegetation if they have to. Mine rarely have to." Gambino steps closer to the massive tank. "Their top and bottom razor-sharp teeth work together like scissors to cut up food."

Toni watches Gambino wave someone into the view-finder. Her eyes widen when a gagged man—his hands bound behind him—steps into her line of vision. Another man steps into the shot. The second man is holding a pair of what looks like garden-variety pruning shears. He wrenches the clenched fist of one of the man's hands open and lightning-quick lobs off his index finger.

Gambino walks over to the man and puts the end of his lit cigar where the blood flows freely. "You've got to cauterize these things quickly," he says. Then he takes the finger and tosses it into the tank. The now-reddened water roils to life as the crazed fish tear at the flesh.

"Contrary to popular belief, piranha only 'frenzy' when they know the meal is dead and they're safe from attack themselves."

Despite her bravado, Toni's stomach flips. There's not much that makes her feel queasy. Moments later, she watches a stripped bone sink to the bottom of the tank.

"Toni, can you guess why this tank is so large?" Gambino asks.

"I suspect it's for when someone makes a much bigger mistake."

"*Bingo!* If your plan works, I'll bump you up a notch in the chain of command. But if it fails . . . Let's just say, I'll add you to the bone pile."

This time when Toni swallows, it's to stop her terror from coming out as a scream.

CHAPTER 8

"You take people, you put them on a journey, you give them peril, you find out who they really are."
—Joss Whedon

M ick, Emma, Libby, and Niall pat shoulders, shake hands, and give hugs amid a flurry of tearful goodbyes as Niall and Joe load the remainder of the guest's luggage in the back of the van. From the looks on everyone's faces, the general atmosphere is one of apprehension. Mick inhales the clean, pine-scented air. *Maureen's devouring Emma with her eyes like this is the last time she'll see her daughter alive.*

The light of dawn gives a magical glow to Pines & Quill. Mick squints against the brilliant sun as it clears the treetops in the east. He notices his dad take Joe to the side, their heads bent close in conversation. *Their faces look pinched and worried.* "Hey, Rafferty, you and Joe are coming back this afternoon, right?"

Rafferty tries to lighten the somber mood. "Not until after I shower. I'd rather you *see* me coming than *smell* me coming." He nods toward Hemingway. "Hemingway may not mind *eau de stink*, but I'll spare the rest of you."

At the sound of his name, Hemingway rolls off his back where he'd been rubbing his shoulders in something, gets on his feet, and trots over to the two men.

Rafferty tousles the wiry hair around Hemingway's ears. The big dog leans into him, basking in the attention.

Mick nods toward his dad and Joe. "It looks like they're having a quick briefing."

"Joe told me he had a colleague he trusts at a neighboring precinct do a little checking. He got a list of tattoo parlors in San Francisco for your dad to investigate first."

Rafferty scratches Hemingway's proffered chin. "Joe and I will check the tattoo shops here. I have a buddy exploring the studios in Seattle. I know that before you and Emma return from your honeymoon in New Orleans, you're going to pursue the Walter and Maxine Williams case to see if you can get a lead on their missing kids, Pam and Kyle. It ties in with busting Gambino. The dead woman with the 'Family First' tattoo on her back—his mark of ownership—impersonated Pam Williams as a writer in residence here at Pines & Quill.

"If there's time to do reconnaissance in the ink shops there, it could prove helpful. Between us, we can cover Gambino's trifecta—the greater Seattle area, San Francisco, and New Orleans. *Somebody's* inking his people in those areas, and one of them might have information on the deaths. Or, for that matter, any of the other crimes he's wanted for."

Before getting into the van, Connor and Maeve walk over to Mick and Rafferty. Connor shakes Rafferty's hand while Maeve hugs her son. "I love you."

"I love you too, Mom."

Then Maeve gives Rafferty a brief hug and a peck on the cheek. "You take care of yourself, young man."

Rafferty blushes. "Yes, ma'am. I will." He notices that Joe, Tom, and Linda are waiting for him in his rental. "Have a safe trip," he says before heading to the car.

With Mick in a bear hug, Connor says, "I love you, son."

Mick squeezes back. "I love you too, Dad." *I hope that Emma and I live long enough to have a relationship like my parents. We've got to put a stop to Gambino.*

In the rearview mirror, Libby sees Rafferty pull his rental car curbside behind the Pines & Quill van in the departure area of the Bellingham International Airport, but her thoughts are elsewhere. *Three people have died at the writing retreat—the woman impersonating Pam Williams, the college student Mick hired to valet cars, and the man who broke into Brontë cottage for Linda Washington's cameras. The July batch of writers in residence arrives tomorrow. I'm grateful that Rafferty agreed to stay in Brontë cottage while Mick and Emma are on their honeymoon. But even with an FBI special agent, are we safe?*

Amid vehicle exhaust, cars jockeying for curbside position, honking horns, and people yelling, Rafferty removes a wheelchair from the trunk, unfolds it, and rolls it to Tom, who transfers himself from the backseat with ease.

Joe starts unloading the luggage from the back of the van, placing it on a trolly.

When Emma's brothers—Eric, Ellery, and Ethan—exit the van, they make quick work of the rest of the baggage and push the trolly across the sun-baked concrete toward the terminal.

Maureen and Philip, Emma's parents, and Sally, Emma's best friend, wait curbside. Maureen blinks to keep her tears at bay.

Libby takes Maureen's hands in both of hers. "I want to thank you again for coming. Your presence made Emma's day. They would have loved seeing you off at the airport, but they're going to see Kevin's parents this morning—the young man who died."

"I'm worried about my daughter. I don't want Emma to get killed."

"We love Emma too, Maureen. Please know that Mick, Joe, and Rafferty, in a joint effort with the police and FBI, are doing everything they can to stop Gambino. I promise to keep you apprised of developments as they unfold."

After their goodbyes, that group heads en masse to the glass entryway. It automatically slides open when they approach, and they step through. After a final wave from Maureen, they disappear from view.

Libby makes her way over to Tom. Taking one of his hands in both of hers, she looks into his blue eyes. "I'm so sorry."

"It's not your fault, Libby. You had nothing to do with that explosion."

"I know, but I'm so sorry that it happened." She includes Linda in her gaze. "I hope you'll come back to Pines & Quill another time. We'd love to see you again."

"I will," Tom says. "But first, I've got to reclaim my life and my mobility. My sense of self requires it." He thumps the top of the right wheel with his palm. "I thought I was farther along than I am." He gives a wistful look at the bag holding his prosthetic legs. "But I've got a lot more work to do."

Libby leans down and hugs Tom. "I look forward to your next visit." Then she turns to Linda. "Thank you for taking the wedding photos. Thank you, too, for being instrumental in identifying the bomber."

Warmth blossoms Linda's cheeks. "It was an accident. He just happened to be part of the candid shots I took."

"Nonetheless, your photos made all the difference."

Tom checks the ticket on his cell. "After we pass through security, we go to Gate E. Then we've got a seven-hour-and-fifteen-minute flight ahead of us. My laptop's in my carry-on. I plan to work on my manuscript." He looks at Libby and smiles. "The next time I see you, it'll be done."

"I'm counting on it," Libby says as she waves them off.

Connor and Maeve are the last to leave. Connor's the first to hug his daughter. *Even though Dad's retired from the FBI, where he was Special Agent in Charge of Marin, Napa, San Mateo, and the main office in San Francisco, he's still formidable. I wish he and Mom didn't have to leave.*

"I love you, Sweetheart," Connor says.

"I love you too, Dad."

Maeve is next to take Libby in her arms. *Mom's a retired criminal psychologist and FBI profiler. She delved into why people committed crimes, particularly violent crimes. With all of the recent deaths, I wish I had her ability to look at the likelihood and timing of the next crime.*

"I love you, Libby."

"I love you too, Mom. And the next time you come to Pines & Quill, I promise to make it *boring*."

"I don't think there is such a thing with the MacCullough and McPherson clans," Joe teases.

"You're right," Maeve says.

After a final goodbye, Connor and Maeve head to the Departures terminal to catch their flight home to San Francisco. Before the automatic doors close, Connor looks over his shoulder and gives Libby a winking grin.

Libby privately resolves to be more like her parents and do a little independent sleuthing. *Niall would be livid if he knew. Mick, too, for that matter. That's why I'm not going to tell them.*

"I know you already know this," Rafferty says, "but it's worth saying again. Your parents are terrific."

Libby smiles and nods her acknowledgment. "They're everything to me. I don't know what I'd do without them."

––––––––

Toni's gaze sweeps the immense Departures terminal, taking everything in like a dry sponge soaks up water. Her nostrils catch the smell of jet exhaust, fast food, and the heady mixture of perfumes and colognes that hang like an invisible cloud over the mass of bustling people. *I wonder where Bobbi is?*

As Toni scans the crowd, she spots him—*her* in this instance—walking across the terminal. Bobbi, one of the best female impersonators in the business, is equally comfortable as a male or female. He'd once told her, "No limits, Toni. Just because I was born in a man's body doesn't mean I can't do both, and exceptionally well, at that."

My God, it's like looking in a mirror. Toni admires the outfit Bobbi chose to impersonate her—a pair of black high-rise stovepipe slacks, black canvas wedges, a white boatneck T-shirt, all topped with a poppy red lightweight trench coat. *Perfect for the weather in San Francisco.*

Toni catches Bobbi's passing glance and gives an almost imperceptible nod. *He better not blow this, or it'll cost us both our lives.*

As promised, Bobbi doesn't acknowledge her as he makes his way toward security.

Toni's flight to Armstrong International in New Orleans leaves an hour later than Bobbi's flight to San Francisco. She locates an airport directory. *They've got a Scotty Browns. I'll have a screwdriver and wait to go through security until that TSA agent takes a break. I don't want her to think I'm going through twice. That would raise suspicion.*

––––––––

Joe sniffs his shirt, then gets into the rental car at the airport. He buckles his seatbelt before responding to Rafferty's comment when he popped the locks. "I probably can't smell *your* stink because *mine's* so bad," Joe says. "Drop me off at my house. After I shower, shave, and catch up with Marci, I'll head over to the precinct. After you clean up and check out of the MoonDance Inn, meet me at the station. We'll see if Judge Watson authorized taps on Toni's home, phone, and possibly tracking devices for her vehicles—both her squad car and Nissan Rogue."

Rafferty lifts an eyebrow. "She drives a *Rogue?* Talk about if the shoe fits . . ."

Both men fall into a comfortable silence, each tending his thoughts.

Joe picks a mental scab. *Gambino wants Mick, but he's going through Emma to get him. There've been three attempts on her life. Mick, Rafferty, and I are working on the same case. Rafferty doesn't have a family. I'm worried that Gambino's going to try to get to me through my wife or daughters. Just thinking about it scares the hell out of me.*

When Rafferty pulls into Joe's driveway, he says, "Are you aware that today's Sunday?"

"Yes, that's why I want to get as much done as early as possible. I promised Marci that I'd go to an afternoon mass with her and the girls."

Rafferty scratches the bristles on his jaw. "Saturday was only yesterday. Mick's and Emma's wedding. So much has happened since then that it seems like a *week* ago." He flips the visor up. "I bet the judge is off today. I wonder about tattoo shops—are they closed on the weekends?"

"I'm pretty sure the judge takes weekends off. It's probably hit or miss with the tattoo parlors. They're open Saturdays, but I don't know about Sundays. Why?"

"Let's focus on one lead this mor—"

Joe's phone buzzes. "Hold that thought," he says, looking down at his cell. "Speak of the devil." He presses a button, then answers, "Bingham." Joe's quiet as he listens. "Yes, sir. Thank you, sir." He disconnects, then digs a finger into his shirt collar and draws a deep breath. "That was Federal Judge Watson. He approved our request for the works—taps on Toni's home, phone, *and* tracking devices for her personal and work vehicles."

"Excellent!" Rafferty thumps the steering wheel with his palm. "Starting with Sam, there have been nine deaths. And they all have a single point of convergence—Gambino. We both know that past behavior is the best predictor of future behavior. So, the sooner we get back to Pines & Quill and make a solid plan with Mick, the more likely we can avert another death."

Tension permeates the vehicle's interior. "Meet me at the station in an hour, Rafferty. We'll check the roster for Toni's schedule. That'll determine the timing of setting our electronic surveillance in place. Then on the way out to Pines & Quill, we'll swing by the morgue and follow up with Dr. Graham."

"The ME? You think she works on Sunday?"

"Count on it," Joe says with confidence. "She's married to her job."

———

Connor and Maeve settle into their seats on the starboard side of the Boeing's four-across cabin. To accommodate his long legs, Connor sits next to the aisle. Maeve is next to the window. The narrow-body model is ideal for short hauls like Bellingham to San Francisco.

Connor touches Maeve's left shoulder, then leans in and whispers in her ear. "Would you do it again?"

"Are you flirting with me, Mr. McPherson?"

"Quite possibly," he says, waggling his eyebrows. "But seriously, would you do it all over again?" He brushes his thumb back and forth on the fabric covering her shoulder.

Maeve lifts her quarter-length sleeve to reveal a small tattoo with black lettering—IABDTL. "You mean this?"

Connor nods. "Yes."

He thinks about the tattoo he got well over fifty years ago. The same day Maeve got hers. Only his lettering is slightly different from hers—IAGDTD.

My lettering stands for "It's a good day to die." Today, the phrase is known for its use in Star Trek. Back when I got mine, it was in light of what I'd learned about the Hunkpapa chief, Running Antelope. He used the phrase to save trapper Fred Gerard and his companions from being executed on Sitting Bull's orders.

When Connor was in training at Quantico, he'd read *The Great Sioux Nation* by Roxanne Dunbar-Ortiz. In it, he'd read that "In the presence of fourteen hundred Indians, Chief Running Antelope mounted a little knoll and electrified the camp with the exclamation: 'This is a good day to die. Who will die with me?' The grand courage of the chief and his thrilling eloquence broke the solid phalanx of warriors. In squads, they came over and gathered close around the fearless insurgent. The rebellion was a success. To avoid a doubtful civil war, Sitting Bull concluded to spare the lives of his prisoners."

That's how I felt—and still feel even though I'm retired—about my role in the FBI. I want to make the world a better place. I want to protect others. And I'll die doing it if that's what it takes.

"Yes, I'd do it again," Maeve says. "But I prefer what my lettering stands for—*It's a better day to live.*"

Connor tucks a loose strand of hair behind his wife's ear. "For over fifty years, you've never failed to tell me to come back to you alive."

Maeve places a gentle kiss on his lips. "And you always have."

Connor looks up as the passenger across the aisle stows a piece of luggage in the overhead compartment. He happens to glance at the small first-class section in the front of the plane.

"Well, well, well," Connor whispers.

"What?" Maeve whispers back.

Eyebrows raised, he nods toward the first-class section. "I wonder what takes Officer Bianco to San Francisco?"

CHAPTER 9

"I'm ever curious about the world. I'm driven to go out and find new things to write about. Having a vivid imagination is also a plus."

—DAVID BALDACCI

Mick knocks on the Pierce's door, then takes Emma's hand while they wait. *I'm here to apologize for the death of their son.* Tilting his head, he blinks rapidly to keep the tears at bay. He sees vapor trails crisscross a cloudless sky on this last day of June.

After a minute, the door opens to a woman with bruised circles under red-rimmed eyes. In one of her hands, she clutches a tissue. She looks like grief has swallowed her whole.

Mick's chest seizes with guilt.

"You must be Mr. and Mrs. McPherson, the newlyweds." The woman takes a step back and opens the door wider. "Please come in."

"Mrs. Pierce," Mick says, "We came to tell you how sorry we are for your loss." He feels the supportive squeeze of Emma's hand as they step through the doorway.

"We can't begin to imagine the pain of losing a child," Emma says, following Mrs. Pierce into the living room.

A man stands when they enter. His clothes are disheveled. "This is my husband, Robert Pierce."

His slouched posture gives the impression that grief's applying pressure to his shoulders.

"Call me Bob," he says, stepping forward to shake their hands. He indicates the couch for them to sit on before he and his wife take their seats. "I understand that congratulations are in order." A note of bitterness taints his words.

"Yes, sir," Mick says. Guilt burns like a hot coal in his heart. "I hired Kevin and his friend Dean to valet and tend bar at our wedding. Sir, I'm so—"

Mr. Pierce cuts him off with the wave of his hand. "I understand Kevin isn't the first person to die out at your place. What's it called again?"

"Pines & Quill. It's a retreat for writers," Mick says.

"Doesn't sound like much of a retreat if people have to be scared for their lives."

"Bob, they've come—"

"Alice, don't interrupt me." He points at Mick and Emma. "*They've* got their whole lives ahead of them. Kevin's life was full of promise. Until yesterday, he had his whole life in front of him too." Burying his face in his hands, the man bends over his thighs. His anger melts into grief as his shoulders shake with sobs.

Alice stands and wrings her hands. "I think it would be best if you go now."

Emma slips her arm through Mick's as the door closes on their retreating backs. "That was awful."

Mick is stricken with the weight of responsibility. "Emma, what have I done? Three people are dead because of me—Sam, Paddy, and now Kevin." He tastes bile in the back of his throat.

Marrying me put Emma in Gambino's crosshairs. What if she's next?

———

Rafferty steps under the hot shower spray in his bathroom at the MoonDance Inn. He tips his head back and closes his eyes. *I wonder how it's going for Mick and Emma as they pay their respects to bereft parents?* He remembers when he and his wife lost their son, Drew, in a car accident just before his sixteenth birthday. *Pamela was inconsolable. I was numb with sorrow.*

Like emotional braille, Rafferty's mind touches the wound. *Drew was a passenger in his best friend's car. The friend, Jack, had just turned sixteen and gotten his driver's license. They were just two young guys—radio on, seat belts on, no one was drinking, and no drugs were involved. Drew was in the front passenger seat, and somehow, without any reason they were able to discover, Jack lost control of the car, and it flipped over and smashed into a tree. Drew was killed on impact. His friend, Jack, died by suicide six months later. The survivor's guilt he felt became too heavy for him to carry, to live with.*

Using the towel, Rafferty wipes the fog from the bathroom mirror. He looks at his face. *Pam and I took an emotional beating. Unfortunately, it led to marital stress and, eventually, divorce. Mick's carrying a tremendous amount of emotional weight. Survivor's guilt, as evidenced by Drew's friend Jack, can become too much to bear. I'm worried about Mick and Emma. I hope he's able to work through this.*

———

Joe hears footsteps echo in the hallway that leads to the "Prairie Dog Farm"—the bullpen at the Bellingham Police station where uniforms sit back-to-back in low-walled cubicles. He looks at his watch pointedly. "Glad you could make it, Rafferty."

"Sorry about that. It took a little longer than I expected. Then I had to check out." He points to Toni's chair. "What have you found out about her schedule?"

"The timing's perfect." Joe holds up a piece of paper. "Chief Simm's left a note taped to my monitor letting me know that my cube mate's unexpectedly out for a couple of weeks. Her mom fell and broke her hip. Toni's flying—or should I say, *already flown*—to San Francisco to be with her." He nods his head toward the wall. "That information matches up with the duty roster. I also received a text from Connor. Guess who's on his and Maeve's flight to San Francisco?"

"You've got to be kidding me," Rafferty says.

"Nope." Joe shakes his head. "And she's flying first class."

"Must be nice," Rafferty says. He looks around the room. From his standing position, he sees that most of the cubicles are empty. "There's no time like the present. I'll be right back."

Joe lifts his eyebrows. "*Now?* We're going to tap Toni's workspace *now?*"

"Yes." He nods his head toward the room in general. "No one's paying any attention to us. We're here just like they are, at the office on a Sunday working our caseload."

Seeing the merit of the plan, Joe agrees. "In for a penny, in for a pound. Instead of stopping by the morgue on the way to Pines & Quill, let's swing by Toni's apartment and see if her car's there. Maybe she took Uber or a taxi to the airport. If it's there, we can—" Joe pauses. "Hey, you *do* know how to install those things, right?"

Rafferty smiles. "I didn't spend twenty weeks at Quantico for nothing." He lowers his voice. "But we're *not* going to bug her apartment while it's light outside; that requires a whole different strategy."

Joe nods. "I agree. We'll save that for the dead of night."

On the west side of Pines & Quill, Libby and Hemingway exit the all-terrain vehicle they use to get around the twenty-acre wooded retreat.

Hemingway's tail wags as he sniffs the ground. Though it's near lunchtime, the shaded areas are still wet with morning dew.

After Libby gathers her supplies from the ATV, she walks up the ramp of Austen cottage. She turns to her four-legged companion. "We already finished getting Thoreau, Brontë, and Dickens ready for the July writers in residence. This is the last cottage." With both arms full of fresh linens, towels, and cleaning supplies, Libby says, "Hemingway, will you open the door, please?"

The big dog clears the ramp in one leap and pushes the door-activation button with his nose. Once the door swings open, they step inside.

I love the welcoming hues of sage and lavender. Libby does a three hundred and sixty-degree turn, appreciating the wheelchair-friendly design with its interior elements spaced for smooth transition.

Hemingway's nails click on the hardwood floor as he checks out the cottage. It reflects the same warm, honeyed tones of a massive beam that runs the length of the structure, parallel with the pitch of the vaulted ceiling.

"Hemingway, since Tom Gordon decided to go back to Philadelphia, this is where Ivy Gladstone and Maggie, her Seeing Eye dog, are going to stay."

While Libby changes the bedding and scours the peaceful space, she has a one-sided conversation with the five-year-old, one-hundred-and-fifty-pound Irish wolfhound. "Just between you and me, I'm going to do a little *seeing* and *eyeing* myself. If I browse a few of the tattoo parlors in town, say that I'm interested in a 'Family First' tattoo, it may shake something loose. What do you think?"

Hemingway dances back-and-forth on his front paws.

"Getting back to Maggie, I'm counting on you to be a gentleman."

Hemingway's ears prick forward.

"I'm serious, young man." Libby gives Hemingway the stink eye. "It wouldn't be nice for you to take liberties."

The big dog sits and dusts the floor with his tail.

"It's not funny, Hemingway. You could find yourself in the mudroom if you don't keep your nose to yourself."

Hemingway rolls onto his back, exposes his belly, and peddles the air with his big paws.

Libby shakes her head. "Men."

Niall peers around the kitchen corner in the main house when he hears Libby and Hemingway come through the mudroom. He wipes his hands on a dishtowel. "I just got back myself." Niall kisses the tip of Libby's nose, then takes the basket of laundry and sets it on the washing machine before taking her in his arms.

Libby wraps her arms around his waist. "Did you get everything on the list?" she asks against the bib of his apron.

Always one for cuddles, Hemingway tries to wedge his muzzle between them.

"I did, and then some. I got everything that our garden doesn't supply for the first week of menus. Speaking of which, I swung by Old Fairhaven Wines for the pairings I've planned, and on the way home, I stopped at the Washington State Liquor Store and bought a few bottles we're getting low on in the Ink Well."

Libby lifts her head and sniffs the air. "What smells so good?"

"The guys should be here soon, so I'm trying out a new recipe for lunch. It's a one-pot sugar-glazed roast that I put in the oven on low before I left."

Libby inhales deeply. "Do I smell onion, garlic, and thyme?"

"You sure do. And potatoes, carrots, and parsnips from our garden. It's in the Dutch oven mixed with pork sausages, bacon, and chicken thighs. I tossed it with a splash of olive oil, cider vinegar, and a pinch of salt."

When the vehicle sensor buzzes, Hemingway nudges Niall and Libby again. "Somebody's here," Niall says.

"Since the phone didn't ring for us to open the gate, it must be Mick and Emma. I loaned them the Prius so they could give their condolences to Mr. and Mrs. Pierce."

Hemingway barks and trots to the front door.

"Hold your horses, Mister," Niall says. "We're right behind you."

When Niall opens the door, Hemingway bolts to greet three cars driving up the lane—Mick and Emma, followed by Joe, then Rafferty bringing up the rear in his rental.

Niall shades his eyes and gazes at the cerulean sky. He inhales the pine-scented air, then turns his attention to the semicircular drive where Hemingway greets Emma then Mick when they exit the car. That's when he notices Mick's face.

Niall bends to Libby. "It looks like someone took the wind out of Mick's sails."

"I wonder what happened?" Libby watches her brother touch his whale fluke pendant—a tell that he's upset. "I suspect their visit to the Pierce's didn't go well."

When Joe and Rafferty exit their vehicles, Hemingway dusts each man's outstretched hand with his whiskers and then herds everyone into the main house.

"What smells so darned good?" Joe asks.

Over his shoulder, Niall says, "You're just in time for lunch. I hope you brought your appetites because you're guinea pigs for a new recipe."

Mick returns Libby's worried look with a slight nod and a smile, his signal for "I'm okay. I'll tell you later," then roughs the fur around Hemingway's neck. "Has anyone fed this big hairy mongrel?"

"Now's a good time," Niall says as he sets the Dutch oven with mitted hands on the trivet in the center of the table. He removes the lid, releasing a savory smell that garners a unison of *oohs* and *aahs*. "It's got to cool a few minutes. I'll be right back." He returns moments later with a massive bowl of tossed salad. "Fresh from the garden. Dig in."

Once everyone's eating, Mick says, "Emma and I leave first thing in the morning." Looking at Joe and Rafferty, he continues. "Now's a good time to cover what we know and make a plan. What did you guys find out this morning?"

Joe fills him in on Toni being on the same flight as Mick's parents to San Francisco. "She'll be gone for two weeks taking care of her mother."

Rafferty brings him up to speed on getting Judge Watson's full approval of electronic surveillance and where they're at with the tapping and tracking devices. "We've taken care of Toni's workstation, the Crown Vic that's her preferred squad car, and her personal vehicle." He cuts his eyes to Joe. "We'll take care of her home another time. We're not sure yet how and when we'll get her cell, but once we figure it out, we'll tap it too."

Joe looks at everyone enjoying their meal. "I won't go into details about our brief visit with the ME. Suffice it to say that Dr. Graham confirmed the identity of the man who was shot last night, Emilio Accardi. And how he died—which was obvious at the scene. She'll let us know when the ballistics report comes back on the casing that one of the techs found."

"Next steps?" Mick asks.

Rafferty sets down his fork. "While you and Emma are on your honeymoon in New Orleans, we'll pursue leads on four people who currently reside in drawers at the morgue: the woman impersonating Pam Williams, Salvatore Rizzo who used Vito Paglio as an alias, Angelo 'Angel' Romano, the owner of Tit 4 Tat Tattoo Studio in Bellingham, and Emilio Acardi, who we now know was a dirty cop. There's another dirty cop that Special Agent Harris in the Seattle office is looking for leads on—the sniper who tried to kill Emma on the whale-watching cruise. His body's at the Snohomish County Medical Examiner facility in Everett."

Mick rattles the ice in his tea. "We're staying a few extra days after our honeymoon to work the Walter and Maxine Williams case and check out some of the tattoo parlors. We know that New Orleans, along with San Francisco and Seattle, is a home base for Gambino—emphasis on *home*. It's where he started."

Joe wipes his mouth with his napkin. "Rafferty has people checking out the tattoo studios in Seattle, and we're going to canvas the ink shops in Fairhaven, Bellingham, and the surrounding area."

Libby's eyebrows raise as she leans in. "There have to be *dozens* in the immediate area alone. You guys need any help?"

Stunned, Niall looks at his wife. "Oh, no," he says, placing his palms flat on the table. "You leave the sleuthing to the professionals. I mean it, Libby."

"Dad's helping them check out tattoo shops in San Francisco," she says.

"Yes," Niall sputters, "but Connor's a retired FBI special agent in charge of practically everything under God's blue sky. He's *trained*, Libby."

"All right already. I just thought I'd offer."

Mick watches his sister and brother-in-law. *Niall and Libby rarely argue. And though I agree with Niall, I'm going to try to take the heat off Libby.*

Mick raises his iced tea glass in a toast. "Here's to Emma and me." He takes her hand and kisses the back of it. Affecting his best Yat accent—the most pronounced version of the New Orleans accent—Mick tries for a bit of levity.

"My *dah-lin'* wife's done her homework. *Naw-lins* is drenched with soul."

"I think it's pronounced *New Or-leenz*," Emma says.

Joe shakes his head. "No, I think Mick's right. I believe the Rs are silent in *Loo-siannah.*"

Mick continues. "The *Be-ug Ee-zee* is one of the top ten honeymoon destinations in the continental United States. We *de-paht* in the *mo-nin.*"

Emma turns to Mick and laughs. "Oh, my gosh. You sound like a nut. Don't try that there, or they'll send us packing."

"*Nah,* they'll just throw us to the *ga-tuhs.*"

Mick leans back in his chair and chews on an ice cube. He shoots a glance at Libby. A grin tugs at her lips. She mouths, "Thank you."

My exaggeration of the Yat accent was an easy diversion to get her off the hot seat with Niall. But if Libby goes to tattoo parlors to try and help with the investigation, my brother-in-law will have to wait in line behind me because I'll throttle her myself. He refills his glass.

"Seriously, though. The clock's ticking. And it's attached to a time bomb—Gambino."

Just then, the buzzer in the kitchen sounds, informing them that a vehicle's at the main gate. A moment later, the phone rings. Being closest, Mick answers it. "McPherson. Yes, just follow the lane. I'll be out front."

"Who's here?" Libby asks.

"Whatcom Courier Service with a delivery that needs to be signed for," he says. "I'll be right back."

When Mick returns, he slits the envelope open with his pocketknife, removes the document, and begins to read. A moment later, his jaw drops open.

"What is it?" Joe asks.

"Mr. and Mrs. Pierce are suing me for the death of their son, Kevin."

CHAPTER 10

"It all begins with a character, usually, and once he stands up on his feet and begins to move, all I can do is trot along behind him with paper and pencil trying to keep up long enough to put down what he says and does."

—WILLIAM FAULKNER

Libby pulls the Pines & Quill van to the curb in the Departures terminal drop-off lane at Bellingham International Airport. After parking, she, Emma, and Mick get out of the vehicle. Libby folds Emma into a hug while Mick removes their luggage. Car doors slam. Travelers pass, pulling wheeled bags that squeak over the pavement. "I know you're going to have a wonderful honeymoon in New Orleans," Libby says. "I've only been there once, but Niall and I *loved* it."

"And when we get back," Emma says, beaming, "there'll be a whole new group of writers in residence for us to meet."

Libby checks the time on her watch. "Speaking of which, the first one, Cheryl Munson, arrives from Philadelphia

shortly. I need to go park and get over to the Arrivals terminal." Her gaze shifts to her brother. "Hey, Mick, you can't
leave without giving your big sister a hug."

Mick lifts Libby off the ground in a bear hug. "Sometime
during the next nine days while we're gone," he says, "our
replacement Jeep may be delivered. In the last conversation I
had with our insurance agent, she said she didn't foresee any
problems." Mick leans back to look into her eyes. "As you
know, we're staying in the Truman Capote literary suite at the
Hotel Monteleone, and I emailed you the gist of our itinerary.
We're still working out some of the details."

Emma's eyes light up. "We'll be there July first through
ninth, which means that we'll get in on their huge Fourth of
July celebration."

"I've heard that Independence Day is tons of fun in the
Big Easy with loads of food, music, and a parade," Libby
says. "Now, you two better get going. You're supposed to be
at the airport two hours before departure, and you're cutting
it close."

She pulls Mick close and whispers. "I know that at the
end of your honeymoon, while you're still in New Orleans,
you're going to meet with Walter and Maxine Williams to
discuss Pam and Kyle, their missing children. I'm scared,
Mick. It's like you and Emma have a target on your backs.
Please be careful. So many people have already died."

Mick nods toward one of the pieces of luggage—a hard-
sided Pelican gun case. "I'm taking precautions."

Libby stiffens. "Oh, my gosh, Mick. Is it legal to carry
guns on an airplane?"

Mick places a reassuring hand on Libby's shoulder. "Don't
worry. Firearms, their parts, and ammunition aren't allowed in
carry-on bags, but guns can be transported in checked bags if
they're properly packed and declared to the airline. I've dotted
my I's and crossed my T's. We'll be just fine."

Libby shivers, but not from cold. "I hope you don't have to use your gun while you're in New Orleans. Watch your backs."

———

Toni lies on her stomach on a towel-covered table, naked from the waist up, at Hell or High Water Tattoo. It's only the first of July, but the humidity level in the lower garden district of New Orleans is already flirting with 80 percent. *I'm glad it's not August.*

Even with the air conditioner cranked up, the combination of heat and ungodly humidity has gotten to Toni. She's cranky as a snake that's rudely woken from a sun-drenched nap. Like a vise, her white-knuckled hands grip each side of the table. Over her shoulder, she complains. "Goddamnit, Rick, are you *trying* to make it hurt worse than normal?"

He shakes his head. "Nope. But if you don't want any evidence that 'Family First' was the original tat, then this cover-up design will do the trick." He pauses for a moment. "But it's intricate. The lines are close. That means it's going to hurt *even more.*" Rick revs the machine for emphasis, then presses the ink-filled needle against the tender skin on her lower back.

Crushing her face against the towel, Toni yells, "Shit!"

———

Libby raises the nameboard for "C. Munson" so it can be seen from a distance as passengers spew into the Arrivals terminal at Bellingham International. The baggage carousel area looks like a piece of candy swarmed by ants.

It's not long before a woman with short, raven-blue hair mingled with strands of silver approaches Libby and extends her hand. A white-toothed smile splits her face. "Hi, you must be Libby MacCullough. I'm Cheryl Munson."

Libby knows from Cheryl's application that she's a professor of sociology at Bryn Mawr College. During a phone conversation, Cheryl told Libby that finishing her book was only *part* of the reason why she wanted to get away from Philly for a while. The other reason, equally important, she said, is that she'd recently broken up with her girlfriend of many years and needs time away to lick her emotional wounds.

Libby takes her hand. "It's so nice to meet you in person. How was your flight?"

"At just over six hours, it was *long*." Cheryl reaches back and rubs one side of her butt. "I'm looking forward to walking all over the twenty acres that I read about on the Pines & Quill website. It looks gorgeous."

"You're going to love it." After collecting Cheryl's suitcases and putting them on the baggage trolley, Libby checks her watch. "The next guest is about to land. Would you like to wait in the lounge while I gather the others?"

"That's a great idea. It'll give me a chance to check my voicemail and email. Should I meet you back here in about twenty minutes?"

Libby nods. "Yes, that's perfect."

Libby holds up the nameboard for "B. Rivers." As passengers from the Oakland flight pour into the spacious baggage area, a handsome man with thick chestnut hair that has flecks of gray at the temples approaches her. "I'm Byron Rivers." Creases radiate from his dark brown eyes and down his face when he smiles.

"It's a pleasure to meet you," Libby says, shaking his extended hand. "How was your flight?"

"With only two hours wheels up, it was quick. I was even able to get some work done in the vineyard this morning before I left."

"Niall, my husband, is somewhat of a sommelier," Libby says. "He's going to love talking with you about your wines."

"I assure you that I'll enjoy it in return."

Libby's gaze takes in the flow of people streaming in.

"Byron, if you'll excuse me a moment, I believe I see the final guest." She lays a hand on the trolley. "Would you mind staying with the luggage while I get them?"

"I'd be happy to."

Libby approaches a woman with high cheekbones, a tapering chin, and shoulder-length, dark brown hair. The giveaway that she's Ivy is the stylish, gray-tinted glasses perched on the dainty nose of her oval-shaped face. That, and her black-and-white, curly-coated dog is wearing a harness with an extra-long handle designed for Seeing Eye dogs. Libby stops about six feet away. "Ivy Gladstone?"

Ivy smiles. "I am. And this," she says, her hand gesturing toward the service dog, "is Sister Margaret Mary McCracken. But everyone calls her Maggie."

"May I pet her?" Libby asks.

"Though it's not a regular practice with service dogs, we're going to be part of your 'pack' for the next twenty-one days, so yes. But let Mags get a good sniff of your hand first."

Libby squats down and extends the back of her hand for Maggie to sniff. "That's quite a name she has. What's the story behind 'Sister Margaret Mary McCracken'?"

Ivy laughs. "As you can see, she's a standard-size Parti poodle. When her trainers described her two-toned coloring to me—black with a white wimple, like a traditional nun's habit—I couldn't resist giving her a nun's name."

Maggie sniffs Libby's hand, gives it a lick, and wags her short tail.

Libby furrows her eyebrows. "Ivy, when we spoke on the phone, I told you about Hemingway, our male Irish wolfhound. I hope he behaves himself."

"I can hear the concern in your voice, Libby. Don't worry; Maggie can hold her own."

"She's about half of Hemingway's size," Libby says. "What does Maggie weigh? About sixty or so pounds?"

"You're good," Ivy says, impressed. "She weighs sixty-five pounds."

"Well, Hemingway weighs one hundred and fifty pounds. He's a huge teddy bear—a lover. That's what concerns me. Even though he's neutered, I'm afraid he might try to get . . . *frisky.*"

"Maggie'll handle it," Ivy says with confidence. "She'll take him down a peg or two and put him in his place."

"Okay then," Libby says, not entirely convinced.

She turns her attention back to the Seeing Eye dog. "Maggie, I got you a big bag of the kind of food your mom told me you eat. It's in the kitchen at Austen cottage, along with food and water bowls. I think you're going to like Pines & Quill. And I guarantee that Hemingway's going to love having you as our guest."

As Rafferty parallel parks his rental car on State Street in Bellingham, he glances at a piece of paper in Joe's hand. "That's a long list of tattoo parlors you've got there."

"Libby was right," Joe says. "There's a dozen in the immediate area alone. After we work our way through it, we'll head over to the morgue and check in with Dr. Graham."

Stepping through the doorway of Chameleon Ink Tattoo & Body Piercing, both men take in their surroundings. Rafferty hears the whine of a tattoo machine start up, and he shivers. "I don't like needles."

"Then it's a good thing we're only here for info . . ."

A man with a shock of red hair and two sleeves of tattoos, all the more colorful because of his pale skin, crosses to them, then looks pointedly at the clock on the wall. "You're a bit early, but let's dive right in. I'm Todd."

Rafferty and Joe steal a subtle glance at each other.

"For starters, yes, it fucking hurts." Todd jams his hands

into the front pockets of his cargo shorts. "Anyone that says otherwise is a fucking liar or on percs. It's the most common question that the non-tattooed ask the tattooed. There's nothing cool about being a 'tough guy' and saying, 'just a little bit.' No, it fucking hurts. Someone is pushing various sizes of needles into your skin over and over again. And if we're talking about the wrist, elbow, close to your armpit, or your ribs—which are the fucking worst—it's going to hurt. Next question?"

Without batting an eye, Rafferty takes the verbal baton and runs with it. "There's a distinct smell in here. What is it?"

"It's Green Soap," Todd says, "a medical-grade soap that tattoo artists use, mainly to clean their clients' skin."

Joe pulls a photo from inside his jacket pocket and hands it to Todd. "Have you ever seen this tattoo?"

Todd's posture stiffens. He removes his hands from his pockets. His eyes widen. "Why do you ask?"

Rafferty and Joe pull out their creds simultaneously and hold them for Todd to inspect.

"You've got to be shitting me. A homicide detective and an FBI agent? With your suits, I thought you were from the *Cascadia Weekly* for the feature story about local ink."

"Sorry to disappoint," Rafferty says. "But it *is* an interview of sorts. What do you know about this tattoo?"

"I only know *one* thing. Stay the hell away from anything to do with it. I've heard rumors. And I'm sure you know that Angel, the owner of Tit 4 Tat, was found murdered in his shop." Todd shakes his head. "I don't know *any*thing, and I intend to keep it that way."

"Mind if we take a look around?" Joe asks.

"Not at all. I've got nothing to hide. You want a tour, or you want to help yourselves?"

"We'll help ourselves, thank you."

When Todd turns to walk away, they see tattoos on the back of his calves. The left one is obvious; it features a flaming skull. But Rafferty can't make out the design on the right. "Excuse me, Todd. I have one more question."

Todd turns around. "Yes?"

"I noticed the tattoos on the back of your calves. I can't quite make out the one on the right."

Todd smiles. "It's a unicorn shitting rainbows." And with that, he turns around and walks to the office area.

Joe turns to Rafferty. "Well, you *did* ask. Carly, my thirteen, going on twenty-one-year-old daughter, tried to talk Marci and me into letting her get a tattoo. One of her many arguments was, 'Just think of it as a form of self-expression.'"

Rafferty shivers again. "Yes, a painful one that's on display for the rest of your life."

It's late afternoon when Toni emerges from Hell or High Water Tattoo. The humidity hits her like a fist. She pinches her already wet shirt away from her skin as she takes in her surroundings, looking left, then right on Magazine Street. *Except for the sirens screaming in the distance, the area has a small village feel to it.*

The Lower Garden District is a large neighborhood that runs roughly from St. Charles Avenue to the river and from Jackson to the Expressway. It has several different sub-neighborhoods, each with its own centers and attractions—Magazine Street between Jackson and Felicity, Magazine Street between Melpomene and Calliope, and St. Charles Avenue—but they all fall under the auspices of this sometimes trendy, sometimes gritty "hood."

Even though the Quarter and streetcars are within walking distance, Toni feels like she'll melt if she walks. With a two-finger whistle, she hails a cab and gives the driver an address. The drive is short but blissfully cool in the air-conditioned cab.

Pushing open the heavy door of Toulouse Dive Bar and stepping through, Toni lets her eyes adjust to the dim interior. *With its unglamorous hole-in-the-wall type of vibe, it fits the description of a dive bar.* Toni remembers the first time she was here and needed to use the restroom. *They're covertly hidden behind the bookcase, which adds to the divey, almost speakeasy charm.*

"Hey, Charlie." Toni nods to a heavyset older man wiping a glass behind the bar.

"Long time, no see, Toni. What can I get you?"

Toni points to her lower back. "I just got some new ink, and it hurts like hell. When in New Orleans, drink the official drink. I'll have a Sazerac—make it a double."

"You got it."

Jazz piped from hidden speakers fills the space—raspy, edgy, rough. Toni watches Charlie mix rye whiskey, bitters, sugar, and herbsaint. Her eyes gaze at the empty place on his right hand where an index finger had once been, then around the bar at the unglamorous, dated decor.

Years ago she'd asked Charlie about the term "dive bar." He said, "It was originally used to describe establishments found belowground in basements—think opium dens. But since much of New Orleans is below sea level, dives have earned the designation for other reasons."

"So what brings you to town, Toni, business or pleasure?"

"Business."

"No need to elaborate," Charlie says, setting the dark amber drink in front of her on the pocked bar.

Toni picks up the glass and slings the liquid to the back of her mouth, visibly shuddering as its fieriness sweeps through her. She presses her lips together and squints her eyes. "You know anybody who can put together a beautiful gift basket? I have friends flying in for their honeymoon, and I want to get them something special."

Charlie lifts his eyebrows a fraction. "Something with a *bang?*"

"No." Toni frowns. "I've got connections at the Hotel Monteleone, so I don't want there to be a mess. I want something that won't leave a trace."

A smile blossoms on the bartender's ruddy face. "You mean like what Shelly Baker did with that hotshot lawyer—what was her name? Pam something or other."

"Yes, like that, Charlie. That's exactly what I mean."

CHAPTER 11

"There are loads of books that use many pages explaining how to write. In my opinion, it comes down to just three things: Read a lot. Write a lot. And tell the truth. These don't ensure you will be a good writer, but you can't be one without them."
—JESSICA NULL VEALITZEK

Emma's mesmerized by the landscape sliding by thousands of feet below her window seat on the flight to New Orleans. The beverage cart rolls up the aisle one last time before they start their descent into the Louis Armstrong International Airport. She hears the hiss from a pull tab on a can of soda as the flight attendant fills another drink request.

"Mick, I'm going to set my watch to New Orleans' time. They're in the central time zone, right?"

"Yes. Bellingham's in the Pacific time zone, so they're two hours ahead of us," Mick says. "Good idea. I'll change mine now too."

"Because we're losing two hours, do you think we'll still be able to find a nice restaurant this late?"

Mick takes Emma's hand. "Almost everything in the Big Easy is open twenty-four seven. Nothing ever closes." He leans in and whispers in her ear. "But I think we might just order room service on the first night of our honeymoon."

Emma's heart flutters, and butterflies dance around in the base of her stomach. "You're right." She places her hands on either side of his face and pulls him in for a lingering kiss.

"Eww," they hear from the seat behind them. "Gross, Mom, they're kissing."

In unison, Emma and Mick straighten slowly, trying not to laugh.

"I'm sorry," comes a woman's voice from behind them.

Emma turns in her seat. "No worries," she says, beaming. "We're on our honeymoon."

She looks out the window again. The Mississippi River winds its way like a long silver ribbon toward the Gulf of Mexico. Now and then, Emma sees lights shimmer on the water—*probably from steamboats and barges.*

Thirty minutes later, their flight is wheels down on the runway. From the speakers, they hear, "Welcome to the Big Easy, where people from every country and culture have come to create the flavorful gumbo that is the essence of New Orleans. Please note that it's eight p.m. local time. We know you have a choice in airlines, so thank you for choosing American Airlines, a proud member of the Oneworld Alliance. We look forward to seeing you again soon."

Mick retrieves their carry-on luggage from the overhead compartment as passengers jockey for position in the narrow aisle. They make their way off the plane, first to the baggage carousel, then toward a shuttle that will take them to the rental car area. A wall of humidity slams Emma and Mick when the glass terminal doors open. It carries a faint scent. At over three hundred years old, somewhat moldy from Hurricane Katrina's remnants and surrounded by muddy water and swamps, NOLA—New Orleans, Louisiana—isn't exactly known for being lemony fresh. The shuttle driver stows their luggage, and they, along with several other passengers, gratefully board the air-conditioned vehicle.

With black lettering on a bright yellow background, the Hertz sign is easy to spot among the others. After they complete the rental paperwork, Emma and Mick receive keyless fobs and instructions on finding their vehicle.

Emma turns to Mick. "How are we going to drive without a key?"

"I rented a Jeep similar to the replacement we're getting. The new models have keyless starts." Mick points to the fob in Emma's hand. "When you press that button, it sends a unique signal to the car's system. Once it's recognized and approved, you can open the door and start the ignition by pushing a button on the dashboard."

Emma draws her eyebrows together. "Does that mean if our Jeep had been keyless, Kevin Pierce, the young man who died at our wedding when the car bomb exploded, would still be alive? The bomb went off when he turned the *key* in the ignition."

"Turning the key is equivalent to pressing that button," Mick says, pointing to the fob in Emma's hand. "Both actions trigger an electrical connection that sends voltage to the spark plugs. The bomber diverted the electrical connection to the detonator that triggered the explosion."

"So it doesn't matter—key or keyless—someone with the right kind of expertise can set off a car bomb?"

Mick squeezes Emma's hand softly. "Unfortunately, that's right."

Emma gazes into Mick's green eyes. "I'm scared, Mick. What if it happens again? Who's next?"

Inside the car rental facility, a man wearing a New Orleans Pelicans baseball cap, pulled low across his brow, leans against the wall pretending to read a brochure. He folds it, slips it back into the clear plastic holder, then types a text message to Toni. "They're heading to their vehicle now." He presses the "send" arrow, and it leaves with a whoosh.

Moments later, his cell phone vibrates, and he reads Toni's response. *Stay on their tail. Deliver the gift basket by midnight tonight. Remember, there are security cameras in every hallway on every level of Hotel Monteleone. Add a cap to the bellhop uniform and pull it low to cover your face. Text me once it's delivered.*

Will do, the man responds.

A moment later, his cell phone vibrates again. This time, when he looks at the screen, there's a photo of a group of alligators. The accompanying text says, *A group of alligators is called a congregation. If you fail to follow my instructions, it won't be the first time I take "dinner" to a congregational meeting in the bayou.*

The man inhales sharply; his hands shake as he types a response. *I understand.* He presses send.

Libby brings the van to a stop in front of a massive wrought-iron entry gate. The overhead sign silhouetted against the cloudless sky beckons, *Welcome to Pines & Quill.* She presses a button on the remote attached to the visor, and the huge entrance gate swings open. She knows the vehicle sensor has buzzed in the main house, notifying Niall of their arrival.

In the rearview mirror, Libby notices her guests' appreciation of their forested surroundings. She uses the automatic controls to lower their windows as she takes the lengthy drive to the main house, slowing so Byron, Cheryl, Ivy, and even Maggie can drink in the beauty.

"I know I read it on your website," Byron says, "but I can't remember how many acres Pines & Quill is."

"The central part is twenty acres, and the adjoining bluff that overlooks Bellingham Bay is ten acres," Libby says.

"So that's why there's a faint hint of salt in the air," Ivy says. "And the pine scent smells wonderful."

"I agree," Cheryl says. "It's a lovely combination."

"In addition to pines," Libby says, "there are several other types of trees. For privacy's sake, we planted trees around each cottage. Austen has blue elderberry, Brontë has Douglas fir, Dickens has big-leaf maple, and Thoreau has western red cedar."

"I can see that even Maggie's nose is twitching apprecia-tively," Cheryl says.

"I suspect Maggie's getting a whiff of some of the wild-life that meanders through our property," Libby says. "We get the usual suspects such as squirrel, raccoon, possum, the occasional skunk, and deer. But now and again, we get a black bear, bobcat, cougar, and coyote."

At the end of the drive, the trees open into a natural space, and the main house comes into view. The two-story home sits on a gentle rise, accentuated by a large circular drive surrounding low, well-maintained shrubs and bushes.

Pointing out the front passenger window, Byron says, "I know that's quince, but what's that?"

"It's flowering currant, but most people refer to it as hummingbird bush. Red flowers bloom in early spring, making them a first stop for the hummingbirds following the Pacific Flyway on their northern migration."

Casual yet elegant, the drive widens at the front door where Niall, with Hemingway at his side, waits.

Libby pulls to a stop and activates the sliding side doors on the van. She unfastens her seatbelt and exits the van, joining Niall and Hemingway as they step forward to greet the new arrivals.

Attuned to the sounds around her, Ivy stretches her hand out through the open door and wiggles her fingers.

Hemingway shifts into a happy, full-body wag and steps forward, plunging his whiskered muzzle into Ivy's hand. She laughs as his cold, wet nose makes contact.

Hemingway's body stiffens when he sees Maggie peer around Ivy. His eyes widen in unabashed interest at the black-and-white standard-size Parti poodle.

When Byron steps out the front passenger door, Niall takes hold of Hemingway's collar with his left hand and extends his right. "I'm Niall MacCullough."

"I'm Byron Rivers. It's nice to meet you. You've got a lovely place here."

Maggie exits through the van's side door and stops. Her tail is a stiff exclamation point as she glares at Hemingway.

Ivy follows on Maggie's heels, her grip firmly on the handle of the harness.

Niall identifies himself, then says, "Let me introduce you properly to this big lummox." He turns to Hemingway and taps his rump. "Sit." He does—his wiry tail dusting the ground ferociously behind him.

"Ladies," he says to Ivy and Maggie, "this is Hemingway. If he becomes a nuisance, point to the main house and tell him to go home."

"May I?" Ivy asks, indicating with her hand that she'd like to pet Hemingway.

"Absolutely," Niall says.

Ivy reaches out and touches the still-sitting Hemingway. "My goodness, Hemingway, you're the size of a pony."

Hemingway takes Ivy's tone as an invitation to stand and take a closer look at the four-legged newcomer.

Half his size, Maggie meets Hemingway's curious gaze without waver.

When he moves to sniff Maggie's ear, she turns, top lip curled, and bares her teeth.

Hemingway opens his jaws into a deep yawn, his tongue forming a pink curl—his tell that he's nervous.

Cheryl walks around from the other side of the van and introduces herself to Niall.

Libby takes charge of Hemingway when Niall starts moving luggage from the van to the back of the ATV. Byron steps in to help with the task.

"Ivy," Libby says, "you and Maggie are in Austen cottage. Cheryl, you're in Brontë. And Byron, you're in Dickens. For those who'd like a ride, Niall will give you a lift in the ATV while he takes your luggage to the cottages, or you can come with me on the pathways."

Without exception, the writers in residence relish the opportunity to stretch their legs and get the lay of the land.

Niall glances at his watch. "While you folks are getting settled in your new digs, I'll put the finishing touches on dinner. We'll see you back here at seven o'clock. That gives you just about an hour to catch your second wind."

"Libby, will you escort Maggie and me to Austen cottage?" Ivy asks, removing a collapsible white cane from her bag that she extends to its entire length. "We'll only need to be shown the way once. After that, we'll have it down pat."

"I'd be happy to," Libby says. "I'm curious. I thought a Seeing Eye dog replaces the need for a cane."

"You're right; that's usually the case. But when I'm outside in new-to-me terrain, I use my cane the first time, so I can *feel* what Maggie sees. And if for some reason I'm ever without her, I at least have some knowledge to work from."

"That sounds like great preplanning," Libby says. "Would it be okay if Hemingway tags along? That way, he and Maggie can have a little more time to become familiar with each other."

"That's a good idea," Ivy says.

Hemingway starts his happy dance, weight shifting back-and-forth on his front paws, practically pirouetting for Maggie's benefit.

Libby looks at Maggie and laughs. "Ivy, you're right about Maggie being able to hold her own. And she's less than impressed. She just gave Hemingway a withering glance and then turned her head away, nose up."

Libby pats the top of Maggie's head. "You go, girl."

Bobbi, impersonating Toni, exits through the doorway of Black Heart Tattoo in San Francisco. He glances at his watch. *It's only 6:00 p.m.; I still have the entire evening ahead of me—all expenses paid.* As promised, he sends a text to Toni. *It hurt like hell, but it's done.*

I know, comes the response. *Your artist, Cody, texted me a photo. It looks good. Check your bank in an hour. The remaining five thousand dollars will be in your account. And remember, you're me. I'm a cop. So be careful of where you go and what you do.* With that, Toni signs off.

Bobbi looks left then right on Valencia Street and decides to turn right where it seems more promising to find a restaurant. *After lying facedown on that table for four hours, I'm starving.*

Connor gazes over the tops of the buildings on the west side of Mission Street. The sun is starting to set, and the gold sky is streaked red and purple. *It's going to rain tomorrow, but tonight's perfect.* He glances at the people hustling and bustling on the sidewalk around him. *This is what I love about San*

Francisco—the adrenaline-soaked hum of the city and towering structures of concrete and glass.

He removes a piece of paper from his pocket and reads the list of tattoo parlors. *I've checked out four of them so far—Cyclops, Frisco, Dermafilia, and Mermaids. No new leads regarding the "Family First" tattoos there. I'm going to stop at one more, Black Heart Tattoo, before I head home.* He smiles. *Maeve promised a picnic dinner on the patio of wine, bruschetta, and antipasto salad. I wouldn't miss that for anything.*

Mick tips the bellhop after he deposits their luggage in the Truman Capote literary suite at the Hotel Monteleone. Before leaving, the young man gives them the required spiel:

"Truman Capote was fond of telling the press that he was born inside Hotel Monteleone. In fact, the hotel assisted his mother with transportation to Touro Hospital, where he was actually born."

On a roll now, the bellhop flourishes his arm toward the balcony. "Overlooking the French Quarter, this beautifully appointed suite reflects Capote's personality—sophisticated and enchanting."

He nods toward the bed and continues. "It offers a king size bed and a comfortable parlor with a dining table with four chairs. The marble and granite bathroom features a garden tub and a separate glass shower. The suite also features a portable telephone, high-speed internet, wet bar and icemaker, refri—"

Mick steps forward and shakes the bellhop's hand. "Thank you *so* much"—he looks at the man's name badge—"Nolan. We've got it from here."

"If you need *anything*, sir, just let me know," Nolan says, backing out the door.

Once the door closes, Emma laughs. "I was afraid he was going to *read* us one of Truman Capote's books."

"The only part of what he said that interests me is the part about the bed." Mick raises his eyebrows suggestively, then pulls his cell from his pocket and turns it off. "I don't want any interruptions."

While Emma turns hers off, Mick makes a beeline for the door they'd entered a few minutes ago. He opens it and secures a small laminated card in the outside lock: *Do Not Disturb*.

Returning, he collects her back into his arms and crushes his lips against hers with intent and heat. His hands slip under her blouse, touching her waist, her back, and continues to roam.

Emma unbuttons her blouse and slips it off; Mick returns the favor. They leave a trail of clothing as they stumble to the bed—their desire growing each step of the way—where they finish undressing each other.

Mick's eyes take in Emma's naked beauty. He can barely breathe for the intensity of arousal filling his bones, his limbs, between his legs.

Emma stretches out beside him and molds her soft curves to the straightness of his masculine lines.

Their eyes lock. Time stops. And they lose themselves in each other, blocking out everything outside their suite.

Connor turns right on Valencia Avenue when he leaves Black Heart Tattoo. His steps smack the sidewalk with urgent excitement as he makes his way toward the parking garage where he left his Prius. Impatient, he foregoes the elevator, taking the stairs to the third level instead. After unlocking the car, he slips into the driver's seat, buckles the shoulder strap, then leans against the headrest to catch his breath. Warm from exertion, he powers the driver's side window down, then removes his cell from his pocket and types a text: *Maeve, I think I may have hit pay dirt. I'll explain when I get there. Do you need me to pick anything up on my way home? I love you.*

While waiting for Maeve's response, Connor's eyes gaze through the opening in the parking garage. Stars blink through gossamer-thin clouds overhead. *I can hardly wait to tell Maeve and the others what I discovered.*

Hugging the shadows, a man in a well-cut suit peers around a cement stanchion on the third floor in the parking garage. He's already checked the area for foot traffic. *None. Everyone's already home for the evening, or they're at a restaurant like I'm going to be in a few minutes.*

His right hand removes a Smith & Wesson M&P 22 Compact with a suppressor from his cross-draw shoulder holster. He supports his right hand with his left, moves the sight to Connor's left temple, slowly lets the air out of his lungs, and squeezes the trigger. *Pffsst*—he smiles at the whisper-soft noise.

The gunman watches as Connor tips forward, his shoulder belt restraining further movement. He steps away from the shadows and scans the garage again. *All clear.* After holstering his gun, he walks to the Prius. *There's no need to check for a pulse. It's obvious he's dead.* He reaches through the open window and removes Connor's cell phone. It buzzes in his hand. Curious, the man reads the screen: *Everything's ready, no need to stop. See you soon. I love you too.*

Following his instructions to the letter, the man sets the cell phone on the garage floor, crushes it with the heel of his shoe, and grinds it into pieces so no one can track its GPS.

He pulls out his cell phone—notices the screen says seven o'clock—and sends a text: *It's done. Unless you need anything else tonight, Boss, I'm heading to dinner.*

His phone vibrates. *Dessert's on me.*

CHAPTER 12

"People try to force things. It's disastrous. Just leave
your mind alone. Your intuition knows what it
wants to write, so get out of the way."
— RAY BRADBURY

Ivy Gladstone and Maggie are the first to arrive at the main house. Not wanting to be late, they left Austen cottage a bit early to have a cushion if they should encounter anything unexpected on their first walk to dinner. Ivy feels the solid wooden door, finds the knocker, and gives it a few good raps. While they wait, she talks with her animal companion. "Maggie, you don't have to let Hemingway ride roughshod over you, but you could at *least* be civil to him."

Libby opens the door. "Hello, ladies, and don't you look lovely?" She backs away from the entrance and invites them in. "Follow me."

Ivy lifts her chin and flares her nostrils. "Oh, my goodness, Libby. We could just follow our noses. It smells delicious!"

"Niall will be pleased you said so, Ivy. As you'll find out, he lives to cook. The scent you're enjoying right now is from the appetizer. Niall's making Manila clams in white wine, butter, onion, tomato, garlic, red bell pepper, and a dash of diced red chili. He's serving it with homemade French baguettes."

"It sounds fantastic. On the walk over, I enjoyed that hint of salt in the air." Ivy gestures toward the surrounding area. "Earlier, you said that Pines & Quill is right next to Bellingham Bay. Are the clams from this area?"

"Yes, they came from Birch Bay State Park," Libby says. "It's a cove between Bellingham and Blaine. In North America, Manila clams are found from British Columbia in Canada to Northern California. But interestingly, they're not native to the area. They were accidentally introduced in Washington State in the 1920s in shipments of oyster seed from Japan."

"Well, it sounds like a happy accident to me." Ivy turns to her hostess. "Libby, is something the matter? I can sense your hesitancy. You've cleared your throat and stepped toward me twice and stopped."

"You can *sense* that?" Libby asks, her voice laced with amazement.

"Yes, I can. Now tell me, what is it?"

"I'm curious about something but embarrassed to ask."

"Please don't be embarrassed. What would you like to know?"

"Your outfit is to *die* for! How does a person who can't see shop for shoes and clothes?"

Ivy lets loose a full laugh. "My best friend, Nora, and I grew up together in a convent. She became a nun and subsequently has limited clothing options. So she loves to shop for me. She says it colors a side of her that would otherwise be drab. And by all accounts, yours included, she does a pretty good job."

"She sure does," Libby says. "The dark mango color of your scoop-neck dress is striking against your light skin tone, and the pin tucks add detail to that flattering little number."

As Libby, Maggie, and Ivy step into the dining area, Niall pops his head around the corner. At the same time, Hemingway stands on his hind legs, his front paws perched on the bottom half of the closed Dutch door. He greets Maggie with a soft woof.

Niall points a warning finger. "Cool your jets, young man."

Maggie's eyes squint in disdain at Hemingway.

"Ivy, can I get you a glass of wine?" Niall opens the under-the-counter wine refrigerator. "I've paired tonight's appetizer with a Merry Edwards sauvignon blanc. It's chilled and ready."

Ivy feels the space in front of her with her free hand until she finds the back of a dining room chair. "Yes, I'd like that. Thank you." Having found a stable spot, she rests her hand while the other holds Maggie's lead.

After Niall pours a glass and sets it by Ivy's place setting, he places the rest of the bottle in an ice bucket in the center of the table with several wine glasses. "Ladies, may I get your chairs?"

Ivy nods. "Yes, thank you."

Once Ivy's seated, Libby sits in the chair next to her.

"Now, go on," Ivy prompts. "There's something else."

"Well." Libby leans in. "*Now* I'm curious why you were raised in a convent. How did that come about?"

"It's a short story. I was born blind, and my parents weren't up to the challenge. They figured God made a mistake, so they returned me to Him. I was His problem from that point forward. Not theirs."

Libby sits back, stunned. "Well, it's their loss. Is that what your book's about? Is it a memoir?"

"No. I'm writing about my favorite subject of all. I'm a special ed teacher. The title of my book is *Splendid Chaos: Struggling Learners & How to Help Them.*"

"Oh, that sounds wonderful."

Both women hear a knock on the door. "I'll be right back," Libby says.

Ivy scoots her chair back and, with Maggie's assistance, takes the opportunity to explore her surroundings. She walks toward Hemingway, who's once again popped his head over the bottom portion of the closed Dutch door. "Oh, I can tell we're going to be fast friends," Ivy says, reaching out and stroking the big dog's head.

Ivy feels Maggie gently tug at the lead. She reaches down to pet her and detects that she's turned her head away in disgust. "Just because I can't see you doesn't mean I don't know what you're doing, young lady." Ivy turns to Hemingway again. "We'll visit again later when Maggie's nose isn't bent out of joint."

Ivy continues exploring the spacious dining area with her free hand. "Niall?" she calls out.

"Yes, Ivy?"

"I'm curious," she says as Maggie helps her back to her chair. "What are the colors in this room?"

"Libby's a fan of *vibrant* colors." Ivy hears a smile in Niall's voice. "She did the dining area in a deep sangria-red, sage, and ochre."

"So *that's* why it feels so good," Ivy says.

"*Feels* good?"

"Yes. Color is simply energy—energy made visible. Each color gives off its own vibe. And though I can't see it, I can *feel* that it's a beautiful room."

"It's interesting you say that," Niall says. "Guests often remark on how this room makes them feel happy."

Ivy smiles. "I'm sure it also has a *lot* to do with the delicious food you serve."

Byron Rivers and Cheryl Munson arrive at the main house at the same time. Careful not to stare, Byron takes in Cheryl's appearance. *Her short dark hair has several strands of silver. I'd wager she's close to my age—a bit north of fifty. And her smile is all the more attractive because it's a little lopsided. It's been a long time since I've made a connection with a woman. Who knows? Maybe it'll happen at Pines & Quill.* "You look lovely this evening," he says.

"Why, thank you. You clean up pretty nice yourself."

Because Byron's holding a bottle of wine in each hand, Cheryl uses the heavy brass knocker that's polished to a subtle glow.

Within moments, Libby opens the big wooden door. "You're right on time, seven o'clock."

Byron holds up the wine. "These are for the chef."

"Thank you. Niall will be delighted. He's in the kitchen putting the last touches on the clams."

"So *that's* what smells so good," Cheryl presses her palms together in delight. "For a minute, I thought I'd died and gone to heaven."

Libby leads them straight through to the massive dining area where Ivy's already seated. "Have a seat, Cheryl. Byron, Niall's just through there." She points.

As Niall bathes the clams in the zesty sauce, he sees Byron. "Well, well." His eyebrows perk up. "What have you got there?"

"Two bottles of zinfandel for the chef." Turning, Byron spots a Wolf range and built-in oven flanked by a stainless-steel Sub-Zero refrigerator on one side and a matching glass-fronted, under-the-counter wine refrigerator on the other. "Oh, man, this kitchen is amazing!"

"It's my 'man cave.'" Niall grins. "Thank you for the wine. I'll pair it with a meal while you're here." Niall opens the refrigerator for an ingredient. "Your vineyard's in Napa Valley. I had that pegged as a white wine area."

Byron watches Niall add butter to one of the pans on the stove. "Although cabernet sauvignon and Chardonnay are the most widely planted, the Napa Valley holds many surprises for wine lovers looking for varieties off the beaten path. From albariño to zinfandel. More than three dozen different wine grape varieties flourish in the Napa Valley."

"Speaking of Napa Valley, how did your vineyard fare during the Glass Fire? That was horrific."

Byron shakes his head. "The Glass Fire erupted late last September and raced across northern Napa Valley, burning buildings at some of the region's most celebrated wineries and vineyards. Ultimately, twenty-seven properties saw structural damage—a figure that far exceeds that of the 2017 fires, which burned six Napa wineries. I didn't lose any structures, but I lost thirty seven acres."

"Oh, man. I'm sorry to hear that." Niall places a hand on his sternum. "But, I'm glad that you're safe, and we're certainly glad that you chose Pines & Quill to write your book. What's it about?"

"It's called *Zins of the Father: A Guide to Zinfandel Wines & Food Pairings.*"

"That's clever." Niall chuckles. "I'll be the first in line to buy a copy."

Both men turn when they hear a sizzle and pop. The cheese-like smell of cooking butter fills the air. Niall grabs a pan from the front left burner before the contents burn. "Hey, Byron, grab that other pan with those hot mitts." Niall nods toward the counter. "Then follow me. Soup's on."

"I'm on it, Chef." Happy to be helpful, Byron follows Niall into the dining area. *Pines & Quill is the ideal place to write my book. I wasn't worried about the wine aspect of things, I've got that down pat. But the food part's a bit outside my area of expertise. Niall's the perfect person to bounce ideas off.*

Cheryl watches the silent interplay between Maggie and Hemingway. *Hemingway's ears stand at full attention, and his eyes are laser-focused on Maggie. She, on the other hand, is acting aloof with her nose in the air and her head turned away— probably to hide a smile. The giveaway is the relaxed wag of Maggie's tail.* Cheryl smiles. *I think she's gloating.*

"Ivy, I'm pretty sure that Hemingway would gladly give up his tail to be out here with Maggie, but she's giving him the stink eye."

Ivy reaches out and pets the top of Maggie's head. "She's a priss, this one."

Cheryl pours a glass of wine. "I love her full name, Sister Margaret Mary McCracken. It's perfect with her black-and-white coloring and a pattern that resembles a nun's habit." She pauses for a moment. "You know what? She's the ideal character for a cozy mystery series. *Please* tell me that's what you're working on."

Ivy laughs. "No, it's not. But it's a great idea; I'll keep it in mind. I'm a special ed teacher. The working title of my book is *Splendid Chaos: Struggling Learners & How to Help Them.* How about you? What are you writing about?"

"Well, I teach at Bryn Mawr College. I'm a professor of sociology."

"That's impressive," Ivy says. "Bryn Mawr's a distinguished women's college."

"I just received tenure, and to celebrate, I'm writing a book; it's titled *Fierce Women: Our Mothers, Our Daughters, Our Sisters, Ourselves.*"

Ivy clasps her hands together in front of her chest. "Oh, that's a perfect title. I love it."

"Thank you. But *now* I feel like an impostor. Like I don't have the credentials to write it."

"Why? Why *now*?" Ivy asks.

"Because my girlfriend of twenty years just broke up

with me. I'm not only here to work on my manuscript but to lick my emotional wounds. I no longer feel like I have the relationship credentials to write a book about women when I've blown it so bad."

"I'm sorry to hear about your relationship, Cheryl. Loss of any kind is hard. At least you picked the right place to come to heal. I may not be able to see it, but I can *feel* the Zen-like tranquility here. It's like a healing balm."

Both women pause to sip from their wine glasses.

"As to the relationship aspect of things," Ivy continues, "you wouldn't be normal—in fact, no one would listen to you if you hadn't experienced not only the ups but the downs too. Perfect people aren't believable. Neither are perfect relationships. In my experience, people want to read about other people they can relate to. We live in a world of flaws. Like secrets, flaws are an integral part of our lives. To my way of thinking, they're part of what makes us unique, special, and beautiful."

Cheryl nods and takes another sip. "I sure hope you're right." *Secrets? What secrets?*

―――――――

Libby gazes at the people around the large pine table engaging with each other. *I wonder what's keeping Rafferty?* "I hope you brought your appetites with you. Niall has a spectacular menu planned. The next item is roasted beet and arugula salad."

As if on cue, an apron-clad Niall sets a huge bowl and serving tongs in the center of the table. "It's loaded with goat cheese, pickled red onions, candied walnuts, and beets. Then I tossed it with a lemon-dill vinaigrette. We serve family-style at Pines & Quill, so please help yourselves." Niall takes a seat at the opposite end of the table from Libby.

With each monthly group of writers in residence, Libby and Niall nod to each other under copper-bottomed pots that hang from the ceiling. In over thirty years of marriage, they've built an extensive repertoire of facial expressions that only they understand.

They settle back—like satisfied cats washing their whiskers—and smile as they watch a small community form. Bonds deepen through conversation as their guests share stories, histories, breakthroughs, and roadblocks, offering advice and feedback, and challenging each other to take risks. This month, the July group of writers should prove no different.

As Libby's about to explain the rest of the evening's agenda—dessert and after-dinner drinks in the Ink Well, followed by each guest drawing a card from *The Observation Deck: A Tool Kit for Writers*—the vehicle sensor buzzes.

"I bet that's Rafferty now. If the phone doesn't ring in a moment, that'll confirm my suspicions; he knows the entry code."

A few minutes later, there's a rap at the front door. They hear it open, and a man's voice calls out, "Honey, I'm home,"

Niall rolls his eyes. "Oh, brother."

Rafferty walks into the room. "Libby, I'm sorry I'm late. Joe and I got caught up. It wasn't until Marci called Joe and told him to get home for dinner that we realized the time."

Libby smiles at Rafferty. *His entire look screams FBI. With a dark suit, a tie loosened at the neck, and disheveled hair, he looks like someone who's had a long, trying day. Behind wire-rimmed glasses are intense, brown eyes. But there's a sadness in them too.*

"No worries. I'm just glad you made it." Libby gestures to the empty chair across from Ivy. "We haven't gotten to the main course yet. Come sit down, and I'll introduce our guests."

When Rafferty steps around the table, he notices a dog on the floor lying next to a pair of shapely legs. "Well, hello there," he says to the black-and-white dog who now stands, her short tail wagging incessantly. "At a little over two feet tall—you must be a standard poodle."

Their interaction elicits a jealous whine from Hemingway.

Rafferty looks at Hemingway, leaning as far over the lower portion of the mudroom's closed Dutch door as he can. He's envious of the attention being lavished elsewhere. "You big lug. I'll come to see you in a minute."

Turning his gaze back to the poodle, he asks, "Who are you?"

Ivy's head tilts up. "This is Maggie. She's my Seeing Eye dog. And you're right, she's twenty-six inches tall."

"May I pet her?"

"As I explained to the rest of the group earlier, it's not a regular practice with service dogs. But since we're going to be together for the next twenty-one days, yes. But let Mags get a good sniff of your hand first."

Rafferty extends the back of his hand for Maggie to sniff.

"Aren't you a beauty?" he says to Maggie, who's now licking his hand.

Ivy smooths the napkin on her lap. "It seems you've charmed her. She's usually a little standoffish with strangers."

Rafferty squats down. "She probably just senses that I love dogs."

"Do you have one? Or should I say, are you *had* by one?"

Rafferty laughs. "With my job and the hours I keep, it wouldn't be fair." He stands up and heads over to Hemingway, stopping at the biscuit jar first. "I fill that vacancy with this big guy." After giving Hemingway the treat, he rubs one of his ears. "Now I better go wash my hands, or Libby will send me to the doghouse too."

"Rafferty, I'll come to the kitchen with you," Niall says. "That way, I can rope you into helping me carry the rest of the meal back to the table."

A few minutes later, Niall and Rafferty return to the table bearing bowls and platters. An intoxicating combination of scents fills the air.

"I knew it," Cheryl says. "I *have* died and gone to heaven. What smells so good?"

"The rest of tonight's meal is wild sockeye salmon drizzled with serrano aioli, balsamic brussels sprouts, and garlic mashed potatoes." Niall places two platters on the table. "Dig in while it's still piping hot."

"I don't mind if I do." Byron lifts a piece of salmon onto his plate. He turns to Ivy. "May I get a piece for you?"

"That would be lovely. Thank you." Ivy feels for the silverware on either side of her plate.

After Rafferty deposits two heaping bowls on the table, he takes a seat. It's quiet for a moment as everyone fills their plates and tucks in.

Niall takes the opportunity to walk around the table and refill wine glasses.

"This is delicious," Ivy says.

Rafferty nods in agreement. "It's incredible what comes out of that kitchen."

Ivy leans forward a bit. "You mentioned that with your job and long hours, it wouldn't be fair to have a dog. May I ask what it is that you do?" She lowered her voice when asking the question.

Rafferty's intrigued by the intimate feel of that. Aware that she can't see him staring, he takes his time gazing at Ivy's features. She's beautiful with her high cheekbones, tapering chin, and shoulder-length, dark brown hair. "I work for the FBI."

"Now *that's* interesting. In what capacity?"

"I'm a special agent who works on criminal cases that cross state lines."

"And you're here writing a book about your experiences?" Ivy asks.

Rafferty wipes his mouth with his napkin. "No. I'm here working on a case with Libby's brother, Mick, a private investigator, and Joe Bingham, a local homicide detective."

From next to Rafferty, Libby interjects. "Just before I picked you and the others up at the airport today, I dropped off Mick and Emma, my brother and sister-in-law." She looks at her watch and sees that it's eight o'clock. "Right now, they're in New Orleans on their honeymoon."

"Oh, I love the Big Easy," Byron chimes in. Raising his glass, he says, "Here's to the newlyweds."

Rafferty joins everyone around the table, lifting his glass in a toast to Mick and Emma. *I hope they've got each other's backs. With so many attempts on their lives, they've been like walking targets.*

Niall, the epitome of efficiency, interjects, "Okay, everyone, it's time to adjourn to the Ink Well. I'll join you soon."

"Thank you for the exquisite meal. I'm stuffed." Byron pats his stomach for emphasis.

Cheryl pushes back her chair. "Me, too."

"Yes, thank you," Ivy and Rafferty say in unison.

"Jinx, you owe me," Ivy says, laughing.

With its floor-to-ceiling bookshelves on either side of the massive fieldstone fireplace, the Ink Well serves as the after-dinner gathering place for guests to continue visiting over dessert while enjoying drinks from the MacCullough's small but well-stocked bar.

With her appetite satisfied, Ivy, with Maggie's help, feels her way through the large cozy room, enjoying its welcoming ambiance.

Rafferty notices coral toenails peeking out of her sandals. The dark mango color of her dress is a perfect foil for her porcelain complexion. That she tucks a phantom strand of hair behind an ear makes him smile—that, and the fact that the soft fabric of her dress caresses her curves.

"Didn't I read something online about a special journal?" Cheryl asks.

"Yes, you did." Libby walks to a thick book on an oak stand, rests her hand on the open page, and continues. "We encourage guests to make entries during their stay. We have entries dating from 1980 when Pines & Quill opened its doors. It's become somewhat of a living legacy, a way for writers to connect with those who've come before and those who'll come after."

Byron smooths the arms of a deep leather chair. "And if memory serves me well, didn't it also say that on more than one occasion, the journal provided clues that helped solve mysteries that occurred here?"

"That's right. And Hemingway too." Libby smiles at Byron. "Snoopy as all get out, he's our resident Sherlock Holmes. But we'll share those stories another evening. I'm curious to know what each of you is working on."

Rafferty feels his cell phone vibrate. Slipping it from his pocket, he takes a surreptitious glance. It's a text from Maeve: *I don't mean to alarm you. Please do NOT say anything to Libby or Niall. Connor texted me well over an hour ago that he was on his way home. He hasn't shown up yet. I've tried calling his cell, but after three rings, it goes straight into voicemail. I'm scared, but I don't want to worry the others if it turns out to be a nonevent. Please call me privately as soon as you can.*

A chill fishtails up Rafferty's spine making the tiny hairs on his arms stand on end, and his heart beats a little too fast. *Maeve would never text me if she wasn't dead certain that something was wrong.*

CHAPTER 13

*"Description begins in the writer's imagination, but
should finish in the reader's."*

—STEPHEN KING

Rafferty lifts his eyes from the display on his cell phone to
see Libby looking at him. *She knows something's wrong.*
"Libby, I'm sorry, but I have to excuse myself. Duty calls."

"Don't worry, Rafferty. With two parents and one brother
in law enforcement, I know the drill."

"If you hear the vehicle sensor go off, it's just me."
Rafferty walks over to Maggie and crouches down to pet the
top of her curly head. "It was nice meeting you, Maggie. I hope
to see you tomorrow." He gazes at her human companion. "It
was a pleasure meeting you as well, Ivy."

Ivy extends her hand until it meets Rafferty's shoulder.
"I look forward to talking with you again. I heard someone
say that you're from Seattle. I'm from there too. Maybe the
next time we meet, we can compare notes."

"I'd like that." Rafferty briefly touches her hand before standing. He turns to Byron and Cheryl. "It was a pleasure meeting you too. Hopefully, I can join you for dinner tomorrow evening. I'd like to hear about the books you're writing."

On his way to the front door, Rafferty detours through the kitchen. "Thank you for dinner, Niall. It was delicious."

"You're welcome." Niall nods toward a serving tray. "Aren't you staying for dessert?"

"I'm sorry, but I got a call that can't wait. I hope to see you tomorrow. I'm heading to the cottage before I leave. I told Libby that if you hear the vehicle buzzer, it's just me."

Niall furrows his brows. "I hope you're able to wrap up whatever's calling you away."

"Me, too. Good night."

Under a starry vault on this first night of July, Rafferty heads toward Thoreau cottage. Malibu lamps work in conjunction with the moon to light the smooth walkway.

Surrounded by western red cedar trees, Thoreau cottage is on the south side of the property. When Rafferty steps through the doorway and flips on the light, he feels the simple, yet full, impact of the natural beauty of the interior's minimalism. Like a magnet, it draws him in.

The south-facing wall is constructed entirely of glass. It frames a breathtaking view of the Bellingham Bay National Park and Reserve, home to El Cañón del Diablo—The Devil's Canyon. So named because of the boulder field at the bottom of a hundred-foot rock wall. *I'm glad it's dark outside and the view's limited because I want to give Maeve my undivided attention when I talk with her. She's not one to cry wolf. Something's wrong.*

———

Libby sets her glass on the antique chest moonlighting as a coffee table in the Ink Well. "Would you mind if Hemingway joins us?" she asks her guests.

"I don't mind at all," Ivy says. "I think it'll be good for Maggie and him to get better acquainted."

Byron and Cheryl, both of them dog lovers, agree.

As Libby stands to get Hemingway, he appears with Niall in the doorway. "I thought I'd check if it would be okay for this big lug to join us."

"Great minds think alike. I was just coming to get him." Libby looks at Hemingway and points to the Turkish rug on the side of her legs away from Maggie. "Come lie down, and behave yourself, young man."

"I'll be right back with the sweet course," Niall says.

Giddy with delight, Hemingway's tail beats the rug. His tongue hangs out of a lopsided grin.

Maggie averts her gaze, seeming to spurn his attention, but her short tail says otherwise.

Niall returns a moment later, carrying a tray laden with dessert, small plates, and napkins. "I hope you saved room for cookies-and-cream truffles."

"Oh, my word," Cheryl says, lifting a black-and-white delight from the tray and setting it on a plate. "Do you share your recipes?"

"I'd be happy to. This dessert is so easy. It only has three ingredients."

While Niall shares the ingredients—"Oreo cookies, softened cream cheese, and melted white chocolate"—Libby makes a dessert plate for Ivy and places it on the side table next to her.

"That's it?" Byron asks around a bite of dessert. "It's delicious!"

"But what do you *do* with the three ingredients?" Ivy asks.

"I crush the cookies and reserve two tablespoons of the mixture for sprinkling on top of the truffles." Niall sets the tray on the coffee table. "Then I stir the crumbs and cream cheese together and chill it for about an hour." Taking off his apron, Niall sits next to Byron. "Once it's chilled, I roll the mixture into golf ball-size portions and dip them in the melted white chocolate, put them on a platter lined with parchment paper, and sprinkle the reserved cookie crumbs on top before the chocolate hardens. That's it."

Libby leans back in her chair and looks at the contented faces of the writers in residence. *They have no idea of the death and destruction that's taken place at Pines & Quill. First, someone shot and killed the woman posing as Pam Williams, a civil rights attorney who came here to work on her manuscript. Then a car bomb meant for Mick and Emma killed the valet, Kevin Pierce, when he turned the ignition key in Mick's Jeep.*

Fear gnaws the pit of Libby's stomach. *I wonder what the text Rafferty received was about? He has a team working on Gambino leads in Seattle. In San Francisco, Dad's following leads at tattoo studios trying to find an artist inking Gambino's mark of ownership—"Family First." And Rafferty and Joe are working the case here in Fairhaven and Bellingham, where two of Gambino's henchmen, Salvatore Rizzo and "Angel" Romano, were killed.*

Libby twists the napkin in her hands. *Please, God, keep my brother and Emma safe on their honeymoon. New Orleans is one of Gambino's three crime headquarters. Mick said that after their honeymoon, while they're still there, he'll try to find leads on the real Pam Williams and her brother Kyle, who are still missing. But I'm scared because, from the attempts on Mick's and Emma's lives, it's evident that Gambino has a contract out on them. And now they're right in his backyard.*

Mick looks at his naked bride and grins. "I've worked up an appetite. I'm starving!"

Emma stretches like a satisfied cat. "I'm hungry too."

"I'll get the menu, and we can order room service unless you want to get dressed and go out?" Mick says.

"Let's order in. I think we'll be *busy*."

When Mick slips back into bed, menu in hand, he notices the clock on the nightstand. *Eleven o'clock.* "Do you feel like eating breakfast or dinner?"

They look at the menu together. "Everything looks good," Emma says. "Why don't we order appetizers so we can try several of their local offerings?"

"That sounds like a great idea."

Once they decide, Mick picks up the receiver on the hotel phone and places their order from the in-house Carousel Lounge and Bar Bite Menu. "We'd like an order of shrimp corn dogs with chow-chow relish, an order of crawfish pies with Creole sauce, an order of oysters Rockefeller, and an order of blue crab and corn beignets with Cajun brown butter and remoulade sauce. And for dessert, we'd like a piece of mile-high sweet potato pie with caramel sauce."

When Mick hangs up the phone, Emma bursts into laughter—it's rich and happy like morning coffee. "They're going to think we're pigs."

"They know we're on our honeymoon, so they know what we've been up to." Mick waggles his eyebrows. "I'm sure we're not the only newlyweds to order practically everything on the late-night menu."

Emma points. Next to one of the chairs is an elegant side table boasting a silver tray with six chocolate-dipped strawberries, two champagne flutes, and an opener. An ice bucket stands table-side with a bottle of bubbly in now-melted ice. "We were so *busy* when we first arrived that I didn't see that," she says. "It could be an appetizer for the appetizers."

"Coming right up, Mrs. McPherson." Mick slips out of bed. The champagne bottle makes a loud pop when he opens it. He pours two glasses and hands one to Emma.

"To us," she says, clinking her glass against his.

"To a long and happy life together." *Please, God, help me keep Emma safe.*

They feed each other the chocolate-dipped strawberries. "Room service said it would be about forty-five minutes before our food is delivered," Mick says.

Emma lifts an eyebrow flirtatiously. "Is that so?"

Mick takes both of her hands in his, kissing them, backs and palms. As their bodies curl toward each other, tender and gentle, to make love, he murmurs her name.

"Emma."

———

Rafferty doesn't place many people on a pedestal. Among the few are Maeve and Connor McPherson. Not only because they're good human beings, but because of their distinguished careers. Before calling Maeve, Rafferty ticks through a mental list of their accomplishments:

Maeve enjoyed a long and distinguished career as a criminal psychologist. Her expertise is the "why" behind criminal activity—the motivation—particularly for violent crimes. When law enforcement agencies try to determine who a criminal is—for instance, a serial killer—they often bring in a criminal psychologist. The CP uses a mix of psychology, pattern recognition, and indicative reasoning to predict a suspect's age, background personality, and other identifying characteristics. The resulting profile is used by law enforcement to narrow down their pool of suspects quickly. Maeve worked with the FBI to help solve crimes by developing profiles of murderers, kidnappers, rapists, and other violent criminals.

Maeve and Connor met at Quantico. She was there training, and so was he. But his area of focus was different. He was there for NAT—New Agent Training with the FBI. To this day, agents recount stories from his long career. Connor worked his way up through the ranks, and by the time he retired, he was the FBI's Special Agent in Charge of Marin, Napa, and San Mateo County offices, and the main office in San Francisco.

Rafferty dials Maeve's number. *Stay on point. She'll appreciate it if I cut right to the chase.*

Maeve picks up on the first ring. "Rafferty, thank you for calling me back so quickly."

"Tell me what you know."

"When Connor pulled out of the garage, I waved to him from the front door like I always do, but he was preoccupied on his cell phone. Then after he left, I noticed his closet door was open. When I went to close it, I saw that his gun and shoulder holster were gone."

Rafferty's impressed with Maeve's succinct briefing. Like bullet points, her information is precise and emotion-free. *Just like we were taught in training—don't waste time.*

"Did you see the list of San Francisco tattoo parlors Connor received from Joe Bingham to check out?" Rafferty asks.

"I did not."

"I'll get it from Joe, then call the locals. I'll have boots on the ground at and near those locations within the hour. Text me a recent photo of Connor. You've already given me a description of his car and what he's wearing. I have his cell phone number, so we might be able to determine the location he texted you from. Maybe even the person he was speaking with on the phone this morning."

Rafferty glances at his watch. *Nine-forty-five.*

"Maeve, I'm booking a flight now. If there's a red-eye from Bellingham to San Francisco, I'll be on it. If not, I'll be on the next flight out. I'll text you when I land. I've got your address. As soon as I rent a car, I'll drive straight to your home."

Maeve loosens the white-knuckled grip on her phone. "Thank you, Rafferty." After he hangs up, she closes her eyes and concentrates on her heartbeat—that even staccato—and the world becomes less blurry around the edges.

I thought the days of constant danger, of not knowing if Connor would live through the day, were behind me. This morning he was excited to "be on assignment" again—this time to help Mick, Joe, and Rafferty with their case by following possible leads to Gambino in the list of tattoo parlors Joe gave him.

And though Connor and I discussed it many times, neither of us can imagine a world without the other.

Maeve sits at the patio table, still set for dinner with Connor, the food long put away. She leans back, exhausted, and looks at the stars pricking the black sky. The moon is down, and the air is cool and still. She rubs her arms.

"Connor," she whispers, "for over fifty years, you never failed to come back to me alive." A tear slides down Maeve's cheek. "I'm counting on you to keep your word, my love."

———

Sitting majestically at the foot of Royal Street, Hotel Monteleone includes the only high-rise building in the interior French Quarter and is well known for its Carousel Piano Bar and Lounge—a rotating bar. Considered a literary landmark, it was a favorite of many southern authors. It boasts five hundred and seventy luxurious guest rooms, including fifty-five luxury suites and literary author suites.

Still family-owned and operated, Hotel Monteleone is staffed by hundreds of employees, but by no means do they all know each other. The visual difference between staff and guests is the distinctive uniform—a burgundy jacket with brass buttons atop a white dress shirt, a gold satin bowtie, matching cummerbund, black pants, and black shoes. The pièce de résistance is a burgundy-and-gold cap set at a jaunty angle. In addition to hotel guests, the staff hustles and bustles on every floor at every hour.

In a first-floor bathroom stall, a man changes into a hotel uniform. After all, a trade has been made; a deal has been struck. After pressing an authentic-looking mustache to the area above his lip, making sure the adhesive holds, he slips on a pair of black-framed glasses. Pulling his cap low, as instructed by Toni, he exits the stall and walks out the restroom door to the kitchen, where by prearrangement, he's been assigned the room service cart for Mr. and Mrs. McPherson.

The delivery cart is draped with a crisp white linen cloth on which sit several gold-rimmed china plates topped with vented silver covers. Before leaving the kitchen, he looks under the linen covering. The cellophane-wrapped gift basket from Toni is there. He remembers what she said. "Deliver the gift basket by midnight tonight. Text me when you're done."

He doesn't know what's in it, nor does he want to know. *A "gift" from Toni could be anything from a bomb to an acid face wash.* He thinks about the photo she texted him with the "congregation of alligators"—his punishment if he fails. *I just want to deliver the package and get the hell out of here!*

He takes the service elevator to the floor with the Truman Capote Suite and notes the time. *Eleven forty-five. Shit!* Filled with fear, he can't even appreciate the scents wafting from the vented plate covers. As the elevator doors open, he removes the basket and carefully places it on top of the cart alongside the covered food plates. The card affixed to the cinched ribbon is written in calligraphy: "For the Newlyweds. Compliments of Hotel Monteleone."

He tries to whistle as he pushes the cart down the hall, but his mouth's too dry. *This is cutting it too fucking close!* When he arrives at the door with a bronze plate above a peephole that reads TRUMAN CAPOTE SUITE, he raps three times then calls out, "Room service."

CHAPTER 14

*"I do not over-intellectualize the production process.
I try to keep it simple: Tell the damned story."*
—Tom Clancy

Mick extracts money from his wallet and wraps a fluffy terry-cloth robe around his naked frame on the way to answer the door. He looks through the peephole and sees a uniformed hotel employee with their room service order.

When Mick opens the door, the delivery man greets him and starts to push the cart into the room.

"I've got it from here, thanks," Mick says, pressing cash into the man's palm. "What's this?" he asks, pointing to the gift basket.

"It's compliments of the house," the man says. "A special treat that newlyweds receive on the first night of their stay."

"That's very generous," Mick says. "Thank you."

"My pleasure. Enjoy the rest of your time at Hotel Monteleone."

Delicious aromas escape the vented plate covers, filling the room with a mixture of savory scents as Mick wheels the cart toward Emma. He bows. "For *madame*. Do you wish to eat at the table or in bed?"

Emma gives Mick a wicked grin. "Let's eat in bed," she says while plumping mounds of pillows against the headboard. She sits cross-legged and leans back to survey the covered dishes. "What's that?" she asks, pointing to the gift basket.

"The delivery guy said it's a special treat that newlyweds receive on the first night of their stay. Do you want to open it now?"

"Sure, let's see what's inside."

Mick wheels the cart next to Emma's side of the bed and picks up the basket. "It's heavy," he says, placing it on the sheet covered mattress in front of her crossed legs.

Emma looks at the card affixed to the cinched ribbon and reads it out loud. "For the Newlyweds. Compliments of Hotel Monteleone."

She scrunches her face in concentration. "You know what?"

"What?"

"I don't want to rush. I want to savor *every single thing*."— Emma emphasizes each word. "Let's enjoy our appetizers first. Then we'll find out what the gift is. After all, we only get one honeymoon. This way, we can stretch out the good things and make them last."

Mick bows from the waist. "As you wish, *madame*."

Emma returns the basket to the cart. "*Madame* wishes for you to get in bed with her." She pats the spot beside her. "Let's eat. I'm starving."

"Me too," Mick says, slipping into bed next to his bride.

Rafferty checks the boarding pass on his cell phone then slips into a spot on the starboard side of the Boeing's four-across cabin. To accommodate his long legs, he purchased an aisle seat. The narrow-body model of this airplane is ideal for short hauls like Bellingham to San Francisco. He looks at his watch. *I'm surprised there are so many passengers on this regional flight at eleven-thirty at night.*

Earlier, when Rafferty called Joe for the list of San Francisco tattoo parlors that he'd given Connor to check out, they agreed to follow Maeve's lead and not call Mick until she gave the word. And while they both understand her desire not to worry him while he and Emma are on their honeymoon, they both know Mick's going to be upset that they held back something this important from him. Nonetheless, they agreed that they'd rather incur Mick's anger than go against Maeve's wishes.

Rafferty takes off his glasses and pinches the bridge of his nose. *Maeve may look innocuous, but I've heard stories from her long and distinguished career as a criminal profiler. Like a tiger, her grace overlays power.* Weary, he slips his glasses back on.

When a flight attendant wheels a beverage cart up the aisle, Rafferty accepts a cup of black coffee. He feels the heat through the Styrofoam and sips it tentatively. As the steam fogs his lenses, he relaxes his shoulders, leans his head back, and looks at the bottom of the overhead compartment. It makes him think of luggage and the adage he lives by, "Travel light, travel fast." Before leaving for the airport, he threw a Dopp kit and a change of clothes into a single carry-on to avoid checking baggage.

Rafferty sets his cup on the tray in front of him and touches the left front side of his suit coat. He feels the shoulder-holstered gun beneath the fabric. *I'm glad that federal agents are allowed to carry weapons on commercial flights. And though I had to declare it at check-in, fill out paperwork, and have an additional screening at the TSA checkpoint, it saves precious time when I land. I can bypass the wait at the baggage carousel and go straight to pick up my rental car. Time is of the essence.*

He'd given the local agents, working in conjunction with SFPD, the list of tattoo parlors Connor was checking out. *They're scouring every square inch in and around each one. There's not a person among us who won't move heaven and earth to locate Connor McPherson. Please God, let them find him alive before I land.*

———

Emma finishes the last taste of their shared dessert, puts a hand on her stomach, and moans. "I think I'm going to explode."

"I'm stuffed too," Mick says. "I don't think I can move. Let's open the gift basket. I hope it's not food."

Emma lifts the basket from the room service cart and once again sets it on the sheet-covered mattress in front of her crossed legs. After untying the ribbon, she pulls back the paper to reveal a bottle of champagne, a bottle of absinthe, a note written on thick ivory-colored cardstock, and a matching sealed envelope.

She reads the note out loud. "Death in the Afternoon, also called the Hemingway or the Hemingway Champagne, is a cocktail made up of absinthe and champagne, invented by Ernest Hemingway. The cocktail shares a name with his 1932 book titled *Death in the Afternoon*, and the recipe was published in *So Red the Nose*, or *Breath in the Afternoon*, a 1935 cocktail book with contributions from famous authors.

"Hemingway loved drinking as much as he did writing. His advice, circa 1935 with this cocktail: 'Pour one jigger absinthe into a champagne glass. Add iced champagne until it attains the proper opalescent milkiness. Drink three to five of these slowly.'"

"Three to five? Good grief!" Emma exclaims before she continues reading. "We hope you'll enjoy both the cocktail and the gift in the envelope tomorrow, Tuesday, July second, along with the other honeymooners staying at Hotel Monteleone."

Emma slips her thumb under the sealed flap of the envelope and opens it. When she pulls out a thick piece of notepaper, two tickets fall out.

"What are they for?" Mick asks.

Emma unfolds the note and once again reads out loud. "There's no better way for out-of-towners to experience NOLA—New Orleans, Louisiana—than on a bayou tour at Swamp Adventures. Let Smith, your knowledgeable and entertaining guide, share his love of Louisiana wildlife, culture, and history with you on your private airboat tour. Here's your chance to see alligators and other swamp creatures close up in the wild on a small, intimate airboat. Please be at the location on the tickets by noon to enjoy this once-in-a-lifetime experience. The honeymoon boat tours are staggered. Yours departs at twelve-fifteen."

Emma turns to Mick. "It sounds exciting. What do you think?"

"If that's what you'd like to do tomorrow, then that's what we're going to do."

"How about you?" Emma asks. "Is it what you'd like to do?"

"I'd like to do *anything* with you, Mrs. McPherson. Anything at all." He looks at the clock on the nightstand. "It's three-thirty in the morning. If we're going to be there by noon, we'd better get some sleep."

Emma places the contents of the gift basket on the room service cart and rolls it away from the bed, then heads toward the bathroom. "I'm going to brush my teeth and get all the sugar from the caramel sauce on the mile-high sweet potato pie off my teeth."

"I'll brush mine when you finish," Mick says.

In the bathroom, Emma looks in the mirror and sees the face of a delighted young woman smiling back. *I've never been so happy in my entire life.*

Rafferty opens his eyes when an announcement by one of the flight attendants comes over the speakers. "Ladies and gentlemen, we've started our descent into San Francisco. Please make sure your seat backs and tray tables are in their full upright position, that your seat belt is securely fastened, and all carry-on luggage is underneath the seat in front of you or in an overhead bin. Please turn off all electronic devices until we're safely parked at the gate. The flight attendants are currently passing through the cabin to make a final check and collect any remaining cups and glasses. Cabin service is now terminated. Thank you."

The plane lands at 1:30 am. *Two hours from wheels up to wheels down. Not bad.* When Rafferty takes his phone out of airplane mode, he sees a text from Jim Beckman, FBI special agent in charge of the main office in San Francisco—the man who took over Connor McPherson's position when he retired. The text says, *Call me when you land, regardless of the time.*

The moment he deplanes and finds a quiet spot, he makes the call. Beckman picks up immediately. "Rafferty, we found McPherson. He's dead."

"Oh, my God," Rafferty says, feeling gut-punched. "What happened?"

"He was shot in his left temple. We found him sitting in the driver's seat of his Prius on the third floor of a multi-level parking garage on Valencia Avenue."

"Why wouldn't somebody parking their car call it in to the police?" Rafferty asks.

"The window's down, so there's no broken glass, and the shoulder strap of his seatbelt's holding him upright. Without closer inspection, he just looks like a man sitting in his car."

"How about security cameras?"

"The footage is being examined right now."

"What's the closest ink shop to that location?" Rafferty asks.

"Black Heart Tattoo. It's probably the last one Connor checked out. His cell phone's on the ground next to the vehicle—crushed. The scene's being forensically processed right now. When they finish, Connor's body will be released to the medical examiner for official identification and determination of cause and manner of death even though it's clear what happened."

"Christ," Rafferty says. *The last time I saw Connor was just the other day. Three of us—Libby, Joe, and I—took a van and a carload of people to Bellingham International to catch their flights home, among them, Connor and Maeve McPherson. Once they stepped through the terminal doors, I told Libby, "I know you already know this, but it bears repeating. Your parents are terrific." She smiled and nodded her agreement. "They're everything to me. I don't know what I'd do without them."*

"I know this doesn't make it any better," Beckman says, "but Connor didn't feel a thing. He didn't even know it happened."

"Does Maeve know yet?"

"No. I waited, knowing that you're personal friends with the family. Would you deliver the news? It might be easier coming from someone close."

"I'd appreciate that," Rafferty says. "I can't imagine that anything will make it easier, but I'll tell Maeve."

Beckman nods. "Dr. Christopher Liverman, the chief medical examiner, will do the autopsy in the morning. I'll text you the exact address later; it's on Newhall Street."

"I'll find it," Rafferty says.

"You know the drill, Rafferty. Even though we all know Connor McPherson—hell, who doesn't?—Maeve still needs to make a formal identification."

"I'm going to pick up a rental car and head to the McPherson's house now." Rafferty takes off his glasses and wipes his eyes with his sleeve. "I'll bring Maeve by tomorrow." His voice catches on "Maeve." *I can't believe this is happening, that Connor's dead.* He replaces his glasses and turns to look at his watch. "Make that *today* once the ME's in. Thank you, Beckman. I appreciate the workforce you authorized for the search."

"You'd have done it too. McPherson was one of our own."

"Yes," Rafferty says, feeling a gut-hollowing loss. "He was the *best* of our own."

Maeve feels movement in the air; it caresses her cheek. She wakes from a dream and sits upright in her living room chair. The dream was so real. She was having dinner on the patio with Connor. They were talking about a book they're reading together, Peter Mayle's *A Year in Provence.*

"Connor?" Maeve whispers. She stands and walks to the light switch on the wall and flips it. The ceiling light comes on then flickers several times before holding steady. "Connor?" she says again, this time a little louder. She feels a gentle touch on her shoulder. It's as if Connor's in the room with her. Then just as quickly as it came, the feeling of his presence is gone. *Is that his way of letting me know he's okay, of helping me to accept the unacceptable?*

Maeve lights a candle and shuts off the lights. As she watches the orange flame, her breathing slows, and her thoughts flow. *Darkness always makes me feel safe like I do under the night sky, like I did in Connor's arms.* "Did." *There, I said it—past tense.* As Maeve feels tears slide down her cheeks, her cell phone alerts her to a text. It's from Rafferty. *Maeve, I just pulled into your driveway. I want you to know I'm here so I don't startle you when I knock on the door.*

Maeve turns on the front porch light and opens the door. She sees Rafferty; light from the streetlamp behind him halos his head. Her heart lurches at the invisible weight pressing down on his shoulders, on her shoulders. The magnitude of it is almost too much to bear.

Rafferty walks toward her; his face is ashen. "Maeve." His voice is low and shaken. "I'm so sorry. So very, very sorry."

Falling between Mick and Libby in age, Rafferty's like another one of my children. If his heart's breaking this much, I can't imagine what it's going to do to them. Maeve steps forward and wraps Rafferty in her arms. "Just before you arrived, Connor told me goodbye."

———

Mick reaches over to the nightstand and slaps the "off" button on the alarm clock. "No way, no how," he says before covering his face with a pillow.

"Oh, no, you don't, Mr. McPherson," Emma says. "You said, and I quote, 'I'd like to do *anything* with you, Mrs. McPherson. Anything at all.' If we're going to make it to Swamp Adventures in time, we've got to rise and shine."

Mick lifts the pillow and squints one eye open. "What makes you so perky this morning?"

Emma smiles. "It's what happens when a woman is satisfied. If you follow me to the shower," she says, leaning forward and finishes on a whisper, "I'll make you a satisfied man."

Mick throws the pillow across the room and jumps out of bed. "Last one in the shower's a rotten egg!"

Later, Mick sees Emma watching him dress. His outfit includes his Glock 22 in a back-of-the-waistband holster clip. It's designed for ultimate concealment.

"Are you expecting trouble?"

"I hope not. But with the attempts we've had on our lives, I'd rather be safe than sorry."

They drive the rental Jeep to Antoine's Restaurant on St. Louis Street. When it was recommended to them, they were told, "It's the oldest family-owned restaurant in the country serving traditional French Creole cuisine since 1840."

Once seated, Mick and Emma are informed that they're too late for the breakfast menu.

Mick grins and gives Emma an unrepentant look.

They order an early lunch of seafood gumbo. It's made with blue crab and shrimp stock, trinity, Gulf shrimp, oysters, crabmeat, okra, and filé. Neither of them is familiar with trinity or filé, so their server explains. "Trinity is two parts onion to one part each celery and bell pepper. Filé is a powder made from dried sassafras leaves; it's a traditional thickening agent for gumbo."

When the server leaves, Mick leans across the table and whispers, "*Lunch* is what you get for dawdling, Mrs. McPherson."

"You didn't seem to be in too much of a hurry yourself, Mr. McPherson."

Mick makes up for lost time on their drive to Swamp Adventures. "Thank God for GPS." Once parked, they walk to the pier. There's only one airboat left. A man in the boat stands and greets them. "You must be Mr. and Mrs. McPherson. I'm Smith."

"I'm sorry we're late, Smith," Mick says.

The man looks at his watch and smiles. "You're not late; it's only ten past noon. You have five more minutes."

Mick nods toward a shotgun near a steering mechanism that looks like a large joystick.

"What's that for?"

The man turns and points. "See those over there?"

"The logs?" Emma asks.

"Those aren't logs, ma'am. They're alligators. Look closely, and you'll see them blink now and again. And while they look kind of lazy right now, they can get—" He pauses. "Well, let's just say they can get *unruly* at times. Got your tickets?"

With one foot in the airboat, Mick feels his back pocket and finds his cell phone. That's when it dawns on him that it's been off since they got to their hotel room.

He turns to Emma. "I just realized our phones have been off since we arrived." Mick switches his on and sees several missed calls, voicemails, and a text that says, *Urgent—call me,* from his mother.

When he turns back to explain to Smith that he needs those five minutes, after all, Mick finds himself looking into the barrel of the shotgun.

CHAPTER 15

"The most valuable of all talents is that of never using two words when one will do."
—Thomas Jefferson

L ibby usually enjoys being alone with her thoughts. But this morning, they're unpleasant. In the night, she'd dreamed that someone tried to kill her brother and his new wife on their honeymoon in New Orleans. The vision—*something to do with water, both of them being pulled under*—keeps resurfacing in her mind's eye. *I'm going to text them to make sure they're okay.*

Libby sits at the patio table just off the dining room of the main house. She's tired from a lack of sleep. *Tuesday morning sure came quickly.* In the distance, she sees Hemingway. His front paws are high up on the bark of a tree trunk. *With any luck, whatever he chased will stay hidden in the branches, well out of his reach.*

The sun is just rising, cut in half by the jagged line of treetops on the eastern side of their property, turning the sky gold and pink.

Let go of your worry, Libby tells herself. She inhales slowly then exhales deeply. *There, that's better.* She pats the arms of her chair. *Summer in Washington State is always gorgeous, and today, the second day of July, promises to deliver. It's perfect for bicycling into town to pick up a few new reads from Village Books.*

She smiles as she remembers when she and Niall decided to add bicycles to the perk list for their guests. They had to reprint the cheerful monogrammed notecards with P&Q, Pines & Quill's initials, that they leave on the kitchen counter in each cottage. Inside it reads:

Pines & Quill offers writers a peaceful, inspiring, wooded setting to pursue the work they love. We aim to encourage artistic exploration, nurture creative thought, and forge bonds between diverse thinkers. Our vision is for you to find inspiration and make progress on your work.

Located between the main house and the garden is a common area that includes laundry facilities and supplies, a printer and paper, and assorted office supplies should you need them.

There are also bicycles with covered saddle-baskets if you feel adventurous and would like to explore the surrounding area or pick up sundries in town. Each basket contains a map of Fairhaven, a brisk fifteen-minute walk or a five-minute bicycle ride from Pines & Quill.

In the crisp air, Libby's breath puffs into clouds. She pulls her thick chenille bathrobe tighter as she waits for Niall. *I'm fortunate to have a husband who loves anything to do with the kitchen.* In the background, beans groan in a grinder; an espresso machine gurgles and whistles. *It's a noisy endeavor, making coffee.*

It was after eleven o'clock last night when Ivy, Cheryl, and Byron returned to their cottages. They'd had a pleasant evening in the Ink Well—the main house living room and after-dinner gathering place for guests to continue visiting after dinner. It's here they enjoy dessert and drinks from their house bar. If the Pines & Quill reviews are anything to go by, their writers in residence appreciate its bevy of comfortable, over-stuffed chairs, floor-to-ceiling bookshelves, and the massive fieldstone fireplace.

With such a late bedtime, Libby's glad that everyone agreed to take a pass on the six o'clock tai chi session this morning. "But we promise to make it a regular habit after that," they said.

Just then, a bathrobe-clad Niall joins Libby on the patio with two large mugs. The rich scent of coffee fills the air. Steam, like the breath of ghosts, wafts around them. "Here's your coffee, love."

Libby cradles the coffee mug with both hands as Hemingway joins them. The look he gives them speaks volumes. *Where's my treat?*

Niall reaches into a pocket on his robe and extracts a biscuit. "I didn't forget you, big fella."

Tail wagging, Hemingway settles at their feet. He sets the biscuit on the pavers between his massive front paws and guards it.

Libby laughs. "Protecting his loot is half the fun for him."

"I think you're right," Niall says. "By the way, I never heard Rafferty's car come back last night. Did you?"

"No, and I was listening for it."

Niall leans forward and tucks a loose strand of hair behind one of Libby's ears. "Are we still expecting Mick's and Emma's replacement Jeep to arrive today?"

"Yes, but the delivery window they gave me is huge, and I was hoping to take one of the bicycles into town to Village Books."

"I'll hold down the fort," Niall says. "I need to work in the garden anyway."

Libby turns and studies his face. Although it's tan and weathered from working outdoors, she loves it.

"Since you're going to the bookstore, will you pick up a book for me?"

"Of course," Libby says. "What's the title?"

"Well." Niall hesitates. "As you know, I haven't been dealing well with Paddy's death. Father Burke at St. Barnabas recommended *The Empty Room: Understanding Sibling Loss.*"

Libby sees an all-too-familiar sadness in Niall's eyes. It's taken up residence since Paddy's death.

Niall picks at imaginary lint on the sleeve of his robe. "Nothing will ever help me to understand why he was *murdered*—why anyone would shoot a priest to death in a confessional. But I'm hoping to learn how to work through my grief, how to live without him. Since I was born, Paddy's always been part of my life. When I lost him, I lost part of myself too."

Libby sets her mug on the patio table. Closing the gap between them, she sits on his lap and wraps the warmth of her body around him, pressing her forehead to his. "I love you, Niall, and I'm so sorry for what happened to Paddy. I loved him too."

"I know you did. And he loved you."

"Between Mick, Joe, and Rafferty," Libby says, "they'll find who killed Paddy and the other people too, including Kevin Pierce, the valet who died in the explosion when he moved Mick's and Emma's Jeep at their wedding. And hope-fully, they'll find Pam Williams and her brother Kyle; their parents, Walter and Maxine Williams, are heartsick."

Niall thumbs a tear from Libby's cheek.

"We're fortunate to still have both of my parents who love you like a son, Mick who loves you like a brother, and our son, Ian, who adores you. The love of family is everything."

There's been so much death. Please, God, keep us all safe.

———

Emma stands on the pier behind her husband. Caught off-guard, Mick has one foot on the deck of the airboat and the other on the dock. Stark terror kicks her heartbeat into over-drive when Emma sees that Smith, their bayou guide, has a shotgun trained on him. Adrenaline floods her veins, trigger-ing a fight-or-flight response.

Emma eases Mick's Glock from his back-of-the-waist-band holster clip. She's familiar with the model because of the target practice she does with her father and three brothers. Their handgun of choice? "I'll take a Glock 22 every time," they practically say in unison, high-fiving each other when they annihilate the range targets with forty caliber Smith & Wesson rounds.

Unlike most centerfire handguns, the Glock doesn't have a hammer that drops to push a firing pin when the trigger's pulled. Instead, it has a striker enclosed within the slide—ideal for rapid-fire.

Emma steps to the right from behind Mick, racking the slide, and fires once, twice, three times in succession. The first bullet pierces Smith's left shoulder. The second one knocks the shotgun out of his hands. And the third bullet hits his right thigh, sending his body over the side of the airboat into the swamp water. He comes up sputtering. "God fucking damn it. Get me out of here." His hands grip the gunnel of the boat.

"I don't want to be eaten by gators." His gaze darts left and right. "Help me!" he yells.

Emma points the barrel of the gun past the boat. "Mick, the alligators are headed this way."

Mick grabs a coil of rope and wraps part of it behind Smith's shoulder blades and under his armpits. "Grab onto the rope."

"I fucking can't," he whines. "Your wife shot me."

"If you don't want to be gator bait, you'll grab onto the rope and help me to hoist you up."

Both men startle when they hear two gunshots. They look in the direction where Emma's pointing the gun. One of the gators rolls slightly then starts to sink beneath the water. It does nothing to slow the other two. Their approach is rapid. One opens its massive jaws emitting a deep bellow. The other alligator submerges, a precursor to a "death roll"—when an alligator rolls its prey under the water violently to bring it into submission before death.

Smith looks over his shoulder. His scream pierces the air.

Horror-struck, Emma watches the water roil beneath him. She moves to get a better shot at the visible alligator, then fires two successive rounds into its gaping jaws. It jolts backward before slipping under the surface, bubbles replacing where its head had been.

The bayou guide's fearful cries blend with the shrieking "ha-ha-ha" from a colony of gulls overhead. It serves as their alarm call. Smith's feet peddle furiously under the water.

Emma sees sweat rolling off Mick's face. His hands slip on the rope—once, twice, creating enough slack for Smith's head to go under. The grip of his white-knuckled hand releases the gunnel.

Emma watches Mick wrap the rope around each hand and pull with everything he has. Then she sees blood in the water. "Oh, God, Mick!"

Smith's head resurfaces briefly. "The bastard's got me. He's pulling me under. Help me; get me out of here!"

Running to Mick, Emma sets the gun on the deck, wraps her arms around his waist, and pulls with him. *It's like a tug of war with Smith in between us and the alligator.* Her nostrils flare at the scent of their sweat—the sour stench of fear.

Their combined effort's enough for Smith to gain purchase. He swings his good leg over the gunnel, but the foot of his other leg is trapped in the alligator's jaws. Its menacing eyes watch them from just above the surface.

"Mick, have you got him? I'm going to let go so I can shoot it."

Mick braces himself. "I've got him," he yells.

Emma picks up the gun and jumps onto the pier to take the shot she needs. Careful not to hit Smith, she squeezes off three rounds.

The alligator bellows, releasing Smith's leg. When he surges forward, Mick falls backward, catching himself before going over the other side of the airboat. Bent forward with his hands on his knees, Mick's chest heaves as he gulps in air.

Smith lies sprawled facedown on the deck; his breath comes in gasps as bloody swamp water spreads out from his body. His untucked shirt exposes a "Family First" tattoo on his lower back.

A gruesome bite mark above Smith's ankle bleeds profusely, and the shoe on that foot is gone.

Mick uses Smith's belt as a tourniquet to keep him from bleeding to death.

Emma maintains her position, gun at the ready, while Mick calls the police and rapidly explains the situation, including the need of an ambulance.

"What the hell is wrong with you? You could have killed me!" Smith glares at Emma—his voice sharp as a blade.

"If I'd wanted to kill you," Emma says, "you'd be dead."

Mick squats on the deck of the airboat in front of Smith. "I want answers. And I want them *now*. Why did you hold a shotgun on us?"

"I wouldn't have done it myself," he snarls, "but I'm under orders."

"Whose orders?"

"One of Gambino's lieutenants. I don't know her name."

"*Her?* A woman?"

"Yes. I was supposed to take you deep into the bayou and force you to jump into the water. You'd have been the first ones I'd ever fed to the gators *alive*. They usually bring me dead bodies."

Repulsed, Mick asks, "When was the last time you fed someone to the alligators?"

"I have no idea, you son of a bitch. It's not like I keep details in a planner."

Mick points to the alligators. "We didn't save your sorry ass just to hit a brick wall."

Mick grabs the back of the man's shirt with one hand and his belt with the other and begins to stand. "I'm not at all above tossing you back in."

"Wait a minute. Wait a minute!" Smith shouts. "It was about a month ago." He pauses. "Yeah, on June first. I remember the day 'cause I got a DUI that night. I was drinking to forget. I've had to get a ride to work ever since."

"What was different about that day? What did you need to forget?"

"It was the first time that Shelly ever brought me a woman's body to dump."

"Who's Shelly?"

"Shelly Baker. She works for Gambino."

"Is she the lieutenant you mentioned a minute ago?"

"No, she's an underling to that lieutenant. The interesting thing about Shelly is that she looks exactly like the woman she had me dump. I mean *identical.*"

"Who was the woman you dumped?" Mick asks.

"I don't know. Some bigwig attorney."

"Does the name Pam Williams mean anything to you?"

Smith's eyebrows lift in surprise. "Yeah. Now that you say it. That was her name. Gambino had us torch her office a few months before Shelly killed her, but it seems she didn't get the message. Shelly said she waited for the woman on the floor in the back seat of her car in the garage. Williams was going to the airport to fly to some writing thing. Shelly used a garrote. She always says, 'No muss, no fuss.' Because they were identical, she took her place. I guess Gambino has a long-term job for her on the West Coast because I haven't seen Shelly since."

Wailing sirens split the air. In moments, two white squad cars with blue detailing, including a star—its five points supporting an elongated half-moon arched over it—screech to a halt. Four car doors fly open, and four officers step out, guns drawn.

"Set your weapon on the pier, ma'am, and step away," one of them says.

Emma looks at Mick, who nods.

"Now you two," the lead officer says, "get out of the boat and don't make any fast moves."

"I can't move fast," Smith complains. "I've been shot twice and mauled by an alligator."

"Then stay put."

He nods at two of the officers. "Go guard that guy, will ya? And you two," he says, pointing his gun at Mick and Emma, "step this way."

When they reach the two officers, the lower-ranking one frisks them. When it's clear they're not concealing weapons, Mick puts an arm around Emma's shoulder and answers the lead officer's questions, only moving his arm when asked to produce his identification and credentials. *Gambino tried to have us killed. Again. What is it he thinks we know or have?* His gaze drifts down to the top of Emma's head. *God, I love this woman. Thank goodness for her quick thinking, or we'd both be dead.*

When the ambulance arrives, the two officers guarding Smith lift him by each of his arms, none too gently. One of the officers wrinkles his nose. "Good Lord! You stink like old crab and wet dog."

Standing on one leg, Smith yells in pain then hurls insults like rocks. "You fucking pigs are going to pay for this. I'm going to call my lawyer!"

Mick looks at Smith and raises an eyebrow. *It seems that the irony of the situation is lost on Smith.* They watch as one of the officers pulls a wallet out of Smith's pocket and opens it. He holds it next to the man's face. "Yep, he matches the photo on the driver's license—Gianni Greco."

After the paramedics load Greco into the back of the ambulance, an officer climbs in with him. When a paramedic closes the doors, he asks the remaining officers, "Which hospital do you want us to transport him to?"

"University Medical Center," one of them says. "I'll follow."

He turns to Mick and Emma. "You said you're here on your honeymoon, staying at Hotel Monteleone. How long do you plan to be in New Orleans?"

"We fly home July tenth, so a little more than a week," Mick says.

"All right. That should be sufficient in the event we need to contact you for more information." After confirming their contact details, he gets in his vehicle, and both squad cars pull away.

Emma turns into Mick's embrace. He rests his chin on the top of her head. "Are you okay?"

"I don't feel sick to my stomach; I feel sick at heart."

"Your quick thinking saved both of our lives."

Emma tips her head back and looks at Mick. "You can thank my dad for that. He *made* me practice with him and the boys. I didn't like it one little bit. Not until I got better than them." Emma grins. "Then it was fun to rub their noses in it."

Walking through the humid air—intensified by the bayou—to their rental, Mick says, "I need to go see Walter and Maxine Williams to let them know what we learned about Pam."

"Do you think Gambino had that done to her brother, Kyle, too?"

"No, I don't believe so. Remember, Kyle came to Pines & Quill to visit Pam. Only none of us knew at the time that she was an impostor. The identical-looking Shelly Baker was posing as Pam. She must have messed up or crossed somebody because, as you know, she was killed—shot through the bedroom window in Dickens cottage. I'm going to call Rafferty now so he and Joe can start working with this information, then I'll call Mr. and Mrs. Williams."

As the newlyweds sit in the parking lot to recover in the Jeep's air conditioning, Mick speed dials Rafferty.

Rafferty picks up on the first ring. "Mick, we've been trying to reach you."

"You and Joe? What's up?"

"No. Me and your mother. She's here with me now."

"My parents are in Fairhaven?"

"No, I'm with Maeve in San Francisco. Hold on. I'm handing the phone to your mom."

Mick hears the phone change hands. "Son, I'm pressing the FaceTime button so we can see each other."

Mick positions the phone so that he can see his mother on the screen. When her face comes into view, he can tell that she's been crying.

"Mom, what's wrong? Why's Rafferty there? Where's Dad?"

"Honey, I just got off the phone with Libby. She's on her way."

Tears start to sting Mick's eyes. "Mom, you're scaring me. What's wrong?"

Maeve's voice catches. "Honey, your father died."

"Oh, my God!" Mick cries out. Tears begin to fall from his eyes and roll down his face. His voice thick, he speaks around the lump in his throat. "Mom, what happened? Was Dad in a car accident? Did he have a heart attack?"

"Mick, he'd been canvassing the list of tattoo parlors that Joe gave him. He sent me a text. It said, *Maeve, I think I may have hit pay dirt. I'll explain when I get there. Do you need me to pick anything up on my way home? I love you.* That was the last time I heard from your father."

"But what *happened?*" Mick pleads.

"It was a hit. Your dad was shot sitting in his car in a parking garage on Valencia Avenue."

Mick struggles to speak. "I can't believe it. I just can't believe Dad's gone. Emma and I are on our way. We'll be there by nightfall."

CHAPTER 16

"When writing a novel, a writer should create living people, people, not characters. A character is a caricature."
— ERNEST HEMINGWAY

L ibby pulls another tissue from the pack; her lap is littered with their crumpled aftermath. *I can't believe that Dad's dead. There has to be a mistake.* As her flight descends through a blanket of dark clouds, she's able to make out the Golden Gate Bridge through her tears and the slashing rain outside the plane's porthole-size windows.

The overhead speakers come to life. "Ladies and gentlemen, we've just been cleared to land at the San Francisco International Airport, where the local time is four o'clock. As you can see, it's raining, which is unusual for this time of year in their quasi-Mediterranean climate. Eighty percent of the rain falls in five months, November through March. April is iffy; often sunny and warm, but it can get rain. The rest of the year, May through October, only gets about five percent of the annual rainfall. That said, in the event of turbulence, please make sure one last time that your seatbelt is securely fastened."

I took pain-relief capsules over an hour ago, but my head's still pounding. Come on. Kick in. Libby closes her eyes and unfists the tissue in her hand. She places one palm on her stomach and the other on her sternum in an attempt to regulate her breathing.

Inhale. Exhale. She senses the passenger in the next seat is watching her.

Inhale. Exhale. She hears the thud of the landing gear lock into place.

Inhale. Exhale. She feels the lump in her throat move, and a sob escapes.

I can't imagine my life without Dad in it. He was such a special man, warm and kind, with a deep sense of personal dignity. He was always there for me, my rock.

Tears continue to slip unchecked down Libby's face. *In less than a day, my life feels like it's careening out of control.*

Mick tightens his arms around Emma in their hotel room as he presses his face into her shoulder. *Dad may have been an FBI agent by day, but he was a gardener, lover of nature, and keeper of the land on his own time. Growing up, I loved watching and helping him tend to our acreage. I'm the person I am today because of his love of these things. I love and protect my family because he loved and protected his.* "I don't think it's a good idea for you to stay behind. We just escaped another hit by Gambino, Emma. Come with me. Forget about chasing these mobsters. I can't lose you too."

"Mick, your dad invested his entire career in bringing thugs like Gambino to justice. And it's why you got your PI license, so that you can assist Rafferty and Joe with criminal investigations without your hands tied by red tape like theirs. Your mother and sister need you, Mick.

"I'll be less than twenty-four hours behind you. It wouldn't be right to share the information we learned about Pam with her parents over the phone. It needs to be delivered in person. So in the morning, I'll check out of the hotel, drive to their home and talk with them, then fly back to Bellingham to help Niall with this month's guests. Libby flew to San Francisco to be with your mom. Niall can't do everything by himself."

Mick zips his luggage closed, then crosses the room to the balcony.

Emma joins him and wraps an arm around his waist. "This is what family does, and I'm part of the family now. Please let me help, Mick."

He turns and gently cups Emma's face, a hand on either side. He feels tears slip down his cheeks. "I love you, Emma. I love that you're my wife, that you're part of my family, and that you want to help. And I understand the need to share the news about Pam in person. But I'm scared. I don't know what I'd do if one more person dies on my watch."

"No one has died on your watch, Mick. You've got to stop blaming yourself for things you have no control over."

"I can't help it. I feel responsible. And I feel responsible for you too."

"Mick, I took care of myself when Alex Berndt held me hostage in that cave in The Devil's Canyon. I stabbed him in the thigh, and then you shot him. We make a good team. And this afternoon, I shot Gianni Greco when he was going to feed us to the alligators. I'm capable."

"Are you saying you don't need me?"

"I'm saying that I need you, but that you need me too. It's a two-way street. We've got to have each other's backs."

Mick tilts his head. "Are we having our first fight?"

"No," Emma says. "We're having a discussion where I convince you to let me help."

Mick pulls Emma into his arms. "Promise me that after you drop me off at the airport, you'll come straight back here and lock yourself in. Then after you visit Walter and Maxine in the morning, you'll go to the airport and fly out."

Emma stands on tiptoe and kisses Mick. "I promise." She lifts her wrist so they can both see her watch. "It's six o'clock. We have to leave now if you're going to catch your flight. And you need extra time because you have to check your gun case."

The burden of survivor's guilt weighs heavy on Mick's shoulders. *I can't believe my dad's gone, that I'll never be able to hug him again or tell him that I love him. I remember buying my first car when I was sixteen—an old Volvo wagon with a stick shift that Dad taught me how to drive. One day when we were out having a lesson, I was nose-first at the top of a hill, and another car pulled up behind us close to our back bumper. I was petrified. "Dad, let's trade seats. I can't do it. I'll roll and hit them."*

"You can do this, son. Just a minute."

Dad got out of the car and walked to the driver's window of the vehicle behind us. When he explained the situation, they backed way up.

When Dad got in the car, he said, "Mick, you've got this."

The car rolled, but I did it. And with Dad's continued encouragement and confidence in me, it wasn't long before I drove on Filbert Street, the steepest street in San Francisco, and nailed it.

Mick gazes at the sky and tries to draw a deep breath, but his chest feels like it's gripped in a vise.

"If we hadn't included my dad in the Gambino case, he'd still be alive."

Niall's stomach twists with worry. *By the time Libby booked a flight and we got to the airport, grief had swallowed her and spit out someone who looked like my wife but was unrecognizable in every other way.* He glances at the kitchen clock. The amount of time since he'd last heard her voice is stacking up with excruciating insistence.

Before dialing each cottage to ask Ivy, Cheryl, and Byron to please let themselves in the main house when they come for dinner, he reminds himself of what Libby said. "Niall, don't wear your heart on your sleeve. Their time away is supposed to be fun for the writers in residence. In the past two months, we've had so much death and heartache at Pines & Quill that if we're not careful, our bookings will dry up. I'm counting on you to be your usual cheerful self."

Cheryl is the first guest to arrive. She pops her head around the corner of the kitchen area. "Hi. Am I the first one here?"

"You are." Niall nods toward the clock that displays six o'clock. "And you're right on time."

She steps closer and inhales appreciatively. "It smells wonderful, kind of"—she searches for the right word—"*fiery.*"

"You've got a good nose." A cloud of steam rises when Niall lifts a lid from one of the pans on the stove. "It's spicy scampi, this evening's appetizer."

Cheryl looks at the simmering contents. "Oh, wow! Now my mouth's watering. What's it made with?"

And though he doesn't feel like it, Niall smiles. "It's sautéed prawns, shallots, butter, garlic, tomatoes, capers, white wine, lemon, and spicy chili pepper flakes. And I serve it with grilled crostini. Speaking of which," he says, pointing to a thickly sliced loaf of ciabatta bread on a cutting board. "While I finish getting this ready, will you please drizzle those slices with olive oil?"

"I'd be happy to," Cheryl says.

"Thank you. The cruet is on the counter to the right of the oven—careful; it's hot. Once drizzled, if you'd pop the slices in the oven and then stand guard, they only get *one* minute on each side."

"I'm on it, Chef. I'll just wash my hands first."

Niall hears Hemingway woof in the mudroom off the dining area. "I've got five dollars that says Ivy and Maggie are here."

"What can we do to help?" Niall and Cheryl turn to see Byron and Ivy accompanied by a self-satisfied-looking Maggie.

"I won't turn down any offers of help," Niall says. "It would be terrific if you'd set the table with four place settings."

Above her shaded glasses, Ivy's brows arch. "Only four?"

"Rafferty hasn't made it back yet, and Libby got called away unexpectedly."

"Okay, four place settings it is," Byron says.

Niall reaches for a serving platter. "You'll find everything you need on the side table."

"I'll join you in a minute," Ivy says to Byron before she and Maggie step toward Niall. "Is everything okay?"

I'm so glad she can't see me. "Yes, everything's fine," Niall says.

Emma pulls curbside at the Departures terminal and steels herself. *Show Mick that you're strong, courageous, and can help with his work even though you're scared.* She unbuckles her seatbelt and turns toward Mick. Emotion tightens her throat. "I love you more than you'll ever know, Mr. McPherson."

Tears well in Mick's eyes as he pulls her into his arms. "Emma, you know I don't want you to stay here by yourself. The only reason I agreed to this is that you promised to fly home the minute you share the news we learned about Pam with her parents, Walter and Maxine Williams."

Emma leans into Mick's embrace and speaks against his neck. "Thank you for believing in me. You help your mom and sister. And when I get home, I'll help Niall. Your family, *our* family, needs us right now."

They walk to the back of the Jeep, where Mick retrieves his carry-on bag and gun case. To keep her unshed tears from falling, Emma tips her head back and pretends to look at the predusk sky.

Mick takes her in his arms; his bear hug lifts her off the ground. After they embrace, they pull back and gaze into each other's eyes. "I love you," they say in unison.

Emma puts on a brave face and blows a kiss to Mick as he turns one last time before stepping through the doorway of Louis Armstrong International Airport. She drives the rental to the cell phone waiting lot, parks at the curb, and lets thick tears fall from her eyes and roll down her face.

Ten minutes later, spent, she looks at herself in the rear-view mirror and sees puffy half-moons under reddened eyes. "All right, Emma, it's time to gather yourself together and get to work." She pulls her cell phone out of her purse and Googles "waiting time for a gun in New Orleans." The results show that the state of Louisiana doesn't have a waiting period for gun purchases.

Next, she Googles the closest gun shop to Hotel Monteleone and drives to Gretna Gun Works on Lafayette Street. *It's only six miles from the hotel and right on the way. And though a concealed carry is illegal without a permit, I don't have time to wait for one. I'd rather take my chances now and have the opportunity to explain myself later than be dead.*

When Emma steps into the gun store, a door entry chime announces her arrival. As she gazes around the space, the faint smell of burned gunpowder pinches at her nostrils. Two walls are lined with firearms—one with handguns, the other with shotguns and rifles. The adjoining area features an assortment of reloading equipment, including canisters filled with various types of gunpowder. A third wall exhibits a selection of hunting bows—long, cross, compound, and recurve—with a choice of arrows for each type. Ammunition, and other hunting accessories, including camouflage clothing, are on display near the cash register. Through the glass upper half of the fourth wall, Emma sees an indoor shooting range. Most of the stalls are occupied with people target practicing.

An older man lumbers from behind a glass case where knives stand at attention in foam displays like soldiers in neat rows. "How can I help you, little lady?"

I know exactly what I want. The same handgun I always use when I practice with Dad and my brothers. "I want a Glock 26, two boxes of 9mm self-defense ammo, a belly band concealed carry holster, and a hard-sided Pelican case for travel."

The look of incredulity on the man's face would be laughable at any other time. Emma nods toward the glass wall. "I see you have an indoor range."

The man's chest puffs up. "One of the finest."

Emma enters the shooting range where the smell of burned gunpowder is no longer faint; it assails her nostrils. She steps into an empty stall, slips on a pair of amber shooting glasses and hearing protection, clips a paper target to the pulley system, and sends it fifty yards downrange. Then, ready to test her new weapon, she loads a magazine with bullets, inserts it into the Glock, racks the slide, and fires ten consecutive rounds.

As she pulls the target back toward her, she realizes that it's quiet—no one else in the range is firing. Curious, she turns around to find the other shooters gathered behind her.

"That's a mighty impressive pattern on your target," one of the men says.

"May I see that?" another one says, reaching for it. Target in hand, he whistles. "It's a tight circle, not more than five inches in diameter over the heart."

"Where'd ya learn to shoot like that?" a preteen boy asks.

Emma nods toward the man—presumably his father—standing next to the boy. "Practice. Lots and lots of practice with my father and brothers."

When the others return to their stalls, Emma loads another magazine, inserts it into the Glock, and puts on the belly band. She tucks in the gun and leaves the store with the remaining items in a bag. As she pulls out of the parking lot, her stomach growls. It dawns on her that she hadn't eaten since Antoine's Restaurant this morning with Mick. *I'm not taking any chances with room service—look what happened last time!* She spots a Popeyes Louisiana Kitchen and uses the drive-through to order dinner, then proceeds to the Hotel Monteleone. Her mind is racing. *I think I know how to locate Pam Williams's brother, Kyle.*

Mick stows his carry-on in the overhead compartment then sits next to the window. Unfortunately, with a last-minute booking, he wasn't able to get a seat on the aisle. He rubs the top of his left thigh. *My leg is going to ache by the time we land.*

He looks at the long line of people as they board, trying to guess which one is the FAM—federal air marshal. Finally, when all the passenger luggage is stowed and everyone's seated, a male flight attendant's voice comes over the speakers. "Ladies and gentlemen, on behalf of Captain Hunter and the entire crew, we would like to welcome you aboard American Airlines flight 1492, with nonstop service to San Francisco . . ."

Mick tunes it out. *The last time I flew with Dad, the two of us went on a fishing trip to Montana. We stayed at the Gallatin River fly-fishing lodge just outside Bozeman. The river is medium-size and flows north from its origin in Yellowstone Park, past the town of Big Sky, through the Gallatin Canyon, then through the pastoral Gallatin Valley to its confluence with the Missouri River. Dad and I fished our hearts out. We enjoyed float fishing and wade fishing, and it was my first time fly fishing. But he was a great teacher. Between his expertise and the high trout density, the river produced fast action and a high catch rate for both of us. And though the Gallatin River isn't known for trophy trout like some of the larger rivers in the area, its beauty and intimate nature made it a favorite of the other anglers we talked with at the lodge. I can't believe I'll never have the chance to fish with my dad again.*

Mick wipes his tears with his sleeve, then glances at his watch. *If we take off at eight o'clock central time, we should land at nine forty-five Pacific time.* Anxious to get going, he drums his fingers on the armrests. *By the time I collect my gun case, rent a car, and drive to the house, it'll be after eleven o'clock. I'm sure Libby's staying in her old room, and Mom's probably put Rafferty in my old room—we can bunk together. No matter how many people are there, the house will feel empty without both of my parents in it.*

An exhausted-looking young woman carrying a sleeping toddler in a car seat sets the child down in the middle seat next to Mick. "Hello." Her voice is weary. "This is us." She nods to the two seats on Mick's right.

"What can I do to help?" he asks.

"If you'd strap the car seat in, that would be nice. And because Jillian's under two years old, the seat needs to face backward."

Mick has it done in a short time.

"Thank you. Not only was that fast, but you also did it right. Are you a dad?"

"Not yet," Mick says. "I used to be a police officer, and believe it or not, it was part of our training."

The woman holds out her hand. "I'm Bonnie. Please don't think me rude if I don't talk during the flight. I try to get some sleep when Jillian sleeps."

Mick shakes her hand. "It's nice to meet you. I'm Mick, and I'll most likely sleep too."

After a few minutes, the speakers activate once again. "Ladies and gentlemen, we have just been cleared for takeoff. Flight attendants, please be seated."

Mick looks at his seat companions to see if the announcement woke the baby. *They're both sound asleep.* Satisfied, he leans his head back and closes his eyes. *Emma will make a great mother. And if I'm half the father my dad was . . .*

Mick swallows a lump forming in his throat. *When I was about five years old, I remember Dad let me use my "muscles" to make strawberry ice cream from scratch with an old hand-crank ice cream maker. It seemed like I turned the handle endlessly. But when he offered to take over, I kept at it. My reward was a huge dish of ice cream. I devoured it so fast that I got a brain freeze.*

Behind his closed lids, Mick's eyes sting with unshed tears. His hands curl into fists. *I've always worked on the premise of justice rather than vengeance. But this time, I'm not so sure.*

———

When Emma enters the Truman Capote Suite, she locks the door and leans against it. As she surveys the lavish space, her gaze drifts to the bed. *The bed Mick and I made love in repeatedly on the first night of our honeymoon. Before Gambino's lieutenant—whoever she is—tried to have Gianni Greco, alias Smith, feed us to the alligators. The bed's made, so housekeeping's been here. I wonder if anyone else has been here or is here right now?*

Emma sets her purse and two bags on the floor before pulling the Glock 26 from her bellyband. She sweeps from left to right with the gun extended, clearing the space, including the bathroom, closets, and balcony. *No one's in the suite.* After holstering the weapon, Emma closes and locks the sliding glass door to the balcony, then wedges one of the table chairs under the door handle. She relaxes her shoulders and exhales deeply. *I didn't realize I'd been holding my breath.*

Emma gathers her purse and bags, carries them to the table, and gets a bottle of water from the suite's refrigerator. Then, exhausted, she collapses into a chair. Tears blur her vision. *Mick's probably halfway to San Francisco by now, and Libby's already there. The loss of their father has crushed them. Maeve's heart is broken at the death of her husband. And I'm on my honeymoon alone.* Overwhelmed with sadness for them all, Emma's throat clenches. She twists the lid off the bottle of water and takes a sip.

As sadness ebbs, anger takes its place. Anger at the waste of innocent lives—Mick's partner, Sam, Niall's brother, Paddy, the civil rights attorney, Pam Williams, and the young valet, Kevin Pierce. Each of them flashes past her mind's eye before she settles on a resolve.

Fortified with determination, Emma opens the fast-food bag and pulls out her meal. She takes small bites and chews slowly, mulling over her plan, then checks her watch. Using her cell phone, she Googles the time difference between New Orleans and Tucson. One hour.

It's seven o'clock mountain time in Tucson. So it's not too late to call.

CHAPTER 17

*"If you want to be a writer, you must do two things
above all others: read a lot and write a lot."*
—STEPHEN KING

Mick's drive from the airport to his parents' home on the outskirts of San Francisco is slow going because of the unusual July downpour. *As much as I'm coming home to lend emotional support to my mother and sister at my father's death, I need their comfort, too, because I don't know what I'll do without Dad. He's always there for me. He's the most important influence in my life.* Mick can hardly tell the difference between the rain sluicing down the windshield and his tears as the wipers work furiously, trying to keep the glass clear. Knuckles white on the steering wheel, he hunches forward to see two feet beyond the nose of the car.

An eternity later, his headlamps sweep across "McPherson" on a mailbox. There are two unfamiliar cars parked in the brick driveway. *One's probably Libby's rental; the other must be*

Rafferty's. The clock on the dashboard indicates that it's ten minutes past midnight. *It's already Wednesday, July third. Emma said to text her when I get here, no matter the time.*

Mick pulls his cell phone out of his pocket and types a short text. He presses "send" and hears the outgoing *whoosh.* He inhales deeply. *I miss my wife. I understand what Emma's trying to do for me, for our family. But it doesn't feel right that we're apart.*

As he walks across the driveway, Mick gazes into the past to see his dad again. He remembers the year he was a freshman in college. *Dad and I tore out the concrete driveway and installed brick pavers. It took us forever—the driveway seemed to grow as we worked—but Mom was so pleased with what she called "aesthetic appeal" that it was well worth the effort.*

Mick's pulled from his memory when the door opens and his mother steps out. In the shadow of the interior entryway, he sees Libby and Rafferty behind her. As Maeve steps toward him, her face crumples, and she cries.

Mick's heart breaks for his mother's pain, for his pain, for their pain. He pulls her into his arms and lays his cheek on her silver hair.

Libby joins the family hug, with Maeve in between them. "I can't believe Dad's gone," she sobs.

Rafferty steps forward and grips Mick's shoulder. "I'm so sorry. You know how much I looked up to your father. Connor McPherson was one of the finest men I've ever known." Stepping back, Rafferty says, "I'll go put on a fresh pot of coffee while you get settled. And if it's okay, I'm bunking with you in your old room."

"That's—" Mick's voice cracks, and he clears his throat. He takes a moment to gather his emotions. "That's great, Rafferty. Thank you for everything."

I've come home to comfort my mom and sister, but it'll take everything I am not to allow the heartache of losing my dad to level me. Besieged by warring emotions, Mick's grief is deep, but his anger is deeper, a black force of revenge uncoiling inside him. He feels a muscle twitch in his jaw. *I'm going to find my father's killer, and nothing will be able to help him or her when I do.*

Emma turns out the light in the Truman Capote Suite, then slips between the crisp hotel sheets. *It's been a long day, and I'm exhausted. I need to get some sleep before my appointment with Mr. and Mrs. Williams tomorrow morning. How can I tell them what happened to their daughter, Pam, without emotionally destroying them? How can I say that one of Gambino's minions, Shelly Baker, used a garrote on her, then drove her body to the swamp where it was fed to alligators to eliminate the evidence?*

Emma lets her gaze drift to the nightstand. The red digits on the clock gleam 2:10 a.m. *The good news is that I might have a way of locating their missing son, Kyle. And while that won't lessen the pain and loss of their daughter, it may give them a shred of hope.*

Just then, her phone dings indicating an incoming text. She takes it from the nightstand and reads. *I just got to the house. I love you. I miss you. Sleep well, darling.* Her heart aches from missing Mick. She smiles as she types a reply. *I was just thinking about you. I miss you and love you too. I'll call you from the airport tomorrow after I speak with Walter and Maxine Williams. Goodnight, love.* After pressing "send," she hears the whoosh of her outgoing text.

Emma laces her arms behind her head and thinks about the phone call she'd made to Tucson earlier. The instructions she received included, "Make sure that it's something personal, something that others haven't touched since he disappeared."

Emma releases her arms and rolls toward Mick's side of the bed. She presses her face into his pillow, imagining that his scent lingers there.

Her eyes widen. *That's it. His pillowcase!*

———

Gambino is agitated. *Heads, I kill her. Tails, I don't.*

He flips a coin, catches it in his right hand, then slaps it on his left wrist. *Tails, I don't.*

He speed dials Toni Bianco. When she picks up, he growls, "Just shut up and listen. When you witnessed what piranha can do in our most recent conversation, I told you that I'd add you to the bone pile if your plan failed. It failed. I was going to put a contract on you, but then something occurred to me. A way that you can redeem yourself.

"I hear that Giani Greco's got diarrhea of the mouth—singin' like a bird to anyone and everyone who'll listen. I'll see to it that he's transferred from the hospital to the jail within the hour. You see to it that he never speaks to another person, that he never leaves jail alive. Make it happen within the next twelve hours.

"Don't think of disappointing me again, Toni. You might be able to run, but you can't hide."

Gambino disconnects the call.

———

Mick accepts a cup of hot black coffee from Rafferty. "I want to thank you again for everything you've done for my family and me."

"I'm glad to be able to help. I know you just got here, but we have an early morning appointment at the morgue." He nods toward Mick's mom. "Maeve knows the options, but she wants to make the formal identification in person. I suspect that you and Libby do too."

"Yes," Mick and Libby say in union.

"All right then, I'm heading to bed. I'll set the alarm for six."

Mick sits on the couch between his mother and sister for nearly an hour, their faces distraught and bloated from crying. The three of them hug, talk, and weep.

Maeve wipes her eyes. "Libby, do you remember the time that Dad played beauty parlor with you and let you put pink sponge rollers in his hair?"

Maeve turns to Mick. "This was way before you were born, dear."

Mick laughs through his tears. "I would have loved to have seen that. I can't even begin to imagine Dad playing beauty parlor. Nor can I imagine his hair being long enough to curl."

"Your dad was part of a sting operation down on the docks at the time. He looked pretty grizzly at that point."

"Curlers wasn't all," Libby says. "While the Dippity Doo gel in his hair set, he let me paint his nails."

"Fire engine red," Maeve smiles. She glances at the clock on the wall and pats the tops of her grown children's hands. "We've got an early start tomorrow. I think we should end on this cheerful note and go to bed. I'll see you in the morning." She stands and kisses the tops of Mick's and Libby's heads before walking down the hall.

Libby scoots toward her brother and leans against his side. She wraps her arms around her waist in a self-comforting hug. "I can't believe that Dad's gone."

Mick puts an arm around Libby's shoulder and pulls her tight against his side. His eyes glisten with tears. "I can't believe Dad's gone either."

Emma hears a crinkling sound when her checkout invoice and a copy of the *New Orleans Advocate* slide under her hotel room door. A quick turn of her wrist informs her that it's eight o'clock. She picks up the paperwork, glad that she made checkout arrangements the previous day. But, then, the title above the newspaper fold grabs her attention: "Another Inmate Dies at New Orleans Jail After Collapsing, Sheriff Says."

Emma pours a cup of black coffee and sits at the table to read.

A man who was incarcerated at the New Orleans jail yesterday collapsed and died early this morning, less than a week after another relatively young man died in an undetermined manner.

Orleans Parish Sheriff Emile Franko's office said 42-year-old Gianni Greco collapsed from an "apparent medical issue" during a "medication pass."

Deputies and medical personnel on duty in his unit treated Greco until paramedics arrived to take him to University Medical Center, where he was pronounced dead, the agency said.

Greco's next of kin was notified. The Sheriff's Office said it's launching an internal investigation, and autopsy results are pending. An Orleans Parish Coroner's Office spokesman said he would likely have more information next week.

Greco's is the second recent unexplained death of an inmate after an unusual, 18-month period where nobody died in the sheriff's custody. On June 25, 27-year-old Edmond Drake collapsed in his day room and was pronounced dead after being transported to the hospital.

The Sheriff's Office didn't immediately answer whether it believes the two deaths are linked to each other.

While the Sheriff's Office has been under federal oversight for most of the past decade, Franko said last month that he thought it was time for the jail to exit its court-ordered reform agreement, known as a consent decree, which was imposed in part because of frequent inmate deaths.

Emma feels her heart racing. She sets the newspaper down on the table. *The way that Gianni Greco was blabbing,*

I bet Gambino had him killed. I've got to get out of here. I can't trust anybody—not even the police.

She looks at the keyring sitting next to her purse. *I don't dare use the rental car; Gambino may have had it rigged with a bomb. So instead, I'll take a taxi to the Williams home and ask them if they can drop me off at the airport. Before I board my flight, I'll call the rental car agency and let them know where the car is and explain that they may want a bomb squad to check it out first.*

Rafferty shuts off the six o'clock alarm. "I'll hit the shower after you," he says to Mick's slow-moving form across the room.

"All right. I'll be quick and then go make a pot of coffee."

When Mick's out of earshot, Rafferty calls Joe in Bellingham, then presses the phone to his ear.

"Bingham. What's up, Rafferty?"

"I received information late last yesterday that I don't want to share in front of Mick. It might make him angry enough to do something he'll regret later."

"What is it?"

"When the FBI team here in San Francisco went over footage from the security cameras in the parking garage where Connor was killed, and from nearby storefronts, they spotted a person of interest."

"Who?" Joe asks.

"It looks like none other than your ex-partner, Toni Bianco. She was coming out of Black Heart Tattoo on Valencia Street. I wonder if she's the "pay dirt" Connor referred to in his last text? Remember, it said, *Maeve, I think I may have hit pay dirt. I'll explain when I get there.*

"She told Bruce Simms, the police chief, that she was going to San Francisco to help take care of her mother who fell. So the location adds up. The suspicious part is the tattoo parlor." Joe's voice has ratcheted up a notch with excitement.

"I agree. And there's a way we can check to see if the *other* part of her story holds water."

"What part's that?" Joe asks.

"The part about her mother falling and breaking her hip."

"What do you propose?"

"Call Toni and say that the precinct chipped together to send flowers to her mom, but you need a delivery address."

"Then what?"

"See if she balks."

"Why don't I just ask Chief Simms to give me her mother's contact information?"

"Because we don't know yet if he's clean or part of Gambino's network. That's why we went over his head to Federal Judge Watson for clearance to tap Toni's home and phone and to put tracking devices in her personal and work vehicles."

"Of course," Joe says. "I haven't had enough coffee yet. Okay, I'll call her. What if she doesn't balk?"

"Then send flowers."

———

Toni, third in line at Pontilly Coffee, looks at her ringing cell phone. Joe Bingham's name is on the display. *What the fuck?* She's tempted to let it go into voicemail, but with all that's happened—a failed attempt on Mick's and Emma's lives and the death of Gianni Greco—curiosity gets the better of her.

"Bianco."

"Hey, Toni. It's Bingham."

"You know I'm on vacation, right?"

"We heard that your mom took a nasty spill and that you're helping to take care of her."

Toni softens her voice a bit. "Yea, it's been rough going, but she's coming along."

"I'm glad to hear that. The precinct chipped in and ordered

flowers for your mom to help cheer her up. But we don't have a delivery address."

Toni's free hand curls into a white-knuckled fist. "Oh, that's nice, but not at all necessary."

"It's already done, Toni. We just need the delivery address."

Shit, shit, shit. "I'll give you the address where I'm staying and deliver the flowers to my mom."

"You're not staying with your mother?"

"No, she's in convalescent care."

"Give me the name of the facility, and we'll have them sent to her there."

"No way, Bingham. You know how those places are. The employees will keep the flowers for themselves. Mom'll never get them."

Toni quickly looks up the hotel address where Bobbi, her impersonator, is staying in San Francisco. "Have you got a pen and paper?"

"I do. Shoot."

I fucking wish I could shoot you right between the eyes. After Toni relays the information, Bingham says, "We'll have them delivered today."

"Please give everyone my thanks, Bingham."

After she disconnects, Toni shout-whispers "Fuck!" garnering several curious glances from the patrons around her. She steps out of line and speed dials Bobby, her friend who headlined at the Baton Show Lounge in Chicago—America's premiere drag showcase. The nightclub features the best of the best female impersonation and male revue.

A male voice answers. "Hello, this is Bobby."

"You need to be on top of your game and soon," Toni says. "The Bellingham Police precinct is sending flowers for dear old Mom, and you—impersonating me—need to receive them on her behalf."

Bobby's voice switches to Bobbi's voice. "Oh, honey. I can do that, and with pleasure."

"And under no circumstances are you to tell them where she's at."

Bobbi winks. "You mean the Baggit and Scat cemetery?"

"That's right. I need to get a little more mileage out of my mother."

Rafferty shows his badge at the front desk of the San Francisco County morgue and signs in four people—himself, Maeve, Libby, and Mick.

The current chief medical examiner, Dr. Christopher Liverman, conducts investigations of violent, sudden, unexpected, and suspicious deaths occurring within San Francisco County or any death where there's no doctor in attendance. The office works hand in hand with local law enforcement and functions as a repository for records, documents, and photographs generated during death investigations.

Moments later, the receptionist says, "Dr. Liverman will see you now." She points down a hall. "Take the first right you come to, then it's the second door on the left."

As Rafferty leads the way, his shoes' soles slap the floor softly with each step, a rhythmic whisper against the seamless, industrial flooring. Finally, they stop in front of a door. The brass plate is engraved AUTOPSY SUITE.

Rafferty turns the handle, then ushers Maeve, Libby, and Mick into the room before him. With his gaze, he sweeps the space when he enters, taking in the tile, stainless steel, and porcelain. Designed for the task at hand, it's completely functional. Everything is polished and smooth. Easy to clean.

The overly sterile smell assaults Rafferty's nostrils, catapulting his mind to the death of his sixteen-year-old son, Drew. He'd been a passenger in a car that flipped over, smashed into a tree, and killed him on impact. Rafferty had gone to King County morgue in his hometown of Seattle to identify Drew's body. His ex-wife, Pamela, said she couldn't handle it. So he'd gone by himself.

Rafferty registers the wall of refrigerated body drawers. *I wonder how many deaths Gambino is responsible for? And now he's dug his claws into Mick's family to exact payment for the loss of over ten million dollars in heroin, first with the death of Niall's brother, Patrick MacCullough, and now with his father, Connor McPherson. I wonder who the next target is and how we can stop him?*

The air conditioner kicks on; its hum fills the air around them.

From behind, Rafferty sees Maeve stiffen her spine as if fortifying herself for what's to come. Libby takes her mother's hand. Mick's arms are rigid at his sides except for his hands. He clenches and unclenches his fists.

Rafferty remembers five years ago when he braced himself to identify his son. *But, then, no matter how many times I'd seen death, there was nothing that could have prepared me for seeing Drew, still and cold, on a morgue gurney.*

Wearing a thigh-length white lab coat over blue scrubs, the medical examiner steps forward and extends his hand to Maeve first, then the others. "I'm Dr. Liverman. I'm sorry to meet you under these circumstances. Special Agent Rafferty said you were coming this morning, so I have the body ready for identification."

Rafferty nods his silent thanks to the ME for his kindness of removing the emotional agony of pulling Connor McPherson's body from a refrigerated drawer. *I hate that Maeve, Libby, and Mick are going through this. Heaven help the son of a bitch who did this to them.*

He remains standing respectfully behind Connor McPherson's family as Dr. Liverman walks them to a waist-high table.

On it, there's a white cloth covering; the outlines indicate a body underneath.

The steady thrum of the ventilation system shuts off, engulfing the space in silence.

Rafferty hears the *ba-boom ba-boom* of his heartbeat pounding in his head. He feels the burn of tempting tears he fights to hold back as he watches the doctor's hands lightly grasp the top edge of the sheet.

CHAPTER 18

"Write until you are not afraid to write."
—SETH GODIN

Emma gazes at the colorful view as the taxi whisks her to Mr. and Mrs. Williams's home in the Carrollton-Riverbend neighborhood in New Orleans. She pulls her blouse away from her skin. At not quite ten o'clock, the morning's humidity level has begun its notorious climb. The weather station on the radio announced it was already 69 percent, heading to 92.

The oak-lined streetcar route, Carrollton Avenue, runs through this busy uptown neighborhood, ending where the Mississippi River bends, and St. Charles Avenue begins. It's not lost on Emma that the lovely scenery is in stark contrast to the ugly news she's about to deliver.

She presses a hand to her chest. *This neighborhood would have been fun to visit with Mick on our honeymoon. I miss him so much.* Emma wipes a tear from her cheek. *I have no experience losing a parent or a husband; it must be gut-wrenching. I hope that Mick, Maeve, and Libby are going to be okay. I'm so glad they have each other for support after Connor's death. Likewise, I'm relieved that Mr. and Mrs. Williams have each other. They'll need one another's help after I share the news about their daughter, Pam.*

The taxi turns right on Dublin Street. In addition to various local shops and small businesses, the area is home to a slew of restaurants featuring global cuisines, including Barcelona Tapas and Lebanon's Cafe. When they were planning this trip, she and Mick had read about southern favorites, such as Brigtsen's and Carrollton Market.

Another turn and the taxi's cruising down Oak Street. Emma sees that it offers its own series of shops and restaurants alongside popular entertainment venues, such as Maple Leaf Bar and Jacques Imo's.

When the car pulls in front of the Williams's home—a raspberry-color Creole cottage with white trim—Emma pays the driver and includes a handsome tip.

"Would you like me to wait?" he asks.

"No. I've got a ride from here, but thank you for asking." She takes a deep breath as she watches the taxi pull away from the curb and maneuver down the street. *I don't know if it's real or I imagine it, but I swear I smell barbecued shrimp.* Then, she hears the blare of what sounds like a ferry on the Mississippi River.

Emma ascends six steps—each one clad with a colorful paisley carpet tread—to the narrow porch that spans the front width of the cottage. The wrought-iron railing is painted white to match the cottage's trim and the divider grills inside the floor-to-ceiling windows.

A few heartbeats after she knocks, an older gentleman answers the door. The scent of cinnamon wafts toward her.

Emma extends her hand. "Mr. Williams, I'm Emma McPherson. We spoke on the phone."

"Yes, we've been expecting you. Come in. And please call me Walter."

He leads Emma to a sitting room that looks out the picture windows facing the street. It feels pleasant and cozy— like home. The walls are a soft pistachio color that lends a serene feeling to the welcoming space. It has a comfortable-looking hunter-green and burgundy plaid couch, two wine-colored wingback chairs, a worn leather recliner, small dark-wood side tables, a few well cared for potted plants, a glass showcase in a corner with trophies, and a bookshelf beside the showcase. *I wonder if the awards belong to their children, Pam and Kyle? Oh, by gosh, what I'm about to say is going to break their hearts.*

Emma crosses the room to an older woman sitting in a wingback chair and extends both of her hands. "Mrs. Williams, I'm Emma McPherson."

"Thank you for coming, dear." She gestures toward a chair. "Please have a seat, and do call me Maxine; everyone else does. I baked this morning. Would you like a cinnamon roll with some coffee or tea?"

"No, thank you. I just ate." Emma's nervous; her stomach constricts. *I can't imagine receiving the news I'm about to deliver. I'm afraid it's going to shatter their world.* She clears her throat. "There's no easy way to say this, so if you don't mind, I'll just start."

Maxine looks at Emma. "We're expecting the worst, dear, so go ahead."

As gently as she can, Emma explains what she and Mick learned about their daughter, Pam. Shelly Baker used a garrote to kill her, disposed of her body in the swamp, and then because she looked almost identical to Pam, took her place at the writing retreat to fulfill a contract for Georgio "The Bull" Gambino.

Emma looks back and forth between the distraught parents. Maxine sits motionless, staring at something only she can see. Tears run down her cheeks; they're a mother's tears. Deep. Raw. A crumpled tissue rests in one of her hands.

Walter bites his lip to keep from sobbing. Unshed tears glisten his eyes as he walks to a side window and points through the glass. "When they were kids, Pam and Kyle used to play on the tire swing I attached to the limb of that tree." His voice has thickened. "They took turns pushing each other, screaming with delight as they tried to touch the clouds with their toes."

Through the window, morning sunlight pours across the hardwood floor, lighting dust motes.

Emma's heart aches for the older couple. "This doesn't lessen the pain of losing Pam," she says, "but the woman who killed and then impersonated your daughter is no longer living."

Maxine turns to Emma. "She's somebody's daughter, too. I'm sorry for her parents, but I'm glad that she's no longer a menace to society. Thank you for telling us. Thank you too for coming and telling us in person about what happened to Pam. Do you have any idea of where Kyle, our son, is or what's happened to him?"

"I don't," Emma says. "But I think I know someone who can find out. May I share a story with you?"

Mr. Williams wipes a sleeve across his eyes. He crosses the room, sits back down in his chair, and leans forward, his elbows on his thighs. "Yes, if it'll help us find our son, we'd like to hear it."

"A few months ago, I was held hostage by Jason Hughes, an alias for Alex Berndt. He worked for Gambino—the mobster who had Shelly Baker kill your daughter."

Walter grips his hands together. His knuckles are white.

"When Alex took me to a canyon cave, I dropped one of my pearl earrings, then the other, along the way, like a trail, hoping that someone would find them. It turns out that Hemingway, our dog, found them and put up a fuss until my husband and brother-in-law caught on to what Hemingway was trying to tell them.

"To keep from contaminating them, they used leaves to pick up the earrings, put them in their pockets, and ran back to the main house to show them to Cynthia Winters, one of our writers in residence at the time. She's also a forensic intuitive."

Maxine's head snaps up. "The same Cynthia Winters who's on television?"

"Yes, the same. She read the energy vibration from the earrings I dropped to locate me."

"Do you think she could find our Kyle?" Walter asks. "Or has it been too long?"

"Kyle went missing in early June," Emma says. "It's early July now, so it's only been about four weeks. I called Cynthia in Tucson last night, and she's willing to try. She asked me to 'get something personal, something that others haven't touched since Kyle disappeared.' I thought that maybe on the way to drop me off at the airport, we could stop by his house, and I could take his pillowcase. Has anyone changed it since he's been gone?"

"No. We've been in his house, but we didn't change any bedding," Maxine says. "We've been in both the kids' homes because we miss them so much."

Emma looks at her watch. "If we leave right now, we'll have time. And while I don't want to get your hopes up just to have them dashed, whatever it is that Cynthia Winters does, works. I'm living proof."

Maeve grips the gurney's edge in the morgue as Dr. Liverman, the ME, gently draws back the upper portion of the white sheet.

Bathed in the surgical light glaring from overhead, Connor McPherson lay on a sheet of cold brushed steel with a lip and channels around the edge.

She momentarily thinks about the drain hole at the other end of the table. Her hand goes to her mouth, and she repeatedly swallows to keep from throwing up.

Maeve feels Mick and Libby tighten their flank on each side. She draws strength from their presence as she looks at her husband, her lover, her best friend, the father of her children. *For decades we lived together, loved together, laughed, and cried together. We experienced everything that two people can except for the death of a spouse. What am I going to do without you, Connor?*

Using an index finger, Maeve traces the letters on Connor's shoulder—IAGDTD. She thinks about the day over fifty years ago that they got their tattoos. She reminisces out loud.

"Connor's lettering stands for 'It's a good day to die.' That's how your dad felt—even after he retired—about his role in the FBI. He wanted to make the world a better place. He always said, 'I'd be glad to die protecting others if that's what it takes.'"

Maeve bends forward and kisses Connor's cold forehead. "I'd do it again, too," she whispers. "But I prefer what my lettering stands for—'It's a better day to live.'"

She directs her tear-filled eyes to the ME and nods. "Yes, Dr. Liverman, this is my husband, Connor McPherson." Then taking each of her children's hands, she says, "I'd like to go home now. It's going to take a lot of time and effort to catch Gambino."

"But, Mom—"

Maeve interrupts Mick. "I've spent my entire working life with the FBI to help solve crimes by profiling murderers, kidnappers, rapists, and other violent criminals." She touches Connor's shoulder again. "Even though I'm retired, this is the most important case I'll ever work. Not just because of Connor, although that's the impetus. But because Gambino's evil is so far-reaching—New Orleans, San Francisco, and the greater Seattle area.

"As a forensic psychologist, I'm not only interested in *why* people commit violent crimes, but I'm trained to look at the prevalence, likelihood, and timing of their next crime."

Maeve levels her gaze first at Mick, then at Rafferty. "I'm *going* to help you catch this monster and put him behind bars before he or one of his henchmen kills another person."

———

An FBI agent posing as a florist delivery person knocks on Bobbi's hotel door.

"Who is it?"

"New Leaf Florist. I have a delivery for Marcella Bianco."

The door opens, revealing a tall, slender woman with short dark curly hair. She looks just like the photograph he was shown of Toni Bianco.

"I'm Toni, Marcella's daughter."

"Wonderful. Could you sign here, please?"

Bobbi, posing as Toni, accepts a clipboard and pen and signs for the arrangement.

The agent, pretending to adjust his shirt collar, uses the button camera to take photographs. Then, after tucking the clipboard under his arm, he hands the flowers to Bobbi.

"Thank you," she says. "These are positively lovely."

The agent smiles. "I hope your mother enjoys them. Have a pleasant day." *And if you're a dirty cop, I hope you rot in hell.*

———

Emma exits curbside from the back passenger side of the Williams's car with her purse and two pieces of luggage. She checks her watch. *It's almost noon. It took longer at Kyle's home than I thought it would. We couldn't find a large enough ziplock bag to put his pillowcase in, so we used plastic wrap instead. And I put my hands inside sandwich bags to keep from touching the fabric and contaminating it.*

She leans over and speaks through the open window on Maxine's side. "I promise to keep you apprised of any developments regarding Kyle."

After they thank her for everything she and Mick have done on their behalf, Emma walks to the Departures terminal. She completes the paperwork for her handgun, checks it with the agent behind the counter, then proceeds to security. The lines are long, but with a TSA PreCheck ticket, she bypasses the stocking-footed walk through the X-ray machine and goes straight to the PreCheck line for expedited entry.

On the long walk to her departure gate, Emma's nostrils catch the smell of jet exhaust, fast food, and the heady mixture of perfumes and colognes that hang like an invisible cloud over the crowd of bustling people jockeying for position in food, coffee, and restroom lines. As she passes Gate B14, she notices that most of the waiting passengers in the boarding area have their eyes focused on a television display. Curious about what's so fascinating, Emma joins the onlookers.

"I repeat, we interrupt this program to bring you a breaking story of an explosion in the 200 block of Royal Street in New Orleans. First responders are on the scene."

The camera pans to a reporter standing in front of a pressing crowd of people.

"Sarah Winston is live at the scene. Sarah, what can you tell us?"

"Jonah, as you can see, it's chaotic. And as of now, the location and source of the blast are unclear. Most of the people I spoke with say it sounded like it came from there." Sarah points in the direction of a multilevel structure. "The parking garage of Hotel Monteleone. But that has not yet been confirmed."

"Sarah, can you tell us if there are any casualties?"

"Jonah, WGNO was the first news crew on the scene, but it's still too early to say. At last count, there are two ambulances and four fire trucks, but I have not seen anyone being treated by the paramedics. I will remain on scene as this story unfolds. This is Sarah Winston coming to you live from the 200 block of Royal Street. Stay tuned to WGNO, New Orleans' Very Own, for updates. Back to you, Jonah."

Oh, my God. The rental car! The muscles in Emma's body clench in panic as her brain scrambles to figure out where she can hide. Alarm twists her heart. *You're safest with a lot of people around. No one will try to kill you in a busy location. Stay in plain sight.* Fueled by fear, she dashes to her departure gate, takes a seat with her back to the wall, and scans the crowd. *Which one of you works for Gambino?*

———————

Gambino presses a speed dial button on his cell. A moment later, he hears Toni's voice.

"Bianco."

"You did good killing Gianni Greco. How'd you do it?"

"Before his death, our former colleague, Andrew Berndt, taught me a lot about untraceable drugs and poisons that cause death."

"Go on."

"Because Greco was transferred to jail from the hospital, I figured he'd at least of had some general anesthesia for the treatment of his gunshot and alligator wounds. So I used suxamethonium chloride, a drug used for that purpose; it would be in his system anyway. But when given in a much higher dosage, it's lethal. It causes paralysis of the entire body, including the respiratory organs, which leads to death by asphyxiation."

"How'd you get it in him?"

"I used one of our guys in the kitchen. Because it's tasteless, he put it in his food."

"A death in jail is going to be autopsied. What about the medical examiner? Won't he get suspicious?"

"The beauty of suxamethonium chloride is that that the body breaks it down quickly, leaving no obvious traces. But still, it leaves clues and byproducts that are indicators of its presence in the bloodstream at some point. But like I said, Greco was at the hospital for treatment anyway. So if the ME does find any traces in his system, he'll chalk it up to that."

"I'm impressed, Bianco. And I've got another job for you. It's in Bellingham. Leave New Orleans today."

Gambino disconnects the line.

Maeve, Mick, and Libby hug Rafferty one more time in front of Maeve's front porch before he heads to the airport. The sky's blue seems exceptionally crisp, almost startling, as it sometimes does after washed with rain. It's at odds with the mounting anger Maeve feels at the loss of her husband.

"I know you've got a flight to catch," Maeve says. She looks at her watch. "It's almost ten o'clock. Will you make it to the airport on time without speeding?"

"The morning rush is over. I'll be just fine."

Maeve is still reeling from identifying Connor at the morgue this morning, from loss. *It's difficult for me to do what I was taught as a forensic psychologist—detach and compart-mentalize. Yet, it's what kept me sane my entire career. But this isn't a stranger, a case number. It's Connor, my husband. It's up close and personal.*

Gambino, a psychopath, had him killed. Serial killers like him are likely intelligent, of at least average IQ, charming, possibly married, outwardly optimistic, manipulative, and they appear to function well within the boundaries of society.

I remember one of my instructors saying, "Psychopaths and sociopaths are different. Not that a psychopath will kill you or that a sociopath won't, but the likelihood of death at the hands of a psychopath is exponentially greater. And in almost every case, they're harder to catch."

With Connor gone, I have nothing to lose. I'm not going to waste time falling apart; I can do that later. Right now, I'm going to help catch a killer.

Maeve sets her resolve as she shifts from her mental reverie. "Thank you again for everything, Rafferty."

"You're so welcome; I'm glad I could help." He takes her hands in both of his. "I shared the lead that Toni Bianco was seen on security footage near the parking garage where Connor was killed. An FBI agent posing as a flower delivery person just left her hotel room where he used a button camera on his shirt to take photos of her. They sent the images to Joe Bingham in Bellingham for a positive ID. While she's still here in San Francisco, Joe and I will tap her house, probably tonight. We already tapped her personal car, squad car, and office phone."

Maeve squeezes his hands. "Rafferty, I'm serious about helping to put Gambino away. I know it's unorthodox, but please send me everything you've got on him and Toni. Profiling Georgio Gambino and Toni Bianco will give me something constructive to do. If you need authorization, contact Jim Beckman, FBI special agent in charge of the main office in San Francisco. As you know, he's the person who took over Connor's position when he retired; he'll approve it."

She pauses to look at the sky. "And Connor will be pleased that I'm working on this case."

CHAPTER 19

"Protect the time and space in which you write. Keep everybody away from it, even the people who are most important to you."

—Zadie Smith

Niall taps the brake pedal. *I need to slow down; I'm driving a little too fast for this road. But I'm worried sick about Libby, Mick, and Maeve, who've just lost their father and husband, Connor. He was my father-in-law—a man I loved and respected. And just two months ago, I lost my brother, Paddy, who was gunned down in St. Barnabas Church. It appears that his death was on the orders of the same person, Gambino. What can I do to help stop this madman?*

Niall steers his car around a bend and stops at the massive wrought-iron entry gate; its overhead sign proclaims *Welcome to Pines & Quill*. He presses the button on the remote attached to the visor. While he waits for the gate to swing open, he admires the blazing sun pinned to an electric-blue sky. *This is my favorite place on earth.*

As he negotiates the long drive, he enjoys the soft breeze blowing through the open windows. Tall trees flank the smooth road—like soldiers—their canopied shade expansive, with a few rays of light piercing the foliage in certain spots. *The effect is mystical.*

The scent of evergreen fills the car as it glides around familiar curves. It carries with it a certain mellowness that only pines bestow.

At the end of the drive, he pulls around to the side of the house and exits the vehicle.

When he opens the mudroom door, Hemingway's there to greet him. The wolfhound's tail whips the air, and he lets out an excited woof before standing on his hind legs and placing his massive front paws on Niall's shoulders—one on each side. One hundred and fifty pounds of full-grown Irish wolfhound leans against Niall until he almost loses his balance. "This is why I didn't bring in the first load of groceries yet, you big lummox."

Niall scratches the big dog's ears as he rubs his forehead against Hemingway's. "Come on. Let's get the groceries in, and then I'll get you a biscuit."

At the promise of a biscuit, the giant dog lets out another woof and runs circles around his human—ears flopping—as Niall hauls in full reusable grocery bags stamped *Community Food Co-op.*

On the third and final trip from the car, Niall hears the phone ring in the kitchen and picks up his pace. He sets a heavy bag on the gray-veined marble counter and picks up the receiver. "Pines & Quill, Niall speaking."

"Hey, Niall. It's Rafferty."

"How's everyone doing in San Francisco?" Niall asks. "I've been worried."

"Under the circumstances, they're holding up well. Maeve, Mick, and Libby started making arrangements for Connor's funeral and memorial service. I'm flying back to Bellingham today but have a job to do with Joe this evening before heading out to Pines & Quill. That's why I'm calling. I want you to know that it's just me when the vehicle sensor goes off in the middle of the night. I don't want you to worry that there's a stranger at the entrance gate."

"Thanks for the heads up. I would have wondered. And please, come up to the main house for breakfast in the morning. It's the Fourth of July, so I'm serving a red, white, and blue meal."

"Thank you. I wouldn't miss it. Can Joe tag along?"

"Absolutely. He's always welcome at our table."

"Are you taking the group into town tomorrow night to watch the fireworks?"

"I thought I'd use the ATV and take Cheryl, Byron, and Ivy out to the bluff overlooking Bellingham Bay. Hemingway and Ivy's dog, Maggie, can run alongside. It's the perfect vantage point for watching the display without the crowds. I hope you'll join us."

"I'd love to."

"Hey, while you're at it, invite Joe, Marci, and the girls to come too. At thirteen and eleven, I don't think Carly and Brianna have outgrown fireworks yet."

"I doubt it," Rafferty says.

"All right then, have a good day. I'll see you and Joe in the morning for breakfast."

After hanging up the phone, Niall gets Hemingway the promised biscuit. "Here you go, big fella. We've got company coming tomorrow night. I know you're not a fan of fire—"

The phone rings again, interrupting Niall's one-sided conversation. "Who could that be?" He picks up the receiver. "Pines & Quill, Niall speaking."

"Niall, it's Emma."

"Oh, it's good to hear your voice. How are you?"

"I miss Mick something fierce, but I'm well. I'm calling to say that I'm flying in this afternoon, and I hope it's okay, but I'm bringing a guest with me."

"Company's always welcome. Do I know them?"

"She's one of your favorite people. Cynthia Winters. We coordinated our flights so we'll arrive at the same time and share an Uber. And with Mick still in San Francisco, she's staying in the guest room in our cabin. So it'll be nice to have company."

"That's wonderful! Rafferty arrives tonight too. He and Joe have something to do first so he'll be late. What brings Cynthia back to Pines & Quill?"

"Remember how she found me in the cave in *El Cañón del Diablo*—The Devil's Canyon—by reading the energy in the pearl earrings I dropped along the way when Jason Hughes, who turned out to be Alex Berndt, kidnapped me? Well, I'm bringing a personal item of Kyle Williams with me from New Orleans in the hopes that she can locate him too."

"That's brilliant," Niall says. "If you two get to Pines & Quill in time for dinner, please join us. Otherwise, we'll see you in the morning for breakfast. Rafferty and Joe are coming. And I hope you'll join us tomorrow night when we watch the fireworks out on the bluff."

"Oh, I'd love to, and I bet Cynthia would enjoy it as well."

"I hope it doesn't stir up bad memories for her." *That's where Jason Hughes was going to shove her off the cliff into Bellingham Bay. But Hemingway got there in time to rescue her, and Hughes went over the cliff instead.*

"Just thinking about it gives me the creeps," Emma says. "See you soon."

Niall hangs up the phone and turns to Hemingway. "We're going to be in good company tomorrow night. Between the writers in residence, Cynthia, and Emma,"—he pauses to scratch the big dog's chin—"an FBI special agent and a homicide detective are icing on the cake." *And let's hope we won't need their services for anything.*

———

Rafferty plows his fingers through his hair as he rushes toward the rental car facility after his plane lands at Bellingham International. *Gambino's tentacles have a stranglehold on this community. Joe and I need to quit aiming at those tentacles— his lieutenants, soldiers, and associates—and go for body mass, Gambino himself, to stop the insidious spread of his influence and control.*

As he opens the door to the rental car office, he realizes that he's glad to be back. *"Glad" isn't something I feel very often.* He pauses a moment, then smiles. *I'm happy to be back because I get to see Ivy Gladstone again. It's been a long time since I felt that way about a woman.*

Rafferty checks his watch—it's just after four o'clock—then speed dials Joe.

"Bingham."

"It's Rafferty. I just landed and am getting a rental car now. Are you at the station?"

"Yes, I'm glad you're back. How's Mick holding up?"

"He's devastated like the rest of us at the loss of his dad. I'm glad he has Maeve and Libby. They're making preparations for Connor's funeral and memorial service. He'll fly back once the arrangements are worked out. Now more than ever, he wants to nail Gambino's hide to the wall."

"Is the service going to be in San Francisco?"

"I'm not sure. But, for a larger-than-life guy, Maeve said that in his will he's adamant about keeping it low-key. He wants nothing more than family and a few friends to gather and celebrate the good times everyone had together.

"When Libby suggested a memorial service at Pines &

Quill, it was the first time I'd seen Maeve smile since Connor was killed. She said, 'Your father would love that.' Plus, Libby said that her son, Ian, and his fiancée, Fiona, would be able to drive over from Coeur d'Alene for his grandfather's service. At any rate, they're working out the details now."

"Have you eaten yet?" Joe asks.

"No, and I'm *starving.*"

"Me too. I didn't have time for lunch. Swing by the station and pick me up. We'll go to the Black Cat, and I'll fill you in while we eat. Then tonight, after it's dark, we need to finish the wiretap Judge Watson approved on Toni. We got everything—cars and phone—except her house."

"Joe, Gambino's minions are expendable; we cut off one tentacle, he grows another." Rafferty lowers his voice. "We need a plan to get Gambino himself—to remove him from the equation."

Toni Bianco's pissed because her flight from New Orleans to Bellingham is delayed—again. She looks at her watch as she paces back and forth in the Departures terminal.

Fuck! It's seven o'clock. With an almost five-hour flight, I won't arrive in Bellingham until midnight. Then again, it's Pacific time there, so I gain two hours. That makes it about ten o'clock, well within Gambino's demand of "today." I've killed for that bastard.

Toni feels an unaccustomed smile break out on her face. *But, more importantly, I've killed for myself.* She takes a seat at the departure gate and thinks through the last few months of rung-climbing, ticking her victims off one by one on her fingers.

Let's see now; there was Andrew Berndt, who became just a little too important to Gambino for my comfort.

Then Niall MacCullough's brother, Father Patrick Mac-Cullough of St. Barnabas Church. I think Berndt gave him a deathbed confession when he was on chaplaincy duty, and I couldn't have that now, could I?

He was followed by Gambino's minion Salvatore Rizzo, who everyone out at The Scrap Heap wrecking yard knew as Vito Paglio.

Next, I had to eliminate Shelly Baker, who impersonated Pam Williams as a writer in residence at Pines & Quill. Unfortunately, she was busy doing a little rung-climbing herself. You can't blame a gal for eliminating the competition, now, can you?

Then, Kyle Williams was ignorant enough to try and visit his sister Pam at Pines & Quill. That goes to show what family love will get you—nothing. He would have blown the whistle when he discovered it wasn't her, so I had to pop him.

I had to axe Adrian Padula, who failed to kill Emma when she and Mick were whale watching in the San Juan Islands. Anyone in Gambino's employ knows that he always sends a message—with me as the messenger—when someone fails.

Then there was Emilio Accardi's car bomb fiasco. The bomb went off all right, but it killed the wrong person, triggering another message to be delivered.

Angelo "Angel" Romano, the owner of Tit 4 Tat Tattoo Studio, would have run at the mouth about the "Family First" ink he did for Gambino's thugs, so I had to off him.

And Gianni Greco, better known as "Smith" in the Louisiana swamp, was chirping like a jailbird, pouring his heart out to anyone who'd listen.

Toni counts nine outstretched fingers on her hands. *Wait a minute. I thought there were ten.* She pauses for a moment. *Oh, I almost forgot Kevin Pierce, the college student who valeted at Mick's and Emma's wedding. And though he wasn't a direct hit of mine, it was a result of my order. He should never have turned the key in the Jeep's ignition.* She chuckles. *I bet he doesn't have guts enough to do that again.*

Emma waits for Cynthia at the designated spot in the bustling baggage claim area of Bellingham International. They'd
scheduled their flights—hers from New Orleans, Cynthia's
from Tucson—to arrive within twenty minutes of each other.

As Emma checks her cell phone for text messages from
Mick, she hears purposeful steps approaching from behind.
Turning, Emma sees Cynthia.

Both women's faces light up when they see each other
before stepping into an open-armed embrace.

"It's so good to see you," Cynthia says, hugging Emma tight.

"I'm so glad you're here. Thank you for coming." Emma
leans back to gaze at Cynthia's face. Her easy smile, white against
olive-toned skin, makes creases at the sides of liquid brown eyes.

As the two women walk to the baggage carousel, the
gauzy fabric of Cynthia's skirt swirls around her ankles, and
metallic threads wink from the folds of bright purple floral and
striped panels. A jumble of silver bangles on each wrist—some
thick, some thin—clank in unison with the rhythmic cadence
of each step she takes on the buffed linoleum floor in strappy,
Greek-inspired sandals.

Emma notices several men follow Cynthia with their gaze.

"They're not looking at me, dear; they're looking at
you," Cynthia says. "You're beautiful."

"How did you know what I was thinking?" Emma asks.
Cynthia merely smiles.

Emma remembers how easy it is for Cynthia to read
people. *When she was at Pines & Quill in May, she'd accurately
read the lines on everyone's palms. Everyone except for Jason
Hughes. He wouldn't let her touch his palm—probably because
he was really Alex Berndt, a lieutenant in the Gambino crime
family. And on his own time, he was a serial killer, having killed
at least ten women.*

Once the women are in the Uber on their way to Pines & Quill, Emma's phone pings; it's a text from Mick. *Rafferty's back in Bellingham. Please call Joe and ask them both to be present when Cynthia "reads" Kyle's pillowcase. They may have questions she can answer while it's fresh in her hands. I miss you. I love you. I'm coming home soon.*

Before responding, Emma shows the text to Cynthia, who agrees. *I'll call Joe and set it up. I miss you. I love you. Hurry home.*

The two women chatter nonstop on the drive from the airport to Pines & Quill. When they reach the entrance gate, Emma gets out of the Uber and keys in the code on the panel. When she gets back in the car, she tells the driver, "Just follow the lane. There's a roundabout in front of the main house. That's where we'll get out."

"It's even lovelier than it was in May," Cynthia says. "The green's so vibrant it practically hurts my eyes."

"Wait until you see the gardens. Niall's vegetables are Paul Bunyan-size, and Libby's flowers not only smell heavenly, but they're gorgeous."

The front door of the house opens when the driver pulls to a stop. "Ohmygod!" he says as a giant dog catapults over the front steps then sticks its anvil-size head through the open window of the back seat.

Hemingway gazes back and forth between Emma and Cynthia with adoration. Then, not able to contain himself, he woofs with delight.

Cynthia roughs his ears. "You haven't changed a bit, young man."

The women exit the car, and the driver begins removing their luggage from the trunk. As he places it on the driveway, Niall bounds down the steps and embraces both women in a bear hug. "Two of my favorite people on the planet. Gosh, but I'm glad to see you."

When he steps back, he sees that he's impressed flour from the front of his apron onto their clothes. "Oh, dear."

"Not to worry," Cynthia says, laughing. "This is the best welcome anyone could ever have."

Niall looks at his watch. "It's just after five o'clock now. Dinner will be ready at six. Will you join us?"

"We won't be able to make it for dinner," Emma says, "but we might be in time for dessert in the Ink Well afterward. I think that Joe and Rafferty are meeting us at the cabin later. We've got a bit of work to do, and then if it's okay, maybe all four of us could come over."

"I'll look forward to it then. Do you want me to keep this big galoot with me, out from under your feet?"

"Oh, no," Cynthia says. "He's welcome to come with us."

"Can I help carry your bags to the cabin?"

"Thank you, but we've got it, Niall. By the way, what's for dessert?"

"One of my summertime favorites, Blackberry Fool with Calvados."

"Now *that* sounds interesting," Cynthia says. "What is it?"

"It's a British dessert of pureed fruit folded into whipped cream. To give it a bit more sophistication, I soak half the blackberries overnight in Calvados—apple brandy, made in the Calvados region of Normandy—then top it with dollops of whipped cream mixed with blackberry puree. The leftover soaking liquid makes a delicious drink when mixed with champagne. It's a bluish color, so I'm serving it with tomorrow's Fourth of July breakfast."

Emma pats her stomach and smiles. "Oh, it's so good to be home." *If only Mick were here with me.*

Joe and Rafferty are seated at a window table at the Black Cat on Harris Avenue in historic Fairhaven. The view from the third floor of the old-world Sycamore Square building showcases Bellingham Bay. The exposed brick and original hardwood floors are lost on the two men bent forward deep in conversation.

Joe's cell phone rings. The screen indicates that it's five fifteen. He'd normally let it go to voicemail, but he sees that the call's from Emma.

"Hey, Emma. I'm sitting here at the Black Cat with Rafferty. We're about to eat a late lunch. How are you?"

"Hi, Joe. When you and Rafferty finish eating, could you come out to Pines & Quill?"

"Sure, what's up?"

"Do you remember when Cynthia Winters read the energy in the pearl earrings I dropped and used it to find me after being kidnapped by Alex Berndt?"

"I'll never forget that. Why?"

"When I went to Walter and Maxine Williams's home this morning to share the news about their daughter Pam, I told them what Cynthia had done and suggested that maybe she could do the same thing to locate their son, Kyle. They thought it was well worth a try, so we stopped at his place on the way to the airport, and I took his pillowcase. I put sandwich bags on my hands, like gloves, so I wouldn't contaminate the pillowcase while I covered it in plastic wrap."

"You've got my attention. Go ahead."

"Well, Cynthia's here with me at Pines & Quill. She said that since it's only been four weeks since Kyle went missing, it might work. Mick texted and said to ask you and Rafferty to be present when she does her thing. He said you might have questions while she's in the process of reading the pillowcase."

"I wouldn't miss it for the world," Joe says. "And Rafferty didn't get to see it when Cynthia did it before. We'll head over right after we eat. Will you be at the main house?"

"We'll be at the cabin because this is something the guests don't need to know about."

"You're right about that. Better to keep it under the radar. See you soon."

After Joe fills in Rafferty, the server brings their lunch—beer-battered cod tacos for Joe and blackened prawn tacos for Rafferty. When he leaves, Joe says, "I brought something to show you." He slips his hand inside his suit coat, pulls a photo from his shirt pocket, and sets it on the table between them.

Rafferty looks at it. "It's a photo of Toni Bianco that the 'florist' took when he delivered the flower arrangement for her mother."

"That's what we're supposed to think. But I was her partner, remember?" Joe taps the photo with an index finger. "There's something wrong with this picture. Something *very* wrong."

Rafferty stares at the photo. His eyes narrow, his brows furrow. "What is it?"

"What hand is 'Toni' signing for the flowers with?"

"Her left. Why?"

"That's the problem. Toni's right-handed."

CHAPTER 20

*"Becoming a writer means being creative enough to
find the time and the place in your life for writing."*
—HEATHER SELLERS

I vy Gladstone and Maggie, her Seeing Eye dog, arrive at
the main house's front door at a quarter to six. "We're a bit
early," Ivy whispers to her companion, "but I want to find out
from Niall when Rafferty's expected back. And I don't want
to ask him with the other writers around."

She takes a deep breath to settle her nerves, pushes her
gray-tinted glasses up the bridge of her nose with a forefinger,
then tips her face up to the warmth of the waning sun. *I may
not be able to see it, but I appreciate it all the same.*

Ivy places a palm on her flat stomach. *I don't know why
I've got butterflies in my tummy. It's normal for people to be
attracted to each other. I know I'm drawn to Rafferty. And I
think—at least I hope—he's interested in me too.* Ivy exhales
the long-held breath. *But what if he's not?*

After locating the brass knocker on the door, Ivy uses it to rap three times in succession.

Maggie—a standard-size Parti poodle with black-and-white markings—wags her five-inch tail in response to an excited woof from inside.

Ivy feels Maggie's tail tap against her legs.

"I know you pretend you don't like Hemingway, but you can't fool me, Mags."

Ivy hears Hemingway burst through the front door when it opens. She feels his body fly past her, over the front steps, before he realizes he overshot his mark. His toenails click on the steps as he bounds back up and begins sniffing Maggie.

"Sit," Niall commands.

And though Hemingway drops to his rump, Ivy hears his tail dust the landing in a frenzy.

Niall wipes his palms on his striped bistro apron. "I'm sorry, ladies. This young man left his manners in the mudroom. Please come in, won't you?"

Ivy hears Niall step aside. Before stepping inside, through the handle of the guide harness, Ivy feels Maggie's shoulders turn. *I imagine she's giving Hemingway a withering glance before she leads me into the house.* Then Ivy's drawn forward.

Ivy's dainty nose detects an enticing scent in the air. "You've done it again, Niall. What smells so delicious?"

"For starters, we have goat cheese bruschetta with mushrooms and capers. But I don't think that's what you smell. I think your nose has detected the mango and smoked chicken summer salad."

"It's incredible. And now my stomach's growling," Ivy says, laughing.

"I'm glad you brought an appetite. Would it be okay if I give Maggie a treat?"

"Yes, she'd love that."

Niall gets two biscuits from the treat jar. "Here you go, Maggie. And Hemingway, you may stay in polite company if you mind your manners. But the minute you become a nuisance, you'll find yourself behind the mudroom door. Is that understood?"

Hemingway *humphs* when he lies down; his tail thumps the floor.

"Speaking of manners," Niall says, "where are mine? Here, Ivy, let me get your chair."

Niall pulls a chair from the table. "May I get you a glass of white wine?"

"Oh, yes, that would be lovely. Thank you." Ivy feels the place setting in front of her. "How many will be at dinner tonight?"

"In addition to the two of us, I expect Cheryl and Byron. But we could have more join us for dessert in the Ink Well afterward."

Ivy leans forward. "Who would that be?"

Niall sets a glass of wine on the table in front of Ivy. "My sister-in-law Emma, and a family friend, Cynthia Winters. And it's possible, though doubtful, that Rafferty and Joe Bingham will join us."

"I thought Rafferty was in San Francisco."

"You're right, he was. But he called earlier to let me know that he expects to arrive late tonight, so when I hear the vehicle sensor go off, not to think it's a stranger. He's got the gate code and will let himself in."

Ivy picks up her glass of wine and holds it to her mouth to hide the smile blossoming there.

———

Cynthia opens her suitcase in the guest room of Mick's and Emma's cabin. She's glad to be back at Pines & Quill, but she's sick about the reason—*yet another missing person. I hope that using Kyle Williams's pillowcase works and that he's still alive.*

She glances at her watch. *It's six-thirty.* Her heart's beating fast, knowing that Joe and Rafferty will arrive soon. *Joe saw me read the energy in Emma's pearl earrings, but Rafferty—a special agent with the FBI—didn't. He's probably skeptical. I would be, too, if I didn't know how accurate it can be.*

During a recent television interview, Cynthia told the viewers, "I recognize that it's difficult for some people to understand what an intuitive does."

The newscaster explained to the viewing audience, "Several law enforcement agencies use Cynthia Winters' skill of *psychometry,* a form of extrasensory perception that allows a person to read the energy of an object."

When asked to explain further, Cynthia said, "Every item has an energy field that can transfer knowledge about its history. As an intuitive, I can 'see' physical places associated with an object, in real time or the past. The detailed imagery I receive often helps law enforcement agencies to locate an item or a person."

After an on-air demonstration, the newscaster wrapped up the interview by asking, "What does it feel like to be an intuitive?"

Cynthia responded, "The work of an intuitive consultant can be draining. In particular, when a missing person is found dead. However, it's rewarding when they're alive, or when the police find the perpetrator."

As Cynthia removes folded clothing from her luggage and hangs it in the closet, she reminds herself, *It is what it is. Wanting to get a reading won't make it happen. It's just that my heart's breaking for Mr. and Mrs. Williams, who've already lost their daughter, Pam. I hope we can locate their son, Kyle.*

With that thought tucked away, for now, Cynthia looks at her surroundings. The soft yellow walls with spruce trim are welcoming. With a bed, an overstuffed chair, a small oak desk with matching stool, and a chest of drawers, the room's uncluttered and comfortable. *It feels like home.*

Opening the top drawer in the highboy chest next to the closet, Cynthia inhales the scented liner paper. The fragrance is a mixture of lemon and lavender with a hint of geranium. *In aromatherapy, these essential oils are used to calm and soothe. So all I have to do is leave a drawer open for a good night's sleep.*

She closes the drawer. *But I don't want to sleep too soundly. With the number of people who've died at Pines & Quill recently, all of us need to stay alert.*

———

Toni sets an empty in-flight drink glass—double scotch, no rocks, thank you very much—on the tray table in front of her. *God, I needed that.*

She checks her watch. *It's eight-thirty. We've been wheels up for a while now, and with any luck, the almost five-hour flight will catch a tailwind and arrive in Bellingham earlier than expected. It's a damn good thing I gain two hours traveling from central to Pacific time. If I land after midnight, Gambino will kill me. It doesn't matter that the flight delays were out of my control. I might as well change the time now because I'm going to be in one hell of a hurry to check in with that bastard when we land.*

Toni changes her watch to six-thirty, then pulls an eye mask over her face, crosses her arms, and settles back into the seat.

Nobody, and I mean fucking nobody, better get in my way before I reach Gambino while it's still July third, or there'll be "fireworks" a day early.

———

Maeve sits at the dining room table with her two adult children. *And while I'm so grateful that Mick and Libby came to San Francisco to help me, I'm having a difficult time holding it together in front of them. I'm desperate to be alone so I can lick my emotional wounds in private. I need time and space by myself so I can fall apart and grieve the way I need to without burdening the kids with more worry. To do that, I need to show them that I'm strong and capable so they'll be okay with returning home.*

Maeve stands and puts her hands on her hips. She pins Libby and Mick with her "brooks no argument" expression. *Connor and the kids call it "The Face."*

"There's no use arguing about it. And while I'm incredibly appreciative for everything you've done, for all of the help you've given me since your dad died, it's time that the two of you go back home to Emma, Niall, and this month's writers in residence."

"But—"

Maeve raises a hand, palming the air at Mick, who's turned his chair around, straddling the seat—*just like his father.* "There'll be no buts. Rafferty is as good as his word. The documents I requested on Georgio Gambino and Antonia 'Toni' Bianco arrived via email. I want nothing more than to 'get down to brass tacks' as your father would say—print it, spread it out on the table, and start reviewing it."

She looks at their faces. The faces she loves so much. The faces that reflect Connor. Her heart aches at his absence.

"I don't expect you to understand it," Maeve continues, "but your father would. And he'd do the same thing, the thing that's going to help me the most right now."

Mick leans forward. "What's that?"

"It's to have something *meaningful* to do. I'm trained to profile killers. So reviewing this paperwork," she says, waving a hand toward her laptop, "will give me something tangible—" She searches for the right word. "Something *purposeful* to direct my focus. And while it won't take my heart and mind off your father, it'll help me to help you, Joe, and Rafferty to catch the people responsible for his murder."

Mick and Libby stand up, walk over to their mom, and fold her into their arms.

"Okay, Mom." Libby squeezes tight. "If this is what Dad would want, then it's what I want too."

"Thank you, dear." Maeve raises her eyebrows at Mick. "And?"

"Well, okay. If it'll really help you, then it's what I want too."

Maeve steps back from her kids. "Now go make your flight reservations for tomorrow morning." She looks at her watch and sees that it's six-thirty. "In the meantime, I'll make spaghetti for dinner and serve it with a nice merlot that we can toast your father with. Being the Irishman that he was, he always did appreciate a good toast—*Sláinte*."

Rafferty's a half step ahead of Joe as they exit the car and walk toward Mick's and Emma's cabin. *On the drive over to Pines & Quill, Joe said he hopes I won't let a "mumbo-jumbo, hoodoo-voodoo" mentality stand in the way of what we're about to see.*

Little does he know that after my son, Drew, was killed in a car accident, I went to see a psychic. She knew things she had no way of being privy to. She said, "They were just two young guys with the radio on, seat belts on, no one was drinking, and no drugs were involved. Drew was in the front passenger seat when Jack lost control of the car and it flipped over and smashed into a tree. Drew was killed on impact. His friend, Jack, took his own life six months later; the survivor's guilt he felt became too heavy for him to carry, to live with." Unfortunately, she wasn't able to tell me why Jack lost control of the car, the cause of the accident.

Rafferty and Joe step onto the front porch of Mick's and Emma's cabin. After Rafferty raps on the door, they look at their surroundings while they wait. The evening is warm and clear. The sun has started its slow descent toward the western horizon, turning the air a flush blue-pink. Give it an hour or so, and the sky will purple with the day's last light.

The hair on the back of Rafferty's neck stands at attention, a sure sign that something's amiss. *Life is all about contradictions. This evening couldn't be any more beautiful, yet Joe and I are about to discuss a missing person, perhaps even murder.*

Emma opens the door. "Hi, you guys. Come in." She turns to the tall, willowy woman with short white hair cropped close to her head like an elf cap and holds out her hand. "You remember Cynthia Winters."

Rafferty and Joe step forward in turns.

Joe shakes Cynthia's hand. "It's good to see you."

Rafferty also takes her hand. "I'm glad to see you again too. And this time I get to see you in action. I missed out the last time."

Emma touches a pendant at her throat. "Speaking of which, come in and sit down. Can I get either of you some coffee or tea?"

Rafferty holds up his hand. "None for me, thanks. We just came from the Black Cat."

"I'll take a pass too," Joe says, taking a seat.

Rafferty realizes his shoulders are tense and relaxes them. "With the remarkable things Joe's told me about your work, Cynthia, I'm eager to get started."

"I'll be right back then." Emma excuses herself.

Cynthia looks back and forth between the two men. "Emma tells me it's been about four weeks since Kyle Williams went missing."

Rafferty takes a seat opposite Cynthia. "That's right. Do you think what you do will work after that period of time?"

She crosses her legs at the knee and folds her hands in her lap. "I think it's worth a try."

"In addition to what I told him," Joe says, "Rafferty's read about the cases you've helped law enforcement agencies solve across the southwest."

Rafferty nods. "The fact that you've lectured at the FBI Academy in Quantico, Virginia, and have worked on hundreds of cases with city, county, and state law enforcement agencies in thirty-eight states in the US and six foreign countries is impressive. I don't even begin to understand it, but your track record speaks for itself."

Flags of red touch Cynthia's cheeks. "Thank you."

Rafferty and Joe lean forward, their forearms on their thighs.

"The most impressive case I've read about so far," Rafferty says, "is the one where you located two dozen women and children locked in an abandoned railroad car in the Mojave Desert. They'd been left without food and water. Apparently their captors were afraid of getting caught and deserted the 'evidence,' leaving them to die. And they would have, too, if you hadn't used your gift to locate them."

Just then, Emma returns, carrying a plastic-wrapped item in one hand and a pen and tablet in the other. She pauses in front of Rafferty to hand him the notepad and pen and then continues to Cynthia, giving her the plastic-wrapped item.

Emma takes a seat. "Rafferty, like you, I've never seen Cynthia do this before. I was the one who was missing the last time she was at Pines & Quill. But I've heard all about how she read the energy in the pearl earrings I dropped along the way when Jason Hughes, who turned out to be Alex Berndt, held me in a cave in *El Cañón del Diablo*—The Devil's Canyon."

Cynthia rests her hands on the plastic wrap. "Rafferty, I suspect that what you'll see hasn't been in any part of your FBI training or experience, so I'm glad you're already aware of the results it can produce."

Rafferty pinches his chin between a thumb and forefinger. "Are you going to go into a trance?"

"That's a good question, but the answer is no." Cynthia looks around the room and continues, "I'm just going to close my eyes and sit with Kyle Williams's pillowcase for a bit. If I receive any energetic pictures, I'll state them out loud. I say this in advance because it might seem disjointed."

Intrigued, Rafferty leans forward. "What do you mean by energetic pictures?"

"An impression. It could be something I see or hear. It might be something I feel, smell, or even taste."

"You said *if,*" Rafferty notes, an unasked question hanging on the end of his statement.

"That's right," she says gently. "It doesn't always work." And with that, Cynthia unwraps the plastic from around the folded pillowcase, lays it on her left palm, covers it with her right palm, then rests both hands on her lap.

All eyes are on Cynthia as she closes hers. A couple of minutes tick by before she speaks. "I." Another minute passes. "Camp."

Rafferty writes the words on the tablet.

Cynthia's words come faster. "Airport. Five. Cement, lots of cement."

The pen in Rafferty's white-knuckled grip captures each word.

Rafferty leans farther forward as Cynthia's voice gets softer. "Jungle. Atlantic. Homeless." Minutes pass, but nothing more comes.

When Cynthia opens her eyes, there's a collective exhale. "Did you get everything?" she asks.

"Yes," Rafferty says, setting the tablet on the coffee table so everyone can see it.

Like a fishing bobber, a memory's trying to surface in Rafferty's mind. He slides his glasses off and pinches the bridge of his nose. *What is it?* He closes his eyes and toggles the pen back and forth between two fingers trying to jog his recollection.

"Can you sense if he's alive?" Emma asks.

Cynthia shakes her head. "No. Not in this case. I didn't feel a sense of life or death, either one."

Emma picks up the tablet. "Let's put the words all together. I, camp, airport, five, cement, jungle, Atlantic, homeless."

"Bear in mind," Cynthia says, "that they're most likely not in any type of order. I call out what I see, sense, or feel as it happens."

Rafferty looks at the perplexed expression on Joe's, Emma's, and Cynthia's faces. He keeps his face inscrutable. Sweat prickles his scalp as the picture surfacing in his brain becomes clearer—his mind races along with the increased staccato of his heart. *I've got it! It's a memory from when I was a newbie, fresh out of Quantico.*

Rafferty slips his glasses into his shirt pocket. "Any ideas?" he asks the group in general, wanting to hear what everyone else has to say before he shares his thoughts.

Joe furrows his brows. "'Lots of cement' and 'Atlantic.' Do you think that maybe he was covered with cement and dumped in the Atlantic?" He shakes his head before anyone can answer. "I doubt it. That's on the opposite coast. Why would anyone do that when we've got a perfectly good ocean right here?"

Rafferty shifts in his seat. "I have an idea, and it won't take long to check out."

"What is it?" Emma asks.

"The words mean something to me because I live in Seattle."

Joe looks at Rafferty. "Go on," he nods encouragingly.

"When I first began in the FBI, I got crap cases as everyone does when they start. My first assignment was a drug bust. We nailed a husband-and-wife team who camouflaged themselves as homeless people. They came and went freely because everyone tuned them out; they became invisible to society."

Emma's brow creases in consideration. "How does that relate to the impressions Cynthia received?"

Rafferty tugs glasses from his shirt pocket, shakes them open, and slides them on. Then he holds out his hand to Emma. "May I?"

Emma places the tablet in Rafferty's outstretched hand. He looks at it for a minute before looking into Cynthia's brown eyes. "You may well have done it again, Cynthia."

"What?" Joe and Emma ask.

Like ticking off a list, Rafferty touches each word on the tablet with his index finger as he speaks. "It turns out that the couple headquartered themselves in a homeless encampment known as 'The Jungle,' under I-5 near Airport Way South and South Atlantic Street, south of downtown Seattle."

Rafferty looks at the astonishment on the faces around him. "Alive or dead, I bet that's where Kyle Williams is."

CHAPTER 21

*"Mystery writing involves solving a puzzle, but
'high suspense' writing is a situation whereby the
writer thrusts the hero/heroine into high drama."*
— IRIS JOHANSEN

Emma's excited that Mick and Libby will be back home
at Pines & Quill in less than twelve hours. Her heart
breaks for them at the loss of their father. And for Maeve at
the loss of her husband. *I can't even begin to imagine losing
one of my brothers or parents. I know it would change me. I
wonder how it's going to change Mick?*

Emma inhales deeply. The scent of pine needles permeates
the air under a cloudless night sky. One minute it's silent; the
next, a rush of wind comes up from Bellingham Bay smelling
of salt and a faint hint of seaweed. *The roar of the leaves in the
surrounding trees is probably as loud as the waves breaking on
the boulder-strewn beach below the cliff.*

Flanked by Cynthia on one side and Joe and Rafferty on the other, the four walk on the low-lit pathway from Emma's and Mick's cabin toward the main house.

Emma turns to Rafferty. "So when you said you've got 'boots on the ground,' does that mean you sent Seattle-based FBI agents to 'The Jungle' to see if they can locate Kyle Williams?"

"That's right," Rafferty says, checking his watch. "It's almost nine o'clock. There's still three hours left in the day. If we're lucky, we might even hear something before tomorrow."

"Speaking of tomorrow," Joe says. "It's the Fourth of July, and I promised Marci and the girls that I'd take the day off. Especially since I've been gone all day and we're going to be out late tonight."

Emma's eyes snap to Joe's. "You guys have plans for *after* we visit the main house?"

Joe nods. "Yes, we have to finish a job we started. But, unfortunately, it's time-sensitive, so it's got to be done tonight."

"What kind of a job?"

"I can't get into specifics," Joe says, "but suffice it to say that it'll get us a few steps closer to nailing Gambino and his minions."

"Mick would love to be here for that," Emma says. "You know that he and Libby are flying home in the morning, right?" *I can hardly wait to see Mick again!*

"Yes," Joe says. "And he said that we're all invited to watch the fireworks tomorrow night from the bluff overlooking the bay. That way we can enjoy the best view without the crowd."

"It's my first Fourth of July at Pines & Quill," Emma says. "I'm looking forward to it."

When Emma opens the front door of the main house, she's greeted by a hairy, anvil-size head that plows its wet nose into the palm of her open hand.

She puts her forehead to Hemingway's and scrubs the big dog's neck with both hands. "I missed you, too, big guy."

When Hemingway realizes that Cynthia, Joe, and Rafferty are here too, his entire body wags in delight.

"Well, hello there," Cynthia coos, reaching over to scratch his back, leaving his head free to greet Joe and Rafferty.

"Hey, Hem. How ya doin'?" Joe says.

Hemingway licks his hand.

Rafferty scratches behind one of the big dog's ears. "Hemingway, it's good to see you. I missed you too."

Hemingway adjusts his head to lick Rafferty's hand, too. Then turning, he saunters down the hall, leading the four of them to the Ink Well, where he shows them off like a blue-ribbon prize to the occupants—Niall and the writers in residence.

Niall's eyes light up. He stands and presses his hands together. "Oh, you're a sight for sore eyes. And you're just in time for dessert. But first, let me refresh the introductions; some of you have already met but others haven't."

He turns toward the writers in residence and gestures with a hand. "This is Ivy Gladstone and her Seeing Eye dog, Sister Margaret Mary McCracken—Maggie for short. They're here from Seattle where Ivy's a special education teacher. She's working on a book about how to help struggling learners."

Emma can't help but notice that Maggie's short little tail is in propeller mode, whirling as fast as it can. *I wonder how she and Hemingway are getting along?*

Niall continues. "This is Cheryl Munson. She's here from Philadelphia, where she's a professor of sociology at Bryn Mawr College. She's writing a book about the societal influence of strong, independent women.

"And this is Byron Rivers. He owns Zendeavor Cellars in Napa Valley. He's writing a book about pairing food with zinfandel wines."

A myriad of "It's a pleasure," and "So nice to meet you" fly back and forth.

Niall turns the other way to introduce the four who just arrived.

"None of you had the opportunity to meet my sister-in-law, Emma McPherson. She and her husband, Mick, left for their honeymoon the day you arrived. Emma's an accomplished potter. You'll find many of her pieces at Hyde and Seek in town. And they just started carrying her work at Current and Furbish—a well-loved boutique gift shop in the heart of historic Fairhaven.

"This is a family friend, Cynthia Winters. You may recognize her from television, where she frequently makes guest appearances. She's a forensic intuitive who helps law enforcement agencies solve crimes. She's visiting from Tucson, Arizona.

"This is another friend of the family, Joe Bingham. He's a homicide detective right here in Bellingham. You'll meet his wife, Marci, and their daughters, Carly and Brianna, tomorrow evening when they join us to watch fireworks from the bluff."

Emma notices the interplay between the two dogs. Hemingway tries to look regal as Maggie pretends not to notice.

Niall continues. "And this is *Sean* Rafferty. We call him 'Rafferty' to keep him sorted from my brother-in-law, *Sean* McPherson, who we call 'Mick' for the same reason. Rafferty's a special agent with the FBI. He's headquartered in Seattle, but currently working on a case with our local police department."

While Niall introduces Rafferty, Emma takes in Ivy's slight blush. That she tucks a strand of shoulder-length brown hair behind an ear and Rafferty straightens his broad shoulders isn't lost on her either.

Well, well, well. Emma grins.

In San Francisco, Maeve sits cross-legged on the carpeted floor by the dining room table. Light from a nearby torchière spills over the paperwork she extracted from the pile she'd printed and placed on the tabletop. She prefers the old-school method of reading paper as opposed to reading a computer screen.

I've always been a tactile person. I like holding a stack of paper in my hands—the feeling of its heftiness of promises and anticipation. But, most of all, I enjoy looking for a mystery waiting to be solved—looking for the prevalence, likelihood, and timing of the next crime. I also like working solo, so I'm glad that Libby and Mick are already in bed because of their early morning flight to Bellingham.

After adjusting her glasses, Maeve reads the heading on the printout: ANTONIA 'TONI' BIANCO. Skilled in the art of research, she scoots back on her butt until her spine rests comfortably on the front of an overstuffed chair. Then, Maeve settles in for the long haul of parsing through the documentation for consistencies, inconsistencies, truths, and lies.

On the floor to her left rests a bevy of highlighters, a clipboard with lined paper, and a pen. Her laptop is on her right.

Part of the information she received from Jim Beckman—FBI special agent in charge of the main office in San Francisco—the man who took over Connor's position when he retired, includes Toni's application from her initial employment as a police officer in San Francisco. It also contains copies of her transfer paperwork when she relocated to the Bellingham Police department. It appears she transferred there after being put on mandatory leave for a weapon's discharge. She was ultimately cleared of all wrongdoing.

Maeve draws her eyebrows together in concentration. The ruler she uses to read line by line slides down each page slowly and deliberately—a trick she learned at Quantico to focus attention and help ensure that nothing gets overlooked.

When she finally takes a break, Maeve glances at the

dining room clock. It's ten-thirty. She taps the paperwork on her lap. *No one in Human Resources ever thinks to follow up on one's parents. And why would they? They're usually only listed for the sake of emergency contacts, nothing more.* She snags her laptop, stands, shakes out her sleeping legs, then sits at the table and composes an email to Joe, Toni's ex-partner:

Joe, you and Rafferty said that Toni Bianco's in San Francisco to help her mother, Marcella Bianco, who fell and broke her hip. That's impossible because Marcella died seven years ago. Research indicates that she's buried in the Lafayette Cemetery in New Orleans.

Using one of the databases Jim Beckman gave me clearance for, I checked Toni's birth certificate. It shows that Marcella Arianna Bianco is her mother. The father is named "Unknown," so Toni has her mother's last name.

Marcella's death certificate lists the cause as a drug overdose, but the manner of death is classified as "Undetermined." Her death certificate was never finalized because there remains a question as to suicide, accidental overdose, or homicide. And we both know that an "accident" isn't always accidental.

Now, here's where it gets interesting. Marcella's birth certificate lists Carmella Celestina Di Lauro as her mother and Paolo De Lauro as her father. Their heyday was before your time, but not mine. Paolo was one of Naples's most powerful crime bosses. He was the head of a criminal clan known collectively as the Camorra.

The FBI never had a reason to keep tabs on the Camorra, that is, not until they came to the United

States, where they stuck their stake in new turf—specifically New Orleans—where Gambino cut his teeth. Brazen, impertinent, and arrogant, he was a punk kid clawing his way up through the ranks at the time.

Years ago, there was an unsubstantiated rumor that "The Bull" was intentionally fathering children to one day groom for his empire—the one that's now spread from New Orleans to San Francisco and now to the greater Seattle area, including Bellingham.

That said, I have three questions. First, is Gambino Toni's father? We'd need DNA from both of them to confirm or deny that. Second, did she come to San Francisco to kill Connor? Third, where is Toni Bianco?

I'm worried. Out of sight doesn't mean out of commission. From a psychopath's perspective, it means freedom to move around undetected to accomplish an agenda.

That begs a fourth question. What exactly is Toni Bianco's agenda?

———

Cynthia's intrigued by the goings-on around her in the Ink Well. She tries not to "eavesdrop" on the private energy radiating from the people around her, but it's not something she can turn off like a switch.

I hope Rafferty's team finds Kyle Williams alive. I'm worried for my friends at Pines & Quill. The recent loss of life has been devastating. I'm concerned that one of the MacCulloughs, McPhersons, or even Joe or Rafferty might be in Gambino's crosshairs and might be next.

When Niall and Emma carry in dessert trays laden with Blackberry Fool with Calvados, in addition to seeing their happy faces, Cynthia *feels* their elation—Niall at Libby's anticipated return and Emma with Mick's.

During a recent television interview, one of the people in the studio audience asked Cynthia, "How do you receive information or 'vibrations?'"

She responded, "Have you ever woken up because you felt someone staring at you?"

The woman in the audience nodded.

"When you did this, you didn't have to see or hear them to know they were there. You knew they were there simply because you could *feel* them. Not because they touched your skin or bumped the bed. But because you *felt* their energy. That's similar to how I receive information."

As Niall and Emma walk around the room offering plates of Blackberry Fool—pureed fruit folded into whipped cream—Cynthia picks up more information about others. Tuning in, she smiles at a memory of what her mother told her when she'd come home from school crying because she discovered she was different.

"Yes, Cynthia, you *are* different from your friends. Most people are 'sensing'—they pay more attention to the reality that one can perceive physically. People with a sensing preference find themselves rooted in the present world. They're practical, logical, systematic, and action-oriented.

"Cynthia, you're 'intuitive.' You focus on patterns that emerge from what you see and feel. Intuitive people can make sense of the abstract and read between the lines. But, above all, they are imaginative, inspired, creative, and always looking at the big picture. You know, dear," she continued, "one of my favorite quotes from Albert Einstein is, 'The intuitive mind is a sacred gift, and the rational mind is a faithful servant. We have created a society that honors the servant and has forgotten the gift.' Einstein favored intuition over logic, and so do I."

Cynthia rests her fork on her plate and looks around the room.

Joe's anxious to complete their unfinished task and get home to his family. He's tired and in desperate need of a good night's sleep.

Cheryl's heartbroken at the recent breakup with her girlfriend of many years. She's even thinking of leaving the July writing retreat early to try to mend their relationship.

Byron's concerned about his financials. His Northern California vineyard took a beating in the fires, and the insurance company hasn't paid anything to date. Apparently, a wildfire is considered an "Act of God," and they exclude coverage for those.

Cynthia watches Rafferty accept two dessert plates and forks, one for himself, the other for Ivy. *It's as if Cupid's hovering above them and admiring his handiwork after shooting love arrows through their hearts—they're smitten.*

Cynthia accepts a plate of Blackberry Fool with Calvados from Niall and takes a bite. Her tastebuds *zing* with pleasure. She closes her eyes and moans in pleasure. "*Mmm,* this is incredible!"

"I'm glad you like it," Niall says. "I only make it in the summertime."

"The blackberries are delicious."

"I got them at the Community Food Co-op yesterday. They're fresh off the vine. That," Niall says, grinning, "and I soaked them overnight in a *wee* bit of apple brandy." He holds his thumb and forefinger a good way apart to indicate that it wasn't so "wee" after all.

Cynthia picks up her plate and clinks Niall's. "Cheers."

After a few minutes of *oohs* and *aahs* all around, Niall and Emma head back to the kitchen.

Joe's cell phone dings, indicating he just received an email. He reads the screen. "Rafferty, I hate to interrupt, but we have to head out."

Cynthia notes the groove in Joe's forehead; it signals concern. She feels his tension.

Rafferty looks at his watch. "You're right. I had no idea that it's ten-thirty."

Byron and Cheryl, who'd been deep in conversation, look surprised as well.

"It's that late already?" Byron says. "I had no idea. I hope we haven't overstayed our welcome. Perhaps it's time we all head to our cottages."

"I'll see you tomorrow at breakfast then?" Rafferty asks Ivy. "It's my day off, so I'll be around all day."

Ivy touches the soft black-and-white curls on the top of Maggie's head. "We'll look forward to spending some time with you."

Maggie stands, letting Ivy know she's ready to guide her back to Austen cottage. They hold back for a moment so Hemingway can say goodbye to Maggie. He sniffs her thoroughly while she holds her head aloof. But her tail's a dead giveaway that she enjoys the attention. Then she and Ivy bring up the rear as Rafferty, Joe, and the writers in residence let themselves out the front door.

Cynthia gathers the remaining glasses, plates, and forks before she and Hemingway head to the kitchen to help Niall and Emma.

"Hemingway," Cynthia whispers, "something's niggling at the edge of my mind, something I can't quite wrap my head around. I don't know the why or how of it—yet—but trouble's brewing. So we need to stay alert."

Joe leans forward in the passenger seat of Rafferty's rental as they turn onto Iowa Street, an artery that funnels them into the Roosevelt neighborhood in Bellingham. It's bounded by Interstate 5 on the west, Whatcom Creek on the south, Sunset

Drive, E. Illinois Street, and the Railroad Trail on the north, and Huron and Michigan Streets on the east.

The gentle slope along the neighborhood's northern boundary creates properties with lovely views of Bellingham and the Bay to the west. Within these boundaries, the Roosevelt neighborhood is, in every sense of the word, diverse. Land use ranges from single-family residential to industrial.

Gazing out the window, Joe sees a concentration of old and new housing units. Styles vary from hundred-year-old single-family homes to modern apartment complexes. The light industrial area is not without its own mix, with uses ranging from automobile dealerships and warehouses to office development.

Joe lets out a low whistle through his teeth. "Holy Toledo! With cars parked bumper to bumper the entire length of the block, somebody's got to be having an early Fourth of July party."

"There's her house." Rafferty says, pointing to a modest slate-gray home with white shutters. He slows to a stop, but there aren't any parking spaces available.

"Drive a couple of clicks farther," Joe says. "This congestion has to thin out at some point."

A couple of hundred yards later, Rafferty parallel parks between two cars. Even though it's approaching midnight, several people are milling about; others walk along the sidewalk. Judging by their zig zag steps, many of them are inebriated.

After both men exit the car, Rafferty fobs the locks. "This foot traffic makes for good cover," he says, nodding toward the merry revelers.

Approaching Toni's house, Joe appraises it. *Someone without the slightest bit of imagination designed this midsize single-story home. A set of concrete steps descends six treads from the door. There's a black metal mailbox to the right of the door and a black rubber mat centered in front of it. Marci's all about flowers; she'd hate its sterile appearance. The only sign that it's occupied is the front lawn—it's green and manicured to within an inch of its life.*

The ambient light from the street lamps illuminates the front porch. As they climb the steps that lead to Toni's front door, Joe turns to Rafferty. "Time to glove up." After each of them discreetly slips on a pair of latex gloves, he continues. "It's a tumbler lock so it shouldn't take long."

Joe slips a lockpick set from his pocket and retrieves a tension wrench and lockpick rake. He applies tension to the lock, inserts the pick rake, and manipulates the inside components using the braille method—solely by what he feels.

"Where'd you learn how to do that?" Rafferty asks.

"The police academy."

It doesn't take Joe long to find the shear point—the location the key pin must reach for the plug to spin and the lock to open. "When all the pins are aligned at the shear point," he whispers, "the plug's free to rotate within the shaft, and the lock will open."

Joe straightens. "Bingo."

"That was fast," Rafferty says, admiration in his voice.

Joe returns the kit to his pocket and pats it. "Damn straight," he says, smiling.

The men slip inside. Each of them turns on a penlight and, in small segments, takes in his surroundings. Joe gets a chill up his spine. "Do you see what I see?"

Rafferty nods. "There's no color. Whatsoever. Every single thing is either black, white, or a shade of gray."

"And the walls are bare," Joe says. "There's no photos, plants, books, or even a magazine. Hell, there's not even a knickknack."

"It's creepy," Rafferty says. "Add a bit of stainless steel and it would look like a morgue."

Joe shudders visibly. "It gives me the heebie-jeebies."

As they set about the task of bugging Toni's house, Joe whispers. "Good thing we have Federal Judge Watson's authorization for this. Do you know how many privacy intrusion laws we're breaking?"

"Says the man who just picked a lock," Rafferty whispers back.

"All right, we're done. Let's get out of here."

Both men extinguish their penlights, then slip out the front door.

Joe turns, retrieves the lock picking kit from his pocket, and bends over the lock.

"What are you doing?" Rafferty whispers.

"I'm relocking it," Joe says. "We don't want Toni coming home to an unlocked door. Rule one in lock picking is CYA—cover your ass."

The moment Toni's plane lands at Bellingham International, she sends a text to Gambino. *Just landed.*

She watches her phone for an ellipsis cloud. Then, a moment later, it dings, and she reads the text.

Yeah, so my guys informed me. You cut that damned close. Take tomorrow off. I've got a job for you to do on the fifth, and it involves travel, so I need you to be at your best. Instructions will be delivered.

Toni waits for a few beats. Then, when nothing more appears on her screen, she calls an Uber, and within five minutes, she's prepaid for the short trip and on her way. When the driver turns onto Iowa Street into the Roosevelt neighborhood, he glances at Toni in the rearview mirror and says, "Looks like someone's having a party."

As the Uber approaches her house, Toni clocks two men on her front porch. *Gambino can't possibly be having instructions delivered already.* "Slow down," she says, gripping the back of the driver's seat. "But don't stop."

She squints her eyes to get a better look. "What the fucking hell?" she snarls.

"Ma'am?" the driver says.

"Keep driving," she hisses, having confirmed the identity of the two men—*Joe and Rafferty.*

Toni's mind races with different possibilities; her heartbeat accelerates to keep up. *They think I'm in San Francisco, so what are they doing here?*

Anger mixed with worry, Toni clenches and unclenches her fists.

Did they just break into my house? What the hell are they looking for? And why?

She cups her hands together in a vice-like grip.

I was Joe's partner, so I know he doesn't act without reason. And from what I gather, neither does Rafferty. What do they know? They're not stupid enough to break and enter without some type of approval from higher up the food chain, so who authorized this invasion of my privacy and why?

The driver points out the window. "But isn't this your address?"

"Shut your fucking mouth and keep driving."

CHAPTER 22

"I don't think you have time to waste not writing
because you are afraid you won't be good at it."
— Anne Lamott

Toni takes off her shoes and, with ninja-like silence, slips through the front door of her home. *I don't want Joe, Rafferty, and whoever the hell else to hear me—to know that I'm home.*

Leaving the lights off, she uses her cell phone flashlight and retrieves a listening device detector she keeps hidden in a boot in the coat closet. Then moving to the kitchen, she gets a sealable plastic bag from one of the drawers.

Seething with anger that Joe and Rafferty invaded her privacy, Toni sweeps every room in her home, placing each bug she finds in the bag. After a third and final round to ensure she found all of the listening devices, she zips the bag closed and puts it in the freezer. *You assholes can listen until your ears bleed, and you won't hear a damn thing.*

In her bedroom, Toni undresses in the dark, then makes her way to the bathroom. Carefully, she peels off the plastic wrap that protects the fresh cover-up tattoo on her lower back. *I wonder how many people actually follow the aftercare instructions?*

After the artist coated her new tattoo with a thin layer of antibacterial ointment and covered it with cellophane, he harped on her. Toni mimics his voice. "Remove the bandage after twenty-four hours and gently wash the new ink with antimicrobial soap and water. After patting it dry, apply a thin layer of antibacterial ointment twice a day to keep it moist, but don't cover the tattoo." Toni makes a puppet mouth with her right hand and says, "Yada yada yada."

She turns on the water in the shower and adjusts the temperature to match her mood—scalding. *I don't give a damn about my new ink.* Then, stepping under the hot spray, she tilts her head back and closes her eyes. After a few minutes, the pounding water begins to ease the tension in her shoulders. *I wonder what job Gambino has planned for me on the fifth? Whatever it is, it only leaves me tomorrow to exact revenge on Joe and Rafferty.*

As Toni massages shampoo into her short dark hair, an idea erupts. Her fingers tingle with excitement when they curl—*like pulling a trigger*—in the wet strands.

Then, after toweling dry and using a tattoo moisturizer on her lower back, she slips into bed.

I know what I'm going to do. A trace of a smile emerges on her face. *By this time tomorrow, there'll be two new body bags in the morgue.*

Niall rubs his hands together in excitement. Not only because of the festive breakfast he's planned this morning for the Fourth of July, but because Libby's coming home. *I can hardly wait!*

He looks out the kitchen window and sees a soft, glowing light in the eastern sky from the sun still below the horizon. Niall glances at his watch. *It's just after five, so sunrise is on its way. The Fourth of July is dawning, and my sweetheart's on her way. By a quarter after, there'll be sunshine—break-of-day glory. But even that doesn't compare to Libby's radiance.*

Niall flips on the backyard spotlights. His gaze drifts toward his vegetable garden, then to Libby's flowers. *I wonder if there are enough blossoms for me to gather a red, white, and blue arrangement for a centerpiece?*

As he slips a blue-and-white striped bistro apron over his head and ties it in the back, he turns to Hemingway. "That's right, big fella. Libby and Mick should arrive home just around breakfast."

Hemingway wags his tail at the mention of Libby's and Mick's names, then pokes Niall with his cold, wet nose.

"I know. I know. You're hungry for breakfast." They walk to the mudroom, where Niall pours kibble into a large stainless-steel bowl, then sets it on the floor.

Hemingway tucks in as if he hasn't eaten for days, inhaling his food with gusto. His long gray tail, flecked with a bit of white to match his bib and one white sock, wags the entire time.

"And I bet you'll still beg leftovers from our guests," Niall says over his shoulder as he returns to the kitchen. "You're like a bottomless pit."

Niall removes the morning's menu from a magnetic clip on the refrigerator and reads it out loud. "Homemade raspberry sauce for the red. Zucchini egg white frittata for the white. And blueberry breakfast casserole for the blue. And in addition to coffee, I'll mix the leftover soaking liquid from last night's dessert—Blackberry Fool with Calvados—with champagne. It's a bluish color, so it's perfect for this morning's holiday breakfast."

Ignoring Niall, Hemingway licks the now-empty bowl, scooting it across the floor. The stainless steel clanks when it bumps the toe space beneath the cabinet. He looks up with an expression that seems to say, "More please."

Niall shakes his head. "Oh, no you don't, you big galoot." Then he turns and whistles as he gathers ingredients, then chops, measures, blends, and stirs. Each movement is precise and efficient. A congregant in his sanctuary—the kitchen— he never fails to find solace from his worries. And he has plenty. Most recently, the murders of his brother and his father-in-law.

A lump forms in Niall's throat when he thinks of his brother, Paddy, a priest at Saint Barnabas Church—shot to death in a confession booth. *A part of me went with him when he died.* His eyes glisten. Pressing a hand to the counter to steady himself, he also misses Connor McPherson, his father-in-law. *We had an excellent relationship because of our common denominator, Libby.*

Niall furrows his eyebrows and jabs at the dough with the pastry cutter. *And they haven't caught the killer yet.*

Mick turns to look at his sister, Libby. They have aisle seats across from each other on the half-empty early morning flight. She's on the port side, and he's on the starboard side of the Boeing's four-across cabin. The narrow-body model of this airplane is ideal for short hauls like San Francisco to Bellingham. "Do you think Mom's going to be okay?"

Libby nods. "I think Mom's handling the loss of Dad better than we are. She told me that she and Dad talked about each other's death so they'd be better prepared if something like this happened.

"But she's also concentrating on helping you, Joe, and Rafferty to nail Gambino. You know she always enjoyed her career as a forensic psychologist. But this case is different— it struck home. This time, she'll profile and help take down

Gambino, the man who put a hit out on Dad. Focusing on this case has given her a reason to wake up each morning."

Mick places his arm on the aisle-side rest. "She told me she's thinking about giving the house and land to Ian and Fiona as a wedding gift and then moving to Bellingham. She said it would help to give them a debt-free start, and with the acreage, it's ideal to open a veterinary clinic."

"I'd love to have her close by."

"So would I," Mick agrees. "Hey, before we're wheels up, I'm going to text Emma and let her know we're on our way."

"Good idea," Libby says. "I texted Niall earlier to let him know we hope to be there by breakfast. By the way, how are we getting home from the airport?"

"Rafferty called me for the arrival details. He's coming to the airport because Niall's up to his nostrils making a special Fourth of July breakfast for the writers in residence, and Emma and Cynthia are going to help him."

Brother and sister, each with their private thoughts, turn their attention to their cell phones.

Mick types. *Emma, we're on our way. I love you and can hardly wait to see you!*

But his heart's heavy. *The people I love most in this world die—first, my partner, Sam. Then Niall's brother, Paddy. And now, Dad.*

He sets his phone on his lap, leans back in the seat, and closes his eyes. *I'm scared for my family and friends.*

Cynthia wakes with a start. Certain she hears a long, low rumble that crescendos to a deafening whipcrack of thunder, she gets out of bed in the guest bedroom of Mick's and Emma's cabin. The air is electric and alive. In the mirror, she sees that her short white hair is standing on end with static.

She walks to the window and looks out at a beautiful day.

It's so calm. The leaves on the trees closest to her aren't even stirring. Still below the horizon, the sun throws a pale pink cast on the chambray blue sky.

Cynthia remembers another time this happened. Two months ago in May, when she was here at Pines & Quill as a writer in residence, she received a clairaudient impression. Inaudible to everyone else, she heard the distinct crash of waves that grew in volume until it filled the air like thunder. She knew with certainty that it was precognitive, a glimmer of something in advance of its occurrence. Something ominous. *And look what happened. Jason Hughes, who turned out to be Alex Berndt, tried to kill me, Hemingway, and Emma.*

She places a hand on her chest. *Something's wrong. Something menacing. It can't be Alex Berndt because he's dead. I wonder how imminent it is?*

Cynthia plants her feet in a wide stance, places both hands on the windowsill, and tries to tune into the energy of whatever it is.

In her head, warning bells begin to clang, putting her heart and head on red alert.

Rafferty's feet haven't even touched the bedroom floor in Thoreau cottage before his cell phone rings. He squints at his watch, but without his glasses, he can't tell the time. The pinkish hue of predawn light filters through the partially open blinds. *Niall calls this the "butt-crack of dawn."* He grabs his cell from the nightstand. "Rafferty."

Sitting up in bed, he puts on his glasses and listens to the caller without interruption. When the person on the other end of the line finishes, he says, "Good work, Granger. Would you please call Walter and Maxine Williams in New Orleans and request the contact information for their son's dentist? If the body you found is that far decomposed, it may be the only way to confirm that it is or isn't Kyle Williams, especially if he doesn't have any prints on file.

"Speaking of prints, check with Microsoft—Kyle's last known employer—in the event they fingerprint their employees. And have the ME print the corpse, then run them through AFIS.

"Also, you said the body you found was nude and rolled up in a white sheet. Please check the linen tag and get the information back to me."

"Sir?" Granger sounds baffled. "I don't understand. How can a linen tag help?"

"Hotels spend huge sums of money on the linen inventory for their rooms," Rafferty says. "They have sheets, pillowcases, and towels. When they're at full occupancy, they need to wash everything every day. They need to stock them and account for the items at all times. Because of that, many hotels use an RFID tracking system. The system uses UHF or ultra-high frequency radio technology to track the items. Each item has an RFID tag that's scanned when the items are about to leave the property and again upon their return. I want to know if the sheet the body was wrapped in is from the Shoreline Hotel—the last known location that Kyle Williams was at, the place where he called Niall MacCullough from."

"Yes, sir. Will do."

"Thanks again, Granger. Call me back with any hits, day or night."

Rafferty slips out of bed and pads barefoot to the kitchen to start a pot of coffee. While it perks, he showers. A waft of the rich nutty aroma teases his nostrils as he dresses. On his way to pour himself a cup, he passes the southern wall. Solid glass, it overlooks Bellingham Bay National Park and Reserve—home to *El Cañón del Diablo*—The Devil's Canyon. The stunning view brings to mind when Emma was kidnapped by Jason Hughes, an alias for Alexander Berndt, and held hostage in one of the canyon caves. *Thank God Mick was able to rescue Emma before Berndt killed her.*

A knock at the door breaks his reverie. Mug in hand, he crosses the living room and opens it.

Cynthia stands on the front porch dressed in her usual habiliment of colorful bohemian clothing—a flowing, purple ankle-length skirt, matching sandals, and a billowy white peasant blouse cinched at the waist with a wide purple belt. Her ears, neck, fingers, and wrists are adorned with chunky silver and amethyst jewelry.

Rafferty raises his mug in greeting. "Good morning, Cynthia. Please come in. I just made a fresh pot of coffee. Would you like a cup?"

"Yes, that would be lovely," Cynthia says. "I'm sorry to disturb you so early, but I have something to tell you that I don't want anyone else to hear."

After Rafferty pours a cup and hands it to her, he gestures toward one of the chairs facing the window. "Please have a seat, and tell me what's on your mind."

Cynthia relays the precognitive warning she received earlier that something ominous is going to happen. "Rafferty, I know it might sound far-fetched, but the last time this happened, Alex Berndt tried to kill me, Hemingway, and Emma."

"I don't discount anything you say, Cynthia." He sets his mug on the coffee table. "Will you please excuse me for a moment?"

When Rafferty returns, he's wearing a lightweight blazer. He opens the left side to reveal a leather cross-draw holster and the butt of a Sig Sauer P229.

"Cynthia, never think for a moment that I don't put tremendous stock in the work you do. I'm going to share what you told me with Mick and Joe so we're prepared."

Joe looks at the faces around the breakfast table at his home, faces that he loves.

Marci, his wife of fifteen years. *I don't know what I'd do without her. She means the world to me. We need to start having date night again.*

Carly, their thirteen-year-old. *She's thirteen, going on twenty-one, overly concerned with her outward appearance, what others think of her, and feeling pressured to imitate her peers to fit in.*

And Brianna, their eleven-year-old. *My soccer-playing, still-happy-to-get-filthy little girl who doesn't give a rat's ass what other people think.*

"It's not often I get to spend an entire day with my—" Joe's interrupted by the ring of his cell phone.

Marci looks daggers at him. "Joseph Patrick, don't you dare," she warns. "You promised us the *entire* day, and this evening we're going to Pines & Quill *as a family* to watch the fireworks."

"That's right, Dad. You promised," the girls whine in unison.

Joe looks at the display on his phone and sees that it's Rafferty. "I'm not going anywhere. But I have to answer it in case it's the information I've been waiting for."

He holds up an index finger to show it'll only take a minute. "Bingham."

He's quiet for a minute, then periodically says, "Right." "Thanks." "See you tonight." Then he disconnects.

He smiles at his family. "What did I tell you? I'm not going anywhere."

The expression on his face belies the sick feeling in his gut after hearing the information Cynthia shared with Rafferty. *Tonight I'm wearing a gun to Pines & Quill in the event something "ominous" happens.*

With unease, Joe remembers what happened the last time Cynthia had a warning premonition. *Oh, God, please protect my family.*

Mick's heart accelerates with excitement about seeing Emma as Rafferty's vehicle approaches the entrance gate to Pines & Quill. "I've got it," Mick says, hopping out the door behind the driver's seat. Then, after punching in the code, he gets back in, and Rafferty drives down the long tree-covered lane that leads to the writing retreat.

Libby sits bolt upright in the front passenger seat.

Mick can see that her hands are in a death grip on her thighs.

"Can't you drive a little faster?" Libby urges.

"Someone's excited to be home," Rafferty teases.

As they reach the roundabout in front of the main house, Libby opens the car door and runs toward the front door.

All humor gone now, Rafferty looks at Mick in the rearview mirror. "I need to tell you something before you bolt too."

Mick's eyebrows furrow as he listens to what Cynthia shared with Rafferty. "Thank you. I'd like to tell Emma so she stays even more alert. She was a target before. I don't want it to happen again."

Rafferty nods. "I already told Joe. He's wearing his gun tonight."

"I will too," Mick says. Then halfway out the car door, he adds, "Thanks for picking us up at the airport. Now I'm going to go find my wife," and he, too, hurries into the main house.

His heart nearly bursts when his gaze finds Emma. Wearing one of Niall's bistro aprons, she has smudges of flour on her face. *She's never looked more beautiful.*

Emma and Hemingway see Mick at the same time and rush him. Their combined impact nearly knocks him over.

Laughing, Mick picks Emma up in a bear hug and twirls her around. Then, he presses his face into her neck and quietly growls, "Woman, I want to be alone with you."

Hemingway barks with excitement. His tail slashes non-stop back and forth through the air.

Next to Ivy at the dining room table, Maggie stands; her short tail communicates her excitement as she adds her voice to the commotion.

The beaming faces of the guests around the table tell Mick that they're happy for his and Emma's reunion. *Niall and Libby are nowhere to be seen. I bet they're lip-locked in the kitchen.*

"Will you excuse us, please?" Mick says to the room in general. "If we don't see you before then, we'll see you at the barbecue before the fireworks."

And with that, Mick swoops Emma up in his arms, turns around, and marches through the front door, passing Rafferty, who's grinning from ear to ear.

Rafferty's attracted to Ivy, and he thinks that the feeling is mutual. Today he intends to find out.

When he enters the dining area of the main house, he sees Cheryl Munson, Byron Rivers, and Ivy Gladstone seated at the table. Ivy's Seeing Eye dog, Maggie, sits on the floor next to Ivy's legs.

At the sight of Ivy, Rafferty feels his heart bump with excitement in his chest.

Before he can walk over to Ivy, Hemingway's massive front paws mash the tops of his shoes. As the Irish wolfhound prances his "hello," his wet nose snuffles the palm of Rafferty's extended hand.

"It's good to see you, big guy," Rafferty says, scratching under Hemingway's bearded chin.

Their exchange throws Maggie into a state of excitement. The brisk wag of her short tail tells him that she wants his attention too.

Rafferty takes two biscuits from the treat jar by the mud-room's Dutch door. After giving one to Hemingway, he walks over to Maggie and squats down. "Hello, beautiful," he says quietly to Ivy. A blush starts at her neck and reaches the top of her forehead.

"And hello to you, too, Mags." He hands the black-and-white standard Parti poodle a biscuit, which she drops onto the floor in favor of licking his hand.

Keeping his voice low, Rafferty says, "I'm sorry, Ivy. I didn't mean to embarrass you."

"There's no need to apologize," Ivy says. "I appreciate the compliment. And I'm not embarrassed. I'm just happy to see you."

Ivy reaches for Maggie and pats the top of her head. "We both are."

Excitement courses through his body. Rafferty stands. "I'm starving," he announces toward the kitchen. "Niall. Libby. I'm giving you two fair warning before I come in there to scrounge for leftovers."

"Oh, all right already," Niall says. "But make it snappy."

It's evident that the guests around the table are delighted at the easy banter.

One day I hope to have the kind of relationship and welcoming home that Niall, Libby, Mick, and Emma have. But, then, he thinks about Cynthia's precognitive warning—"something ominous is about to happen."

On his way into the kitchen, Rafferty discreetly pats the holster hidden beneath his jacket. *I already lost my son, Drew, in a car accident. And then when Pamela and I couldn't hold it together because our combined grief crushed our relationship, we got a divorce. I won't let that happen again. If I'm fortunate enough to get a next time, I'll do whatever it takes to protect my home, my family, and the people I love.*

CHAPTER 23

"Everybody walks past a thousand story ideas every
day. The good writers are the ones who see five or
six of them. Most people don't see any."

—Orson Scott

Toni Bianco fumes as she ends her second attempt to call Smyth. *Goddamn his lazy ass!*

She uses a burner phone to call the nonemergency number of the precinct. After two rings, she hears, "Bellingham Police Station, how may I direct your call?"

She identifies the watch commander's voice and alters hers not to be recognized. "May I speak with Officer Smyth, please?"

"One moment while I transfer you."

Agitated, she looks out the window while she waits. The sky is crayon blue. Toni hears a series of clicks, followed by "Smyth."

"Don't say my name out loud."

"I thought you were on vacation."

"I am. Why the hell didn't you answer your burner? I tried. *Twice.* But it just kept ringing."

"Yeah, well." He pauses. "Let's just say it had a problem. What do ya need?"

From the smacking of lips on the other end of the line, Toni knows Smyth's talking around a mouthful of food. It's followed by a slurp when he washes it down. She pictures him at his messy desk, scarfing down a donut. In her mind's eye, he has a liberal dusting of powdered sugar on the front of his shirt. *I told Gambino he's not worth the ample space he takes up.*

"Yes, I'm still on vacation. But I need some information."

"What kind?"

"Check the duty roster and tell me who's on deck today."

"Anyone in particular?"

"Bingham. Is he working?

"I can answer that without even getting up," Smyth says, sounding relieved. "I overheard him and that fibbie guy talking."

"Fibbie?" Toni asks.

"Yeah. It's slang for FBI agents who take cases away from local jurisdictions, botch 'em up, and then blame said local jurisdictions for the screwup."

"I *know* what 'fibbie' means," Toni snaps. "I just can't believe you said it. Just say what you mean—FBI Special Agent Rafferty."

"Yeah, him. They're both off today. Apparently, they're going to some *porcupine* place to watch the fireworks from a cliff that overlooks the bay."

"By any chance, was that *porcupine place* Pines & Quill?"

"Yeah, yeah, that's it." He laughs. In the background, Toni hears what she presumes is his beefy hand smacking his thigh. "I knew it had something to do with pines and things with quills."

"Thanks, Smyth." *You imbecile.*

Toni checks the City of Bellingham website that details local news, events, and services to determine when the fireworks start. Then she makes another call.

After one ring, a man answers. "Tommaso." His voice is deep and just this side of gravelly.

"I need a set of wheels. Something that looks sedate, but can haul ass if needed."

"Are you picking up, or am I dropping off?"

"How about a little of each?"

"What do you have in mind?" His voice sounds wary.

"You drop it off in the parking lot of Stemma Brewing Company on Moore Street in the Roosevelt neighborhood. I'll walk there and pick it up. I'll meet you inside, buy you a beer, and get the key. You'll need to find a ride home, though. I've got work to do."

"It's a deal."

After Toni disconnects, she removes her gun cleaning kit from the closet, opens it, and lays the items one by one on the table: cleaning rod, loop, patches, a cleaning brush, solvent, degreaser, lubricant, protectant, an old toothbrush, a bore guide, a cleaning pad, and a few picks and swabs. She handles each item like a mother caressing her baby.

She debates about whether to add a cleaning cradle but decides against it. *I'm walking to Stemma Brewing tonight because the assholes—Bingham and Rafferty—probably bugged and tagged my vehicle with a GPS locator. That, and so no one recognizes my car—a dead giveaway that I'm back in town. I can't easily conceal a rifle, so I'm not going to use one tonight.*

Before sitting down at the table, Toni gets her 9mm Glock 19 and lays it next to the cleaning supplies. Then she removes her holdout, a Beretta Laramie, from her ankle holster. She starts with the Glock. As she breaks it down, she remembers something one of her instructors at the police academy said.

"The most common motivations for murder are love, hatred, and money."

Well, he'd be right on all three counts, Toni muses. *Nothing comes close to the thrill of the kill; I love it. Bingham, Rafferty, and Mick are the bane of my existence; I hate them because I'm trying to climb the chain of command to Gambino, and they keep getting in my way, knocking me back two rungs for every one I climb. And Gambino's going to pay me one hell of a lot of money when I score all three hits tonight during the fireworks.*

Mick catches a glimpse of their naked bodies in the steamy mirror as he and Emma emerge from the shower in their cabin.

He pulls Emma into his arms before the towel she starts to wrap makes its way around her slender figure. "I don't ever want to be apart again."

"I don't either, Mick." She places her arms around his neck and speaks against his chest. "But it was essential that you be with your mom and sister in San Francisco after your dad died. And it was the right thing to do for me to speak in person with Mr. and Mrs. Williams about the death of their daughter, Pam."

Mick sets his chin on the top of Emma's head. "I know you're right. It just felt awful being apart."

After drying off, they move to the master bedroom. The disheveled bed in the center bears witness to their previous lovemaking.

"It looks like a storm blew through," Emma teases.

Mick waggles his eyebrows. "It did. Hurricane Emma."

Emma throws a pillow at Mick. "Seriously though, why do they name hurricanes?"

"I don't know. Let's find out. Alexa," Mick says, directing his question to the room at large. "Why do they name hurricanes?"

From a speaker, they hear, "According to the National Hurricane Center, hurricanes are named to streamline messaging and communications. Short, distinctive names are more easily identifiable and cause less confusion when sharing critical information across weather stations, the media, and the general public about a storm's tracking, path, and predicted impact."

"Well, now we know," they say in unison.

As they finish dressing, Mick adds a clip holster to the inside of his waistband. Designed for ultimate concealment, it'll keep the Glock 22 he slips in it out of sight. Then he stashes a magazine with fifteen additional rounds into his back pocket.

When he turns around, he sees Emma watching him. Her eyebrows are hiked practically to her hairline.

"Are we expecting trouble at the barbecue or fireworks tonight?"

"As a matter of fact, we might be."

Reaching for something on the top shelf of the clothes closet, he explains what Rafferty shared with him. "Cynthia had one of her precognitive warnings this morning. The last time it happened, Alex Berndt tried to kill her, you, and Hemingway. She's concerned that something ominous is about to happen." When Mick turns around, the gun he's holding in his hand points toward the floor.

"I was going to ask you to carry this." Butt end first, he hands Emma his ankle carry—a Sig P938.

Instead of taking it, she says, "We've been so busy"—her face blushes to the roots of her hair—"*catching up*, that I haven't had a chance to show you what I bought after you left New Orleans and before I met with the Williamses."

Emma opens the closet door on her side, reaches to the far right behind her hanging clothes, and backs out carrying a hard-sided Pelican case.

Mick whistles softly through his teeth. "Well, what have we here?"

"After dropping you off at the airport in New Orleans, I stopped at Gretna Gun Works on the way back to the hotel and bought a pistol."

Mick places the Sig P938 back on the closet shelf. "May I?" Mick says, raising his eyebrows as he points at the case.

"Yes. It's what I'm use to shooting with my dad and brothers."

Mick opens the Pelican case, revealing a Glock 26. "Impressive, Mrs. McPherson. I've seen you use this model. You know how to handle it better than most."

Emma walks to her nightstand, opens the drawer, and pulls out two boxes of 9mm self-defense ammo and a concealed carry belly band holster. "If you're gunning up tonight, I am too."

Mick feels love for this woman course through his veins. But they also course with fear. *She's been a target three times now. First in one of the caves in Devil's Canyon below Thoreau cottage. Next, when we were whale watching on The Odyssey in the San Juan Islands. And most recently, at our wedding, a car bomb meant for us killed the valet driver instead.* For Emma's sake, Mick puts on a brave face. "I wouldn't have it any other way."

He takes Emma's hand and leads her toward the kitchen. "I, for one, am starving. So I'm going to make us breakfast." And though he's smiling on the outside, his heart clutches. *I hope that Cynthia's wrong about her feeling that "something ominous is about to happen."*

As they pass through the dining room, Emma looks at the clock on the wall. "We've been *catching up* for a long time. We're well past breakfast, Mr. McPherson. It's time for lunch."

"Then lunch you shall have, Mrs. McPherson."

———

Rafferty's steps are buoyant as he thinks about today's plans with Ivy. Deep within, he feels the mild stirrings of a slow-burning excitement.

When he enters the warm kitchen of the main house, he stops and inhales deeply through his nose. The aroma of yeast from freshly baked bread fills his nostrils, that and herbs. *I think it's a combination of basil, rosemary, and oregano.* "It always smells delicious."

Niall turns. "That's because I love to cook. Speaking of which . . ." He turns and lifts an old-fashioned picnic basket from the counter.

"Thank you for helping a guy out," Rafferty says, taking the basket. "I really appreciate it."

"Any time," Niall says, patting his shoulder. "The appetizer is capri bites—skewered grape tomatoes, mozzarella cubes, and basil leaves. That's followed by two panini sandwiches—a delicious mix of chicken, pesto, veggies, and fontina cheese melted together on fresh-from-the-oven focaccia bread. For dessert, I used my mother-in-law's recipe for lemon bars. And to wash it all down, you have a chilled bottle of Peyrassol Rosé. This particular blend of grenache, cinsault, and Syrah has a refreshing touch of greenness on the palate—a perfect pairing with this picnic lunch."

"Oh, man, it sounds fantastic." But then Rafferty winces. "May I please beg one more favor?"

"Sure, what is it?" Niall asks.

"I haven't done this for so long, and I'm nervous. Can I please take Hemingway along as my wingman?"

"Done what?" Libby asks, walking around the corner carrying a basket of line-dried laundry.

"Oh, well, crap!" Rafferty says. "I was hoping to be gone before I got caught."

"Got caught doing what?" Libby continues to tease as she balances the laundry basket on a hip and lifts the lid of the picnic basket. A huge grin blossoms on her face.

Rafferty pushes his glasses up higher on the bridge of his nose. He feels a flush of heat on his face.

"Come on, Libby," Niall says. "Give the guy a chance."

All innocence, Libby asks, "A chance for what?" Then, walking toward the stairs leading to the second story, she turns and smiles. "Rafferty, I hope you and *wingman* here," she says, nodding toward Hemingway, "have a great time with Ivy and Maggie."

"Thanks, you two. I figure with the dogs along, at least if I run out of things to say, I can steer us to pooch talk, or we can take them on a walk."

As Rafferty and Hemingway step through the open doorway to the mudroom, Rafferty turns around. "I'll probably fall flat on my face—literally and figuratively—and nothing will come of it, so I don't want anyone to know."

"Our lips are sealed," Niall says. "We won't say a word to anyone."

Rafferty and Hemingway follow the path to Austen cottage. "Now you behave yourself with Maggie," Rafferty says. "To even have *half* a chance of getting those two women to like us, we've got to be gentlemen. Do you know what I'm saying, Mister?"

Hemingway runs ahead of Rafferty, then turns around in an excited crouch and barks. His tail wags back and forth like a chef slicing vegetables on a mandolin. He's ready to play.

"Well, now that you've announced our arrival, you might as well go ahead. I'll catch up in a minute."

As Hemingway's backside disappears around a bend, Rafferty thinks, *I've got to settle down. Ivy may not be able to see me, but she's going to hear my heart thumping inside my chest.*

When he rounds the bend and sees Ivy, an avalanche of emotion hits him. She's sitting in an Adirondack chair on the front porch of Austen cottage with her dog seated at her side. The picture of composure, Ivy's shapely legs cross at the knee. Her feet are in open-toed sandals. The sleeveless, fiery orange sundress with embroidery at the neckline and bodice is the perfect foil for her shoulder-length brown hair that frames the creamy complexion of her oval face.

Hemingway's long tail dusts the floorboards in broad sweeps.

Maggie's short tail swishes back and forth.

When Ivy stands and smiles, Rafferty's gaze takes in the whole of her. Her figure is outlined by the supple fabric that emphasizes her petite frame. He swallows.

"Hello, Rafferty," Ivy says. "We're glad you and Hemingway are here."

"Hel—" Rafferty's voice catches in his throat. *What's the matter with me? I feel like a tongue-tied teenager.* "Hello, Ivy."

He continues walking toward the porch. Ivy's smile radiates warmth. That, along with her personality and confidence, is what, in his eyes, makes her beautiful.

Rafferty reaches the bottom step of the porch and looks up. *She's the most captivating woman I've ever met.* His heart clenches with a fierce instinct to protect her. While Rafferty's left hand holds the picnic basket, his right hand affirms the presence of his shoulder holster and gun.

This is one time when I hope Cynthia's precognitive impression is wrong. But if something ominous does happen tonight, at least three of us are prepared.

Gambino picks up the ringing cell phone from the antique table next to his leather wing chair. After looking at the display, he accepts the call. Silence is his way of answering.

"It's Tommaso, sir. You told me to let you know when someone borrows a car from the fleet. I'm loaning one to Bianco tonight."

The tips of Gambino's manicured fingers glide over his white mustache as he stares out the massive plate glass window overlooking Lake Whatcom. The sunshine on the lake's surface glistens like the silver sequins on the dress of his most recent conquest.

Not nearly as massive as his high-rise in Seattle, this well-hidden luxury residence is nestled in the woods. He bought it through a shell corporation a few years back when he realized that Bellingham Bay, just west of here, is ideal for his purposes. And though there's a long boat dock with two boats moored at the end, they're primarily for appearance's sake. This multilevel home has a helo pad on top. Flying is his preferred mode of transportation.

"Did she say what she needs the car for?"

"She said, 'I've got work to do.' But she didn't say what."

"Thank you, Tommaso. Please keep your schedule clear this evening. I may need you later." And with that, Gambino disconnects the call.

What are you up to, Antonia Bianco? You better not double-cross me like your mother, Marcella, did.

Gambino sets the cell phone down and picks up a pair of binoculars to track a bald eagle he'd been watching while on the phone. He uses the center focus knob to bring clarity to the bird of prey. He watches as the raptor swoops down, catches its mark, and then soars skyward.

Gambino nods and his face breaks into a basilisk smile— *just like me.*

CHAPTER 24

"Get it down. Take chances. It may be bad, but that's the only way you can do anything really good."
—WILLIAM FAULKNER

Emma feels the gun tucked in her well-concealed belly band. On high alert because of Cynthia's premonition that something ominous is about to happen, she scans the tree-lined perimeter of the main house, looking for movement or anything that's not part of the natural landscape. But the gray-green dusk settling over the woodland foliage is ideal camouflage, making it easy for anyone who wants to hide. As she takes in the surroundings, her gaze rests on Rafferty and Ivy.

Emma nudges Mick's back with her plate, then nods toward the pair sitting side by side in lawn chairs, heads tilted toward each other, holding hands. Surrounded by a profusion of color from Libby's wildflower garden, including blue camas and yellow avalanche lilies, they make a lovely couple.

Then standing on tiptoe, Emma leans against Mick's back and whispers in his ear. "It looks like Rafferty and Ivy are having a *very* good time together."

Hemingway and Maggie lie at Rafferty's and Ivy's feet. Turned away from each other, they're gnawing on toys that Niall got for them at Mud Bay, a pet store in Bellingham.

"I agree," Mick whispers as he scoops potato salad from the buffet-style picnic on Niall's and Libby's patio. "It's about time he has someone in his life, something pleasant to think about besides work."

Emma gives Mick a crooked smile and whispers, "Says the PI with a gun in his waistband."

Mick leans down and whispers in Emma's ear, "Says the wife of the PI with a gun in *her* belly band."

Emma looks down at her outfit and then smiles up at Mick. "Do you like it?"

In addition to a denim skirt, Emma chose this particular indigo tank top because the crochet-and-ruffle hem that transitions to a curved, tulip crossover in the back is ideal for concealing her weapon.

"Emma, on *you*, a cardboard box would look fantastic."

Libby looks at her watch. "It's seven thirty," she says to the merrymakers gathered on the patio. "Sunset tonight is nine seventeen, and the fireworks start at nine thirty."

Niall nods. "We should start heading over to the bluff at nine o'clock."

Libby uses a fireplace lighter to ignite the citronella-fueled tiki torches, then lights the wicks of citronella candles in several hurricane lamps. The undulating flames add to the festive atmosphere, that and the orchestra of night sounds—summer crickets chirping, leaves rustled by a gentle onshore breeze, the distant waves below the cliffs, and a raft of sea birds overhead scouting a roost for the night.

Byron and Cheryl fill their plates in line in front of Emma and Mick. Joe, his wife Marci, and their two daughters, Carly and Brianna, stand on the other side of the buffet table, with Niall and now Libby bringing up the rear.

"Niall's outdone himself," Cynthia says, in line behind Emma. She looks down at her cinched belt. "I should have worn something with an elastic waistband."

"Hey, you two," Niall calls to Rafferty and Ivy. "You better get over here before it's all gone."

Rafferty lifts a hand in acknowledgment. "We're on our way."

"Maggie's off duty now," Ivy says, removing a collapsible white cane from a bag next to her lawn chair. She extends it to its entire length, then she and Rafferty make their way to the buffet table.

Ivy adjusts her gray-tinted lenses. "Niall, my mouth's watering. What smells so delicious?"

"I hope you brought an appetite," Niall says. He ticks items off his fingers as he names them. "For meats, we have crispy fried chicken and back porch slow-cooker meatballs. The salads include grilled firecracker potato salad and watermelon feta salad. And the side dishes are grilled green beans, barbecued baked beans, smoked deviled eggs, watermelon slices, and homemade sweet and spicy pickles from cucumbers in our garden."

Byron turns to Cheryl. "I intend to try every dish."

"I second the motion," she adds.

Libby nods toward a covered table. "And there's the desserts."

Carly and Brianna raise their eyebrows. "What *kind* of desserts?" Brianna, the younger of the two, asks.

"Well, let's see now," Niall says. "There's individual Mason jars with mixed berry shortcakes topped with whipped cream, lemon blueberry bars, strawberry cheesecake bites, and star-spangled sugar cookies drizzled with white chocolate and raspberry sauce."

Both girls grin, as do several of the adults.

Emma looks at the faces around her, each filled with delight. Fear churns her stomach. She's scared because, in her experience, Cynthia's premonitions have always come true. *If Cynthia suspects that something terrible's going to happen, a possibility becomes a probability. Will probability turn into certainty this time?*

Pines & Quill should be a haven. But because of Gambino, people have died here. Shelly Baker, posing as Pam Williams, was killed in Dickens cottage. Kevin Pierce, the valet at our wedding, died from a car bomb meant for Mick and me when he moved our Jeep for the bakery truck. And Jason Hughes, who turned out to be Alex Berndt, tried to kill Cynthia, and he almost killed me.

I hope Mick, Joe, and Rafferty can stop Gambino before anyone else gets hurt or killed.

Toni walks through the Roosevelt neighborhood of Bellingham. Observant of her surroundings, her gaze takes in everything from car dealerships to condos. The mixed use of the property is what drew her to this area in the first place. She enjoys hiding among humanity going about its business because their comings and goings helps her blend in and hide.

When she enters Stemma Brewing Company, she finds Tommaso sitting at a pub table. He's sipping from a pint glass that reads, "Craft with Character." After she takes a seat across the table from him, he hands her a set of keys.

"You're shitting me," Toni says. She sends her eyebrows spiking with her disbelief. "Of all the cars you could have taken from the fleet, you got me a *Taurus?*"

"You said 'sedate, but can haul ass if needed.'" A smug self-satisfaction settles on Tommaso's face before he picks up his pint again and takes another sip of beer. "The Taurus SHO is the *ultimate* sleeper car that nobody expects. It's ruthlessly fast, powerful, and efficient, with all the mechanical capabilities of a hardcore sports car—but *none* of the persona."

"You're *sure* it can move?" Toni asks.

Tommaso nods. "The third generation SHO has a V8 under the hood built as a collaborative effort between Yamaha and the legend that's Cosworth."

"I don't know what 'Cosworth' is," Toni says.

"It's a British automotive engineering company that specializes in high-performance racing engines. But in this case," Tommaso says, nodding toward the keys in Toni's hand, "the high performance is hidden under an unremarkable exterior. Instead, it's content to let sports cars attract police attention while you fly undetected under the radar."

Toni tosses the keys up and catches them in one hand. "Thanks for this. I owe you one."

"I don't know what 'work' you're doing this evening, and it's none of my business," Tommaso says. "But you know that each car in the fleet has a tracking device on it, right?"

"Thanks for the warning," Toni says. "I appreciate it. But what I'm doing tonight will make Gambino happy. *Very* happy."

She checks her watch. "It's eight forty-five. I've got to go."

Walking across the parking lot to the car, Toni looks up. The sky's transitioning from pale to deep indigo. The first stars have come out.

It's showtime.

Mick stands and claps his hands. "Okay, everyone," he says to the well-fed group on the patio. "It's time we head to the bluff to watch the fireworks. Niall's taking the lawn chairs in the ATV."

267 LAURIE BUCHANAN 267

"What's an ATV?" Brianna, the eleven-year-old, asks.

Mick looks into Brianna's eyes. His heart drums with anxiety. He doesn't want his imagination to go there, but he thinks about the myriad of ominous possibilities that could happen when children are part of the equation. His mind, wary, circles the thoughts, probing them the way a person explores the hole left by a missing tooth. *There are no acceptable outcomes. Brianna and Carly must be protected at all costs.*

"It's an all-terrain vehicle that we use for just about everything outside at Pines & Quill."

"How are we going to find our way in the dark?" Brianna and Carly ask at the same time.

Mick points to a washtub at the end of the patio. "Everyone take a flashlight as you leave. But let's stay together."

He turns to Ivy. "Are you going to put the harness on Maggie, or are you going to use your cane?"

"I'm going to let Maggie play with Hemingway. It's not often that she gets this kind of freedom. Between Rafferty and my cane, I'll be fine."

Rafferty puts his arm around Ivy's waist. "I've got her."

"Okay then," Mick says.

He turns and whistles for Hemingway and Maggie.

When they drop to their hind ends in front of his feet, he attaches a collar light around each of their necks. Maggie's is yellow. Hemingway's is green.

"Oh, that's cool," Brianna says.

"What's cool?" Carly asks, joining them.

"I put collar lights on these guys," Mick says. "They have LED lights that shine brightly in the dark, making them visible at a distance. This way we can keep our eyes on them if they decide to wander."

"That's brilliant," Ivy says.

"But, Ivy," Brianna asks. "How are *you* going to see?"

"You've asked a good question, Brianna. One that a lot of people wonder." She reaches out her hand and places it on Brianna's shoulder. "It's dark for me all the time, so this won't be any different."

With her other hand, Ivy holds up her white cane with the red tip. "When Maggie's not on her harness being my eyes, this helps me to scan my surroundings for obstacles." She turns and pats Rafferty's arm. "But tonight, this guy's offered to be my eyes."

"Cool," Brianna says.

Niall pulls the ATV loaded with lawn chairs alongside the group. "I'll meet you guys there."

The lit collars on Hemingway and Maggie bounce up and down in the dark as they follow Niall.

The trees and bushes come alive with the musical thrumming of field crickets, katydids, and the occasional cicada as the group and the moon-white beams of their flashlights pass by.

"Be careful of the thorny raspberry vines," Mick calls out. "They have a way of reaching out and grabbing you."

"And the blackberry shrubs," Libby adds. "If a prickly vine catches your clothing, it'll trail you until you rip it away or cut it free."

Mick, Joe, and Rafferty catch each other's gazes in the moonlight. They nod in tacit confirmation to the private agreement they'd made at the picnic—*everyone stays on full alert.*

Worry and fear eat away at Mick's gut. All the horrible possibilities of what might happen fill his mind—along with the guilt and recrimination that accompanies survivor's guilt. *My best friend Sam is dead, and it should have been me. My dad and Paddy are both dead because Gambino's after me. I've got to stop him.*

Apart from the great horned owl perched on a high limb in one of the Douglas fir trees on the east side of the property, no one else is aware that Pines & Quill has an uninvited guest.

The owl watches the woman with short, dark, curly hair step with care between tree trunks, stopping periodically to survey the surroundings. Then, after pressing his needle-sharp talons into the tree's flesh, the owl rotates his head on his flexible neck to get a better look with his large yellow eyes.

The owl isn't the only one schooled in the predator-prey dynamic. The woman hugs the shadows, blending with the night, easing over root heaves and through fern shoots as she makes her way toward the bluff.

The Lhaq'temish, the local Native American tribe who live on the Lummi reservation, believe that owls think like humans—only far better. The owl wonders if the woman is the predator or the prey. With its impressive wingspan, the large bird glides through the branches into the sky, aware that the night will tell.

Mick looks up at the stars prickling the black sky before he takes a seat next to Emma. He smiles in the dark. *Dad loved the Fourth of July. When I was a kid, he always warned me, "Be careful, son. Don't blow your fingers off."*

Emma squeezes his hand. "What are you smiling about?"

"I'm remembering fireworks with Dad." Mick's heart stabs with the bittersweet pang of the memories. Bitter because of the loss, there'll be no more. Sweet because the time he spent with his father was precious to him.

"I wish he was with us," Emma says. "I'm glad your mom's thinking about relocating to the Fairhaven area. When she visits at the end of the month, she wants to look at some condos. I'd love for her to live nearby."

"Me, too." *If we have a child, having a grandmother close would be beneficial for both of them. For me, too. And Mom living by herself in San Francisco, one of Gambino's "business" locations, worries me because he goes after his enemy's family and friends—the people they love most in the world. So having her close by would make it easier to keep her safe.*

The first spray of fireworks, red, silver, green, and gold, pop against the dark sky.

Mick turns his attention to the base of the tree line across the clearing. When he angles his head for a better look, he sees that Rafferty's and Joe's gazes are fixed on the perimeter as well. He shifts into a heightened state of awareness, using the ambient light from the fireworks to help him see.

Brianna and Carly's squeals of delight blend with the whistle, whoosh, and whiz of the firecrackers. "Look at the pink one!" "Look at the silver one!"

About forty feet in the distance, he sees the bright collars—green and yellow—on Hemingway and Maggie. *Many dogs are skittish around fireworks. But not these two.*

In between the booms and ear-splitting whistles, Mick hears Rafferty describe to Ivy the color of each firework, how bright it is, and how fast it's moving. Then, in the illumination from the bursts, Mick watches Rafferty demonstrate the size of the firework by putting his hands over Ivy's and moving them apart to fit the dimension of what he sees in the sky. The sight brings a hitch to Mick's heart.

"A huge neon red firework is whizzing by in front of us." Rafferty expands the width of Ivy's hands. "It's shaped like a star!"

As the show crescendos toward the grand finale, the night erupts with dazzling explosions launched high in the sky, offering an impressive pyrotechnic display covering Bellingham Bay. The reflection in the water doubles the beauty of the display.

Suddenly, the *oohs* and *aahs* are pierced by Ivy's scream as Rafferty's body is blown backward in his lawn chair.

———————

That'll teach you to not fuck with me, Rafferty. Toni congratulates herself on her plan. *The thundering noise of the fireworks during the finale will drown out the gunshots when I kill Rafferty, Joe, and Mick.*

She lives for moments like these—the delicious blink of time before squeezing a trigger.

Toni smiles as a scream—loud, piercing, and terrifying— is swallowed by the report of fireworks.

Toni moves her gun to get Joe in her sight, but there aren't any silhouettes. Instead, everyone's lying on the ground.

Then in her peripheral vision, she sees a movement.

Oh, shit! That goddam dog's spotted me, and he's closing the distance fast. Toni's heart hammers in her chest.

She turns to run, but in the denseness of the now-dark forest, she's become disoriented. The trees stand saturnine in weak moonlight filtered by thick overhead leaves.

That damn dog's getting closer.

She stumbles from the path, losing her way in the shrubbery. Toni shoves her way through the bushes, struggling to fight off rising panic as branches scratch her face and tear at her clothes. The smell of pines and damp vegetation fill her nostrils.

The mashing of paws on dead twigs and the snap of branches behind her are close.

As Toni turns, raises her gun, and gets Hemingway in her sight, a bullet rips through her right shoulder, tearing a fiery path through muscle, ligaments, and cartilage.

The gun flies out of her hand on impact.

She lands on the ground at the same time it does, but it's out of her reach.

As Toni tries to stand, Hemingway lunges and lands over her torso—two large paws on either side of her body. His chest is heaving. Saliva drips from his panting mouth.

"It's okay, Hemingway," Toni coos. "I've got a treat for you," she continues in a sing-song voice as she extends the hand of her undamaged arm toward her ankle holster.

<hr />

Mick reacts on pure adrenaline. Rolling off Emma to Rafferty, he two-fingers his carotid artery. "He's alive!" *This is the ominous thing Cynthia's premonition was about.*

Joe calls in an "Officer Down" and orders a Life Flight helicopter.

Mick turns to Emma. "I love you. Stay safe." Then springs to his feet and bolts. And though his gait's uneven, it doesn't slow him down as he follows the vivid green light around Hemingway's neck, diminishing to a glow as he charges across the vast space.

"He's after whoever shot Rafferty," Emma's voice calls.

He turns to see her close behind.

"Go back," Mick shouts.

As they draw closer, he sees a person aim a gun at Hemingway.

Mick takes a shot, and the assailant falls backward. But the lone person's only down momentarily. They get up and scramble into the thicket, out of sight.

Hemingway disappears into the underbrush behind the shooter.

"Shit," Mick says. "Hemingway's going to get himself killed."

The woods are dark, and the brambles sharp as Mick and Emma plunge into the thicket. "Keep your light off," Mick pants through gritted teeth as pain from the old injury sears through his hip bone and shoots needles down his leg, immobilizing him for a moment.

In these very woods of Pines & Quill, where he'd worked to cultivate peace of mind while recovering from the accident that took the life of Sam, his partner, evil now lurks.

A branch snaps. And then another.

Mick squints against the sweat that runs from his forehead into his eyes.

He looks at Emma and points.

She nods as they ease deeper into the underbrush, keeping their profiles low as the briars tear at their clothes.

A deep-throated growl.

A gunshot.

A howl of pain.

CHAPTER 25

"You can always edit a bad page. You can't edit a blank page."

—JODI PICOULT

Rafferty's conscious, but he can't seem to open his eyes more than a sliver. *What happened?* The smell of salt air fills his nostrils, that and the strong, sharp, almost painful smell of blood. In the distance, he hears the low and mournful cry of a foghorn. The one thing he knows for sure is that he hurts like hell. *The upper left side of my chest feels like it's on fire.* His previous experience informs him he's been shot.

A fist of fear squeezes his heart. He tries to speak. "Is Iv—" His voice is nothing more than a whisper.

He feels a hand circle his arm and another one slip under the back of his neck.

Ivy leans in close and speaks into his ear. "I'm right here."

Her voice, the heat from her body, and her scent—a blend of citron, apples, and bluebells—as she bends over his torso floods Rafferty with a warm, familiar feeling . . . *like home.*

Whump-whump-whump. Rafferty hears rotating helicopter blades long before seeing the navigation lights, bright against the black sky, through his eye slits. Then, as it comes closer, a spotlight gathers him and the group huddled around him in its beam. The prop wash pummels them as the helo sheds altitude.

Two flight paramedics exit the bird, transfer him to a stretcher, and load him onto the Life Flight copter, where a flight nurse checks his wound and takes his vitals. "We're taking him to St. Joseph's. It's the closest hospital with a helipad," one of them yells.

"Can I come?" Ivy calls out over the deep rhythm of the idling helo.

"I'm sorry, ma'am, but there's only room for the triage unit and the patient," a paramedic hollers.

"We'll be there as soon as we can," Libby shouts back.

The noise is deafening as the turbine gears up for liftoff.

Rafferty's last conscious thought is of Ivy before he lets himself fall into oblivion.

———

Toni sees Emma and Mick approach from the thicket, weapons drawn. Wisps of moonlight filter through the silhouette of leaves and branches overhead, washing their faces in an eerie pattern.

A ball of fear gathers momentum and rolls through Toni's body. *Gambino just might forgive me if Rafferty's dead. But if not, it's a guar-an-fucking-tee that I am.*

She tries to aim her gun, but her arm is trapped. Hemingway's limp body lies across her. His hundred and fifty pounds of dead weight pins her to the ground.

Mick separates his feet into a bladed stance and draws a bead on her. "I wouldn't if I were you."

As Emma takes Toni's gun and tucks it in her belly band, Hemingway whimpers.

"He's alive, Mick!"

Toni shoots death glares at Mick and Emma. "Goddamn fucking dog."

Mick uses his cell phone. "Call the vet, Dr. Sutton, and have him meet us here. Hemingway's been shot."

Toni hisses through clenched teeth. "What about *me?*"

Mick presses the cell to his ear. "Yes, that's right. You heard *two* shots. The second one was when I shot Bianco." He pauses. "Yes, *Officer* Bianco."

She struggles to free a hand. *There! The stupid dog's blocking their view of my free hand. If I can get one of their guns, I'll kill them both.* Toni's gaze takes in their every move. *I just need them to slip up once.*

Mick squats down and inspects Toni's shoulder wound. "She's going to live," Mick says, "but call an ambulance for her. If you bring the ATV over to the tree line, we'll find you, then drive to the entrance gate to meet Dr. Sutton and the ambulance."

Emma's outstretched arms form a triangle. She aims her gun at a rustling in the underbrush as Joe steps through.

Now! Toni thrusts her left hand out from under Hemingway, grabs the barrel of Mick's gun, and twists, trying to snatch it away. They wrestle it between them until a shot rings out.

Toni watches Joe lower the business end of his gun from the sky to her. The blue in his eyes cools. Two icebergs chill her to the bone.

"That was a warning shot. The next one won't be." Joe squats down next to Mick. "What happened?"

"Mick shot me, Joe!"

He looks at Toni, his face filled with disgust. "I wasn't talking about *you*. I was talking about Hemingway."

Mick and Joe stand as Joe calls Bruce Simms, the police chief.

From this angle, Toni sees the white sliver moon suspended in the sky. *I wish Gambino had Simms in his pocket,
but unfortunately, he doesn't.*

Her left hand brushes against the cargo pocket on her
pant leg. *My knife!* She maneuvers the billet aluminum handle
into her palm—a spearpoint, plain-edged blade, its length just
shy of four inches.

"I'm sorry to disturb you, Chief," Joe says, "but there's
been an incident involving Toni Bianco."

Clocking her captor's movements, Toni eases her way
out from under Hemingway's weight. Her heart races with
anticipation.

Joe details the events of the evening to Simms, including
the fact that she shot—*and hopefully killed*—an FBI agent.

Toni rolls into the underbrush, crouches to all fours, then
dashes in the direction she thinks she parked the car. Seething
with anger at herself for getting caught, mixed with fear of
Gambino's retribution for a botched job that she didn't bother
to get permission for, propels her forward. Leaves crunch and
twigs snap underfoot. A tree branch snaps sharp as it comes
into contact with her face, then swishes down and thumps
the ground. *Fuck the noise! If I can make it to that Taurus, I
can get away.*

The thudding of feet on the ground behind Toni draws
close. Sweat slicks her face as she keeps running. *I wish I still
had either of my guns.* Tucking her thumb under the thumb-
stud, she pushes it up and out, baring its razor-sharp edge. She
whirls around, throws, then continues running.

Toni's body lurches forward, and she hits the ground
face first.

"You missed, Bianco." Mick straddles her waist and
wrestles her arms behind her back.

"Get off me, you asshole," Toni screams as pain from
Mick's well-placed gunshot sears her right shoulder. She tries

to roll away, but a pair of shoes topped by khaki pant legs block her midsection, stopping her.

When Toni cranes her head, she's looking into the barrel of Joe Bingham's gun.

———

Rafferty knows from the terse conversation around him that his wound is life-threatening.

When the Life Flight chopper lands on the helo pad on the roof of St. Joseph's Hospital in Bellingham, Rafferty slits his eyes open. The triage unit offloads him, transfers him from stretcher to gurney, and rushes him through doors that open automatically.

Though Rafferty's in the early stages of inflight sedation, he can still recognize a hospital elevator when he sees one. It's rigged to linger for a significant amount of time on each floor when it stops. It's geared for slow movers—people on crutches, in wheelchairs, or with IV poles attached to their arms.

The second time the doors open, his gurney's wheeled out. He seemingly flies past Mylanta-blue walls as a cacophony of institutional blips, beeps, and whirring barely register.

Kind brown eyes above a surgical mask and below a scrub cap look into Rafferty's. "I'm Doctor Janet Morrison." As she speaks, she inserts a needle into one of his veins. "I'm going to remove the bullet from your chest."

Rafferty feels himself start to go under. He blinks once and holds her gaze. Twice, and barely holds on. By the third blink, he's gone.

———

The ambulance transporting Toni to St. Joseph's Hospital pulls into the circular drive designated for emergency vehicles. Two paramedics place her in a wheelchair and usher her into the building. They turn her over to an orderly who looks like

William "The Refrigerator" Perry, the former American football defensive lineman who played in the NFL for ten seasons, primarily with the Chicago Bears.

Homicide detective Joe Bingham follows on their heels.

The loss of blood hasn't lessened her temper. Or her fear. She's spitting mad at herself and her captors for getting caught. But more importantly, she wonders what's happening with Rafferty. *If that bastard dies, I might still have a chance.*

Toni's wheeled to pre-op, where two grim-faced nurses meet her. "I don't fucking want or need surgery," she barks. "Just bandage me up and let me go home."

One of the nurses tries to insert a needle into Toni's flesh, but she flails her good arm and kicks her feet. The other nurse and "The Refrigerator" grab and hold her. The nurse with the syringe jabs it into her arm and pushes the plunger. "Hold her to my count of ten."

"Bianco, you're making this harder than it needs to be," Joe says.

"Goddamn you to hell, Bingham!"

The count is at five. She tries to stand, but sits back down—hard.

She glares at Joe. "You bastard," she tries to shout, but it comes out as a whimper.

A physician dressed in pale green surgical scrubs joins them. He directs his comment to Toni. "I'm Doctor Richard Dunham. I'm going to remove the bullet from your shoulder if it's still in there, and then repair the damage."

He looks at the nurses. "Get her prepped. Surgery's in suite four in ten minutes."

Dr. Dunham turns to Joe. "I've been apprised of the situation. I understand you'll be present during surgery and then there'll be a police detail stationed at the door of her post-op room afterward."

Joe nods. "That's correct."

The surgeon nods toward a door down the hallway. "You can change into scrubs in there, Detective." He looks at Joe's shoes. "Including shoe covers," he adds. "Then continue down the hall to suite four. It's marked."

"Thank you," Joe says as Toni's wheeled down the hallway. Beyond her control, Toni's chin hits her chest. *Fucking hell.*

Mick looks at Hemingway's body on the surgical table inside Fairhaven Veterinary Hospital. "Is he going to be okay?"

"Hemingway's fortunate," Dr. Sutton says while washing his hands under a faucet at a stainless-steel deep sink. "The bullet entered the front and exited the back of his upper right thigh, missing the deep femoral artery." He nods to reassure Mick and Emma. "In this case, a miss is as good as a mile. Hemingway's going to be sore as hell for a while. Maybe even have a slight limp. But he's going to be fine."

"Then we'll be twins," Mick says, patting his leg that still throbs from the earlier chase across the bluff.

The doctor chuckles.

"We appreciate you helping us in the middle of a holiday night," Emma says.

"I'm just happy this big guy's alive for me to help," Dr. Sutton says.

Mick watches the veterinarian's old hands feel through Hemingway's blood-soaked, wiry coat and then insert the bevel of a needle into a vein in his neck. "Hey buddy," Mick makes his voice soft. "Thank you for catching Toni. I'm so sorry she shot you." He rubs the silky part inside one of Hemingway's ears." You've got to get better because when this is all said and done, you'll get to see Maggie."

Hemingway's tail thumps the surgical table once. He holds his doe-eyed gaze—filled with trust—on Mick's face as the vet's calloused thumb eases the plunger down the syringe barrel, easing sodium pentobarbital into the bloodstream where it travels throughout his system. Then, eyes too heavy to keep open, Hemingway closes his lids and drifts off to sleep.

"He'll be much better off anesthetized while I wash and tend to his wounds. And so will we for that matter," he says, his eyes smiling through craggy brows. "You're holding up well," he continues. "Care to help me get him cleaned and stitched up?"

"I'm at your service," Mick says. "Tell me what to do."

Libby stands on the patio of the main house, where everyone's waiting for word. She stifles a yawn and turns her wrist. The readout indicates that it's one fifteen in the morning on July fifth.

Her gaze drifts to Niall. With a platter in one hand and a coffee pot in the other, he moves from guest to guest. She knows that feeding people is his way of self-soothing.

When she sees the glow of the headlamps tunneling the long drive, she calls out. "I think Mick and Emma are back."

A pickup truck and horse trailer with *Fairhaven Veterinary Hospital* stenciled on the side pulls through the roundabout drive. When the front passenger door opens, the dome light reveals Dr. Sutton at the wheel, Emma in the middle, and Mick exiting the vehicle. She watches as they say goodnight and wave as the trailer's red taillights disappear into the darkness.

When her brother and sister-in-law near the patio, Libby steps forward and hugs them both at once. She whispers rapid-fire in Mick's ear, "What's happening? How's Rafferty? How's Hemingway? And what's going on with Toni Bianco?"

"I'm pretty sure that's what everyone wants to hear," Mick says. He puts an arm around his sister's waist on one side, Emma's on the other, and looks at the assembled group. His gaze takes in the eager faces of Niall, Marci, and her daughters Carly and Brianna, Cynthia, Byron, Cheryl, and

Ivy with her Seeing Eye dog, Maggie, sitting attentively at her side.

"Because tonight's events have escalated to an active investigation," Mick addresses the group, "I can't share the details, but I can give you the broad strokes of what happened. You already know that Sean Rafferty was shot. I spoke on the phone with Joe Bingham who's at St. Joseph's, and he said that Rafferty's prognosis is good."

Ivy stands. "He's going to be okay then?"

"According to Joe, he's expected to make a full recovery."

Ivy sits back down. Relief washes her face.

"How's Hemingway?" Carly and Brianna ask simultaneously.

Maggie stands at the mention of Hemingway's name and wags her short, curly tail.

"Dr. Sutton, the veterinarian, said he's going to be sore when he wakes up," Mick says, "maybe even have a limp like me. But he's going to be his same old good-natured self."

"Who was the other person?" Byron asks. "The one who shot Rafferty?"

"I can't share that information right now," Mick says. "But suffice it to say that that person also had surgery and is expected to make a full recovery. But there's a huge difference. This person has a police detail monitoring them and will be taken into custody once they recover enough to leave the hospital."

Mick and Emma walk over to Marci and the girls as the group mingles to discuss the news. "Joe, Emma, and I would like you to stay in Thoreau cottage tonight since Rafferty won't be using it."

Marci nods and taps the cell phone in her hand. "Yes, Joe texted me to let me know." She looks at her daughters. "I think we'd all feel better staying here tonight."

Carly and Brianna nod their agreement.

"Thank you for asking. We're going to head over to the cottage now. I, for one, am exhausted."

Mick and Emma make their way over to Ivy and Maggie. "Ivy," Mick says. "Would you like to come with Emma and me to the hospital tomorrow morning?" He stops and looks at his watch. "Make that later *this* morning after breakfast to visit Rafferty?"

"I'd love to. But will I be allowed? I'm not family."

"I'm pretty sure that between the combined persuasive efforts of an FBI special agent, a homicide detective, and a private investigator, you'll be allowed to visit."

A doctor in surgical scrubs walks along a post-op hallway in St. Joseph's Hospital. And though his covered shoes are quiet against the tile flooring, the closer he gets to his destination, the more gingerly he walks. He attributes the distinctive "hospital smell" that assails his nostrils to death and disinfectant.

In the distance, two women in pink scrubs sit at the nurses' station. Their backs are to him. Black hands against the stark white background of the clock above their heads indicate that it's almost one-thirty in the morning—*the graveyard shift.*

He pauses in front of a door where a police officer sits slumped in a metal folding chair playing a game on his cell phone.

"Hello, Smyth. How's the patient?"

Smyth looks up and winks.

The "doctor" opens the door with his hip because one of his gloved hands holds two syringes, the other has one.

He walks over to the side of Toni's bed and appraises the surroundings. The overhead fluorescents are out. Instead, soft light illuminates the sterile room. Chalky blue walls and pockmarked ceiling panels envelop a hospital bed, side table, and a single vinyl chair.

His gaze drifts to Toni. "Frail" isn't a word he associates with her, but that's how she looks post-op with her hands resting on top of a white sheet and a thin green blanket folded over her legs. From an IV pole, a clear bag of fluid hangs half empty with a tube running to the inside of her right arm.

He places the syringes on the bedside table, careful to keep two of them together and the third one separate.

Toni's eyes start to flutter open. *Shit!* He uncaps the first needle, inserts it into the IV's access port, and pushes the plunger.

Her eyes are fully open when he turns back, so he removes the surgical cap and pulls the face mask below his chin. "Hey, Bianco."

Toni's eyes narrow in concentration before they widen in recognition. "Aren't you the new transfer?" she mumbles.

"Yes," the impostor says. "I'm the newest transfer at the Bellingham Police station. We met just before you went on vacation to San Francisco, where I used to work."

Her face floods with relief. "So you've come to get me out of here?" She tries to sit up but falls back against the pillow.

He purses his lips and nods. "I suppose that's one way of looking at it." He pauses for a moment, then continues. "In addition to being police officers, we have another thing in common. Alexander Berndt taught both of us a few of his tricks. I've already injected enough calcium gluconate in your IV to initiate a lethal heart attack."

Toni's eyes fill with panic as she attempts to sit up again. When she reaches for the call button, he jerks her back against the pillow and covers her mouth to silence her scream. Toni moans, but the hand over her mouth makes it unintelligible.

"Your skin's already flushed," he whispers. "And you're starting to sweat. Can you feel the trickles of perspiration rolling from your temples? Don't try to answer," he taunts. "It was a rhetorical question to pass time." He nods toward the clock on the wall. "It'll only be another minute before you won't be able to struggle."

He watches as Toni's body becomes lax, then he leans in close. "I've got to say, when Gambino chose *me* to kill his own daughter, I felt honored."

Toni's body momentarily stiffens from shock before it softens again, and a defeated look settles on her face. All fight has gone out of her.

"I was wondering if you knew," he says. "Apparently not."

He takes the second syringe from the bedside table. "Alex taught us that if we're in a hurry—'an impatient disposal' he called it—we can add a second medication." Then looking at the now uncapped needle, he says, "You already know it's potassium phosphate."

This time, he inserts the needle into Toni's vein and presses the plunger.

As he stands by the bed, listening to her moans weaken, he replaces his surgical cap and mask. Before leaving, he recaps the empty syringes and slips them in a scrub pocket, then takes the third syringe from the table.

The moment he opens the door, he drives the needle into Smyth's neck and thumbs the plunger. "Gambino says you're useless."

The officer grabs his chest as he slides off the chair onto the cold tile floor. His eyes bulge, his legs kick, and his breath rattles, then his movements stop.

As the killer walks down the hall, he hears a piercing alarm in the nurses' station followed by a code blue alert over the PA system.

He smiles. *Toni just flatlined.*

CHAPTER 26

"What I try to do is write. I may write for two weeks,
'The cat sat on the mat, that is that, not a rat.' And
it might be just the most boring and awful stuff. But
I try. When I'm writing, I write. And then it's as
if the muse is convinced that I'm serious and says,
'Okay. Okay. I'll come.'"
— MAYA ANGELOU

R afferty thrums his fingers with excitement on the white hospital bedsheet. *I get to see Ivy this afternoon after I'm discharged!* He's making a good recovery at St. Joseph's Hospital in Bellingham, where he's been for the past two weeks. He looks up when someone knocks on the door and opens it.

Mick and Joe stick their heads through the doorway.

"You're a sight for sore eyes," he says. "Come in."

Rafferty picks up the remote and mutes the wall-mounted television. The news ticker scrolling across the bottom of the screen indicates the date—July nineteenth. *It's been two weeks since Toni was murdered, and the killer's still at large.*

Mick and Joe have visited Rafferty daily, but today's the first time since he was admitted that he's meds free; no more painkillers. *Finally, I'm clear-headed enough to hear details and track the conversation.* "Lay it on me, guys. I may hurt like hell, but I want to know what's going on with the case. Start at the beginning, and don't leave out anything."

Mick and Joe each pull a chair to Rafferty's bedside and settle in for the long haul.

Mick leans forward and rests his elbows on his thighs. "Toni Bianco shot you during the fireworks finale to cover up the sound. I'm sure Dr. Morrison's already told you that the surgery she did to repair your lung and remove the bullet was successful." Mick shakes his head. "That was a close call. It just missed your heart."

Rafferty closes his eyes and blows out a sigh of relief.

"She also shot Hemingway, who's making an excellent recovery. When it's all said and done," Mick says, rubbing his thigh, "he may have a slight limp, like me, but it's too soon to tell."

Joe leans back in his chair and crosses his legs at the ankles. "Chaos broke out when Bianco flatlined, triggering a code-blue alert. I was one floor up in your room when a post-op nurse notified me. Tess Morgan, the officer on watch outside your door, took my place, and I ran downstairs where a rapid response team was trying to revive Smyth and Bianco—both to no avail.

"There was a syringe sticking out of Smyth's neck. When I asked if it was something the rapid response team had administered, they said no. So I sealed Toni's post-op room until CSI got there.

"Smyth's autopsy revealed a deadly combination of cyanide, strychnine, and KCl—potassium chloride in his system. They also found a 'Family First' tattoo on his lower back."

Joe nods toward Mick. "And though Mick's shot to Toni's shoulder wasn't life-threatening, she died. After a brief examination, Dr. Dunham, the attending physician, said, 'It appears she suffered from a heart attack after surgery to remove the bullet.' But due to the extenuating circumstance of Smyth's murder, Toni's body was also autopsied."

Joe uncrosses his legs and leans forward. "Now, *here's* where it gets even more interesting. You know Dr. Jill Graham, the medical examiner. She agreed with the physician's conclusion, saying, 'The cause of death *is* a heart attack. But we both know that doesn't mean she wasn't murdered.'

"Two days later, it turns out that Graham's suspicion was supported not only by what forensics found in Toni's IV bag—the presence of enough calcium gluconate to initiate a lethal heart attack—but security camera footage picked up a 'doctor'"—Joe makes air quotes with his fingers—"in full surgical scrubs, including cap, face mask, and latex gloves. He enters and exits Toni's post-op room. When he leaves, he sticks a syringe into Smyth's neck.

"The 'doctor' was picked up on camera *again* when he left the hospital parking garage on foot. And though experts have reviewed the footage repeatedly, he's covered in medical garb. So, besides average height and weight, there's nothing else to even hint at an identity."

Rafferty rubs the back of his neck. "Regardless of who he is, there's a better than excellent chance he works for Gambino. I suspect his job was to prevent Bianco from turning state's evidence against Gambino if she was tried for attempting to murder me. Solution? Remove the possibility."

"I agree," Mick says. "But how did he find out so fast that Bianco was in the hospital?"

"That's easy," Joe says. "Gambino's proven time and again that he has people in even the most inaccessible places to do his bidding."

"You think someone who works in the hospital tipped him off?" Rafferty asks.

"There's not an echelon of society where he doesn't have a toehold. My ex-partner, Toni Bianco, worked for him, and she was a *policewoman*, for God's sake. She came and went as she pleased, and no one was the wiser, myself included. So, yes, I think there could be one or more people working in this hospital who are in Gambino's pocket."

"The one thing that all of Gambino's minions have in common," Rafferty says, "is their 'Family First' tattoos."

"I'm glad you brought that up," Mick says. "When we questioned the ME about the presence of tattoos on Toni, she said, 'Toni Bianco's body has a large, freshly inked butterfly on the lower back. It appears to be cover-up work, but I can't tell what's underneath. That's why I requested an expert. When forensic inquiry is applied to tattoos, not only can it assist in the identification or capture of criminals or missing persons, but an expert can tell what's under a cover-up tattoo.' And you know what they discovered?"

Rafferty holds up a hand. "Don't tell me. A 'Family First' tattoo under the butterfly ink."

"Bingo!" Joe says. "And because of that and the other 'Family First' tattoos in the Gambino cases, Chief Simms has agreed to initiate a surprise inspection of *all* personnel at the Bellingham Police station. He's already run it through HR for approval. They'll be the ones to oversee the process to maintain compliance with whatever rules and regulations there are, ensuring that no one's rights are violated."

Rafferty temples his fingers in front of his mouth. *I wonder if any of the people I work with at the FBI, or any other branch of the government for that matter, are on Gambino's payroll?*

Mick rubs his jaw. "We also heard from your guy Granger in the Seattle office who led the FBI team following Cynthia's clues. They found a decomposed body in a refrigerator-size cardboard box in 'The Jungle'—a homeless encampment under I-5 south of downtown Seattle. Because the corpse was so far gone, they used dental records and got a positive ID for Kyle Williams.

"The room he stayed in at the Shoreline Hotel in Bellingham before he was murdered was wiped spotless—no prints, no luggage, no personal belongings. It was as if he'd never been there. He checked in and then disappeared. He was never seen at the hotel again."

A brief knock on the door is followed by the entrance of Dr. Morrison. She focuses her gaze on Mick and Joe. "Gentlemen, if you'll excuse us, I need to check Mr. Rafferty to see if he's fit to be released this afternoon."

"What time can we pick him up?" Mick asks.

The doctor twists her lips in thought as she considers her watch. "If he's got a clean bill of health, let's say four o'clock. That way he'll be home in time for dinner."

After the door closes behind Mick and Joe, Rafferty listens to the doctor run through a list of instructions and dire warnings. At the same time, she removes a series of post-surgical wraps and binders that immobilize his left shoulder and chest.

"Yes, Dr. Morrison." He nods his acknowledgment. "I understand. And when I come for my recheck in a week, you'll see that I've been careful and followed your instructions."

On the tail of this promise, Dr. Morrison agrees to discharge Rafferty and leaves the room.

Relief floods through his body as he leans back against the pillows and closes his eyes. He reviews the conversation with Mick and Joe before letting his mind drift away from work to a much more pleasant topic. Rafferty replays his favorite memory from his hospital stay. In his mind's eye, it appears in real time.

Mick, Joe, and Libby bring Ivy to visit him. But, prior to leaving the two of them alone, Joe lowers the bedside rail and places a visitor chair close to the bed.

Before Ivy sits down, she asks Rafferty to take off his

glasses. After he does, she takes his head in her soft hands and says, "I'm going to *read* you."

"What does that mean?" Rafferty asks.

"Feeling the head and face of a significant person in our life, like a family member or romantic partner, is a technique some blind people use to 'see' what someone looks like," Ivy says.

She starts with his hair. The feel of her fingers threading through his thick strands almost undoes him.

"Short and unruly," she says. "I like that." Then she begins to massage his scalp. "What color is your hair?"

"Brown," his voice cracks.

She moves her hands to his face, where she feels every square inch ever so softly, ever so slowly.

The feel of her hands sets his skin on fire and sends tingles of excitement shooting through his veins. His heart accelerates. *It's been so long since I've shared this kind of intimacy with anyone.* Mere inches away, he watches Ivy. *I love the tiny divot in her chin and the way her cheeks crease when she smiles. She's beautiful.*

"What color are your eyes?"

"Brown," he whispers. Rafferty's only seen Ivy's eyes once. It was when she removed her tinted glasses while speaking with her sister on the phone. *She was animated and unselfconscious as she talked. That's when I saw her alluring, pale-gray eyes.*

He did a bit of internet research about gray eyes after that and learned that an individual is said to have gray eyes when the dominant color falls between blue, brown, and green, casting off a mystical look that's highly desired. Over the centuries, many people have attributed the trait of gray eyes to supernatural abilities. He smiles to himself. *It must be true because I'm definitely under her spell.*

Then in her slow and deliberate way of speaking, she says, "Yes. It's as I thought. You're handsome. Incredibly handsome. The kind of handsome that makes hands clammy and stomachs flip in a million summersaults."

Then she kisses me just as slowly and just as deliberately on my lips. The combination of Ivy's warm skin, the gentleness of her touch, and her moist mouth wires my body's tension so tight that I clench my fists to keep from detonating. We've got to get out of here!

Cynthia marvels that it's still so light after six o'clock—dinnertime at Pines & Quill. She looks at the happy faces around the massive pine table in the dining area of the main house, glad that she's been able to assist her friends on another case. But that doesn't diminish her worry. *Gambino's still out there, and until he's caught and locked away, Mick, Joe, Rafferty, and the people they love will remain in his crosshairs.*

Cynthia lifts her chin, closes her eyes, and inhales deeply through her nostrils. "Do I smell mint?"

"You've got a good nose," Niall says, setting two platters of appetizers on the table. He points at one. "These juicy little baby bella mushrooms are packed with diced parsley, mint, and sun-dried tomatoes. And these cherrystone clams," he says, pointing at the other platter, "are stuffed with bacon, onion, parsley, and Parmesan cheese."

"Before we dig in," Libby says, nodding toward Rafferty, "Mick and Joe are going to open some bubbly to celebrate your recovery and release from the hospital."

As the two guys cannon off corks and pour champagne into the flutes, Libby continues. "As you know, tomorrow is July twentieth, your last full day at Pines & Quill. On the twenty-first, we'll drive you to Bellingham International Airport, where you'll catch flights back to your homes."

Libby raises her glass. "It's been such a pleasure having you here. *Sláinte!*"

The guests around the table lift their glasses in response. "*Sláinte!*" they chorus in unison.

After taking a bite of a mouthwatering cherrystone clam, Cynthia relishes the gritty texture and nutty taste of the Parmesan cheese. "You've outdone yourself again, Niall," she says around the delicious bite.

"Hear, hear," the others around the table agree.

Niall makes a slight bow at the waist. "I'm glad you're enjoying the appetizers. Be sure to save room for the meal."

Cynthia takes a bite of a stuffed baby bella mushroom and enjoys the divine combination of ingredients. While savoring the delicacy, she indulges herself in a quick read of the energy of the dining room's occupants.

The day after tomorrow, Ivy Gladstone, her Seeing Eye dog, Maggie, and Rafferty head back to Seattle. And though they live in two separate homes, the three of them will spend a lot of time under the same roof. She notices Maggie's short, curly tail wag as she gnaws on her chew toy while keeping an eye on Hemingway. *And though he's twice her size, Maggie's established a rock-solid friendship with the Irish wolfhound.*

Cynthia shifts her gaze. *Byron Rivers will return to Zendeavor Cellars, his vineyard in Napa Valley. After much persuasion, the book he was attempting to write on his own,* Zins of the Father: A Guide to Zinfandel Wines & Food Pairings, *is now being coauthored by Niall.* Cynthia's aware that Libby's the only person Byron and Niall have shared this information with so far. *Their combined knowledge will make the book a huge success.*

Cheryl Munson won't get back together with her girlfriend of many years as she plans. And she's going to be devastated. Cynthia smiles to herself. *But then, a new professor will join the ranks at Bryn Mawr College. They'll fall in love, and life will be good, very good, for both women.*

Cynthia watches as Niall and Libby enter the dining area again. The warm, exotic fragrance of ginger wafts through the room.

"I hope you brought your appetite, Rafferty," Niall says, setting down two platters of seared ahi tuna steaks seasoned with ginger and sesame seeds on a bed of steamed fresh spinach.

At the same time, Libby places a platter of tomato and sliced avocado salad at one end of the table and another with Margherita flatbread topped with fresh vegetables at the other end. The presentation of each dish is photo-worthy.

Rafferty places a hand on his flat stomach. "Oh, man. You have *no* idea how much restraint I'm using right now after two weeks of hospital food to not shovel this delicious-smelling feast into my mouth."

Cynthia laughs with the rest of the guests, then continues her perusal. The Dutch door to the mudroom is open, and she sees Hemingway busy with a chew toy. His long tail thumps the floor periodically when he looks at Maggie. *And though no one else knows it yet, they'll have plenty of opportunities to visit with each other.*

Her gaze drifts to Joe and Marci. Much like Libby and Niall, they have a love-filled marriage based on respect and trust. *I can't see what it is, but they're going to need every ounce of strength in their relationship to help them weather something difficult that's coming up.*

She glances at their daughters, Carly and Brianna. *The same is true for the girls.* Cynthia furrows her eyebrows, trying to get closer to what's hidden from her. All she knows is that the girls are going to have to draw on everything they've learned from their parents.

Cynthia turns her head toward Byron when she hears him say her name. "I'm sorry. What did you say?"

"It looks like you were somewhere else there for a while," Byron teases. "I asked what your plans are after you leave Pines & Quill."

"Don't mind me." Cynthia waves her hand. "I was just

daydreaming. To answer your question, when I get back to Tucson I have some guest appearances to tape, and then I'm taking a monthlong sabbatical in September."

"Oh, that sounds interesting," Libby chimes in. "What are you going to do if I may ask?"

"I'm going on a silent retreat at the Amritapuri Ashram."

"Where's that?" Cheryl asks.

"It's in a remote fishing village on a small island off the southern tip of India where it's cradled between backwaters and the Arabian Sea." Cynthia smiles. "I'm looking forward to thirty days of silence. Thirty days of no connectivity to the outside world. And thirty days to recharge my personal batteries."

"Are you saying you need a break from this noisy bunch?" Niall teases, opening his arms wide to encompass the entire group.

Cynthia laughs. "Not at all. It's just that what I do drains a lot of energy—physical, mental, emotional, spiritual—and I need to plug in. I'm kind of like an electric car. I need to be recharged periodically."

"That's a good analogy," Byron says. "But I don't know if I could be quiet for that long."

"Ditto that," Niall says.

"I don't know if I could be unplugged for that long," Cheryl says.

"I try to do it each year," Cynthia says. "It's amazing what intentional disconnection can do for a person."

"I'd love to know," Byron says. "What are some of the benefits?"

"Well, for starters, silent retreats redirect a person's energy for inward communication. And because it silences our 'monkey mind,'—restless mind chatter—it offers new perspectives." Cynthia sets her fork on her plate. "As we spend time with ourselves, we observe that our inner landscape has both peaks and troughs. This simple recognition that we're not perfect and acknowledging our shortcomings breeds an unmatched power of compassion within us. It increases our ability to connect on a deeper and spiritual level with others and ourselves as well. We seek to understand instead of judge. And it empowers the practice of mindfulness and meditation."

"That's an impressive list of benefits," Libby says.

As Niall pushes from the table to get more champagne from the kitchen, Emma stands. "Niall, you've been working on this meal all day. Please let me get the champagne."

"I'll join you," Cynthia says.

Once they're in the heart of the kitchen, out of earshot from the others, Emma says, "I'm tickled pink for you, Cynthia!"

"And I'm tickled pink for you, too."

"Yes, I'm so happy that Mick and I are married."

"That too," Cynthia says.

Emma tilts her head to the side. "What else do you mean?"

"Can I give you a great big fat hug?" Cynthia asks.

"Of course," Emma says.

Cynthia uses the hug to confirm the earlier peek at Emma's energy. "Congratulations, Mrs. McPherson. You're going to be a mother."

Emma steps back, eyes wide, holding Cynthia at arm's length. "I'm pregnant?" she whispers.

"You most certainly are, my dear," Cynthia says. "When I saw that you didn't drink any champagne, I thought you knew."

"No, I've just been feeling queasy. And the clams—well, they nearly pushed me over the edge. And I usually love them!"

Cynthia hugs Emma again. "That's because you're pregnant, Emma."

———

Mick takes Emma's hand as they walk under the night sky with Hemingway toward their cabin. Looking up, he sees a sprinkling of stars through the silhouette of overhead leaves and branches. He looks at Emma in the moonlight, and his heart inflates with the helium of love. *This woman's presence in my life, her love for me, and mine for her is everything.*

Hemingway takes the opportunity to meander, sniff bushes, and mark his territory.

"I'm glad that Stewart Crenshaw, Rafferty's boss, ordered him back to Seattle for a month of recuperation," Mick says.

"And Ivy told me that she takes the month of August to prep her curriculum for the school year." Emma says. "Apparently, it starts right after Labor Day."

"I don't know how much recuperation he's going to get with Ivy." Mick waggles his eyebrows. "But I'm sure glad they found each other."

Mick pulls Emma into his side. "You're practically floating," he says, laughing. "I need to anchor you."

When they reach the cabin's porch, Mick opens the door and flips the light switch. The interior is welcoming with indigo, cream, and a few splashes of soft yellow. With reading as a favorite pastime, their well-used books fill the built-in shelves.

Emma leads Mick to a French club chair and ottoman with worn leather upholstery that faces the stone fireplace. The rustic interior's exposed logs and wooden beams create a restful atmosphere. She taps the chair. "Have a seat, Mr. McPherson. Hemingway and I will be right back."

Mick cocks an eyebrow. "What are you two up to?"

"You'll find out in just a minute," she says over her shoulder as she and Hemingway saunter out of the room.

Mick relaxes back into the chair and closes his eyes. His mind is a jumble of thoughts that include everything from work, to friends, family, and completing the schooner he's been commissioned to carve.

He opens his eyes when Hemingway's wet nose snuffles his palm. "Hey, Mister." As Mick rubs his fingers through the big dog's wiry coat, he finds a scroll-like note attached to Hemingway's collar. "What's this?"

Hemingway nudges him again.

"I can take a hint."

Mick removes the note, unrolls it, and reads it out loud. "Hurry up and finish the schooner you're working on. You need to build a cradle."

As realization dawns on him, the tingling sensation of joy starts traveling from the base of his feet to the top of his head. A brilliant smile lights his face. He looks up to see Emma peeking at him from around the corner. *The love of my life is more than glowing. She's incandescent.*

Mick leaps from the chair. "I'm going to be a dad!"

He picks Emma up, twirls her around, and they both laugh as Hemingway prances around them, barking with delight at the joy of his humans.

Turn the page to read an excerpt from
Iniquity: A Sean McPherson Novel, Book Four

PROLOGUE

"Start with a question. Then try to answer it."
—MARY LEE SETTLE

Gambino draws a blade across the tip of his left index finger, then presses his thumb into the flesh below the cut. A line of blood beads across his mutilated pad. *I still don't feel any pain.*

He lost most of the feeling in the tips of his fingers decades ago when he tried burning his prints off with cigarettes. When that didn't work, he used hydrochloric acid. *It hurt like a sonofabitch, and I couldn't use my hands for days.* And though it was somewhat successful, the ridges of his prints are still faintly visible.

I'm too smart ever to have been caught, and I've never done time, so my fingerprints aren't on file. But one can never be too careful. That's why I have an army of people in Seattle, New Orleans, and San Francisco who do my bidding for me—most of whom are expendable.

In the privacy of his Seattle penthouse, Gambino wipes blood from the blade, staining what had been a pristine white handkerchief. He folds the knife into its handle and turns off the table-side lamp. In the darkness of the elegant room, he sucks the blood from his wounded finger. The metallic taste doesn't faze him as he relishes the surrounding luxury that satisfies his every whim.

Though off tonight, built-in lights usually add focal accents to the predominantly neutral interior. Each area has its own artwork or an entire array of sculptures. Gambino enjoys the most extensive private collection of Richard Stainthorp's wire sculptures—naturally, he makes his acquisitions under an assumed name.

Stainthorp's a UK-based artist whose specialty is sculpting humans so lifelike they look like they may come alive at any second. As Stainthorp's representative told Gambino, "Wire is a perfect medium for re-creating the look of the human body. Its many strands can be used to mimic its muscles and curves and the finished result is beautiful."

Gambino's most treasured Stainthorp piece is a man in free fall—*he looks to have just been pushed from the top of a tall building.*

Even more so than his wire sculpture collection, Gambino's favorite focal point is the backlit three-hundred-gallon aquarium with red-bellied piranha swimming back and forth looking for prey. *They've proven effective in eliminating evidence of people who cross me.* When fully grown, red-bellied piranhas get a reddish tinge on their belly. Each piranha can weigh up to eight-and-a-half pounds and reach twenty inches in length.

Gambino lifts the aquarium lid with his left hand and swiftly draws his right index finger across the water's surface, leaving a trail of blood, then pulls his hand out and shuts the lid as the piranha frenzy. He feels a stirring in his groin. *Their bloodthirsty passion never fails to excite me.*

With four en suite bedrooms in addition to the master bedroom with its massive skylight above the bed, his residence also boasts an indoor swimming pool clad in sparkling blue Italian mosaic tiles. Another distinct feature of Gambino's penthouse is the dizzying, suspended Lucite staircase. And there is, of course, a terrace with a teakwood seating area overlooking Seattle.

But tonight, he's settled back in his leather chair in the living room with the piranha nearby. He shifts his gaze out the floor-to-ceiling penthouse windows—one of the many perks of being "king of the hill." *Aah, the city—close to it, but above it all.*

His glass-enclosed top floor boasts a three-hundred-and-sixty-degree panoramic view of Seattle. Downtown and Mount Rainier to the south. Puget Sound and the Olympic Mountains to the west. Mount Baker and Lake Union to the north. And Bellevue and the Cascade Mountains to the east.

During the day, a flood of natural light, horizons of mountains, and water are there for his viewing pleasure. In the evening, he views the city dressed in lights. The Space Needle, one of the most recognizable landmarks in the world, presents an imposing figure at any time of day. Uplit against an evening backdrop, it's awe-inspiring. *It makes me think of a flying saucer.*

Built for the 1962 World's Fair—the Century 21 Exposition whose theme was "The Age of Space"—the Space Needle's futuristic design was inspired by the idea that the fair needed a structure to symbolize humanity's space-age aspirations.

Anger stirs in Gambino's chest. For him, it serves as a motivator. He clenches his fists and lets it build to rage. *And though the triumvirate of Mick, Rafferty, and Bingham didn't kill Toni Bianco, I hold the three of them responsible for me having my daughter killed. I couldn't take the chance that she would turn state's evidence against me. Her death—that sin—is on their heads, not mine. She was a rising star, one of the most lethal people in the ranks who work for me. And she didn't even know she was my kid. Toni didn't need grooming; it came to her naturally.* He rubs the cut on his finger. *It must be in the blood.*

It's taken me two months to devise a plan that will bring McPherson, Rafferty, and Bingham to their knees, that will pit them against each other, that will make them wish they were dead. Gambino presses his thumb under the cut on his left index finger, causing it to bleed again. He walks over to his favorite Stainthorp piece—the man in free fall—flips on the spotlight, and wipes his finger on the sculpture, smearing it with blood.

What's that saying? "God visits the iniquity of the fathers on their children." He presses his cut finger against his pursed lips. *Well, what's good enough for God is good enough for me. So be it.*

Reviews and word-of-mouth are instrumental for a book's success. If you enjoyed *Impervious*, please post a review on Amazon. You don't have to purchase a book from Amazon to post a review there. People who buy books elsewhere, receive them as gifts, or check them out from the library can still post Amazon reviews.

To be among the first to hear about *Iniquity*, book four in the Sean McPherson series, please subscribe to my newsletter at www.lauriebuchanan.com, where you're always welcome to stop by and say hello.

ACKNOWLEDGMENTS

A heartfelt thank you goes out to:

You, the reader, for choosing *Impervious*, posting reviews, and emailing me to let me know you enjoy my books. I appreciate your ongoing support and encouragement.

The Sean McPherson Street Team—advance readers who help spread the word. Your cumulative efforts transform a snowball into an avalanche of visibility. Thank you for everything you do on my behalf.

Brooke Warner and *Lauren Wise*, publisher and associate publisher at SparkPress. My hat is off to you for being indomitable liaisons between your authors and every aspect of the often-daunting book publishing industry.

Mimi Bark and *Tabitha Lahr*, talented cover and interior designers at SparkPress. Your artistic flair attracts readers with what every book needs—arresting cover art and an interior that stops people in their tracks, urging them to take a closer look.

Lisa Grau, book publicist at Grau PR. The difference between a bestselling book and a book that sells a handful of copies can be summed up in one word: *publicity.* Thank you for securing influential placements for the Sean McPherson novels.

Professional sources—a crime fiction book is only as good as it is accurate. Thank you to *Vickie Gooch,* detective in the Major Crimes Unit of the Idaho State Police. *Rylene Nowlin,* DNA specialist at the Idaho State Police Crime Lab. *Dr. Glen Groben,* forensic pathologist. *Danny R. Smith,* private investigator and author of the Dickie Floyd Detective novels. *Camille LaCroix,* forensic psychiatrist. *Chuck Ambrose,* psychologist. And *Anthony Geddes,* chief public defender and lead counsel in death penalty cases in Idaho. Your individual and collective insight is invaluable to the storylines in the Sean McPherson novels. Any procedural inaccuracies are entirely mine.

Christine DeSmet, writing coach. I can't imagine writing a book without your mentorship. Your feedback is respectful, honest, and objective—always with my best interest at heart, invariably enhancing my writing voice. Publication after publication, your literary savvy translates into award-winning books for me.

Andrea Kerr, beta reader extraordinaire. Your insight added the pièce de résistance.

Candace Johnson, copy editor. Your exceptional eye for detail and patience to wade line by line through my manuscripts, correcting grammar, sentence structure, resolving inconsistencies, and anything else that's amiss helps me deliver the most polished books possible.

Len, my husband. I'm grateful that we're old enough to remember the duck-and-cover drills we practiced in school during the Cuban Missile Crisis. So now, when bombs go off in the writing studio and "it" hits the fan, you know exactly what to do.

ABOUT THE AUTHOR

photo © Len Buchanan

L aurie Buchanan writes the Sean McPherson novels—
fast-paced thrillers set in the Pacific Northwest that
feature a trifecta of malice and the pursuit and cost of justice.

A cross between Dr. Dolittle, Nanny McPhee, and a
type-A Buddhist, Buchanan is an active listener, observer of
details, payer of attention, reader and writer of books, kindness enthusiast, and red licorice aficionado.

Her books have won multiple awards, including Foreword
INDIES Book of the Year Gold Winner, International Book
Award Gold Winner, National Indie Excellence Awards Winner,
Crime Fiction/Suspense Eric Hoffer Awards Finalist, PenCraft
Award for Literary Excellence, and CLUE Book Awards finalist
Suspense/Thriller Mysteries.

Laurie and her husband live in the Pacific Northwest, where
she enjoys long walks, bicycling, camping, and photography—
because sometimes the best word choice is a picture.

To learn more, please visit Laurie's website at
www.lauriebuchanan.com.